Refuge Of The Mystic Counsel

The Red Cloth Rebellion

Saga One

Author
Anthony James Owens

&

Permanent Coffee Stain LLC
Publishing

Editor
Cassian Drayle

Illustrator
Miriam V. Dawlish

Cover Artist
Anthony James Owens

Table of Contents

PUBLISHERS INTRODUCTION AND COPYRIGHT INFORMATION 2

   Copyright Information 2

DISCLAIMER ACKNOWLEDGEMENT & DEDICATION 4

   Acknowledgement 4

   Dedication 4

MESSAGE FROM THE AUTHOR 5

REFUGE PRELUDE | THE FALL OF PETRICHORE & THE BATTLE OF GOA ... 6

CHAPTER 1 | ARRIVED AND ARMED 10

   The Conqueror I 53

CHAPTER 2 | ORDER TO CHAOS 58

   The Conqueror II 81

CHAPTER 3 | FUGITIVES WITH GUIDANCE 85

   The Conqueror III 111

CHAPTER 4 | BIRTH OF MYSTICS 118

   The Conqueror IV 152

CHAPTER 5 | TIME WELL SPENT 159

   The Conqueror V 179

CHAPTER 6 | LOST THEN FOUND 183

   The Conqueror VI 210

CHAPTER 7 | PROJECT IS COMPLETED 216

   The Conqueror VII 251

CHAPTER 8 | RED FOR REBELLION 256

   Chapter 8 Continued | Red For Rebellion 298
   The Conqueror VIII 317

NOVEL CAST AND CREDITS 321

POST CREDIT SCENE 324

DELETED CHAPTER SCENES 327

REFLECTIONS FROM THE AUTHOR 346

FUTURE PUBLISHINGS 348

Publishers Introduction and Copyright Information

Permanent Coffee Stain LLC is a dynamic and forward-thinking book publishing company based in New York, USA. Dedicated to the art of storytelling, we embrace all genres, from thought-provoking literary fiction to compelling non-fiction, poetry, fantasy, science fiction, mystery, and beyond. Our mission is to amplify diverse voices, champion creative expression, and bring captivating narratives to readers worldwide.

With an unwavering commitment to quality and innovation, we support both emerging and established authors, ensuring their work reaches the right audience through expertly curated publishing, marketing, and distribution strategies. At Permanent Coffee Stain LLC, every book is more than just a publication—it is a legacy, a conversation, and a lasting imprint on the literary world.

Copyright Information

Published in the United States by Permanent Coffee Stain LLC, New York

For permissions, inquiries, or publishing opportunities, please contact:

Permanent Coffee Stain LLC

pcspublishing@permanentcoffeestain.org

ISBN 979-8-9985717-4-9

Disclaimer Acknowledgement & Dedication

This is a work of fiction. Names, characters, places, and events are either the product of the author's imagination or used fictitiously. Any resemblance to actual persons, living or dead, or real events is purely coincidental.

The publisher and author make no representations or warranties regarding the accuracy, completeness, or suitability of the content for any particular purpose. This book is intended for entertainment purposes only. The author and publisher assume no responsibility for any interpretations, actions, or consequences resulting from the reading of this work.

Published in the United States by Permanent Coffee Stain LLC, New York

Acknowledgement

I would like to extend my deepest gratitude to everyone who played a role in bringing this book to life. To my family and friends, thank you for your unwavering support and encouragement. To my editor and publishing team at Permanent Coffee Stain LLC, your dedication and insight have been invaluable. To my readers—thank you for taking this journey with me. Your love for stories is what makes writing worthwhile.

Dedication

"To those who have always believed in me—especially my daughter, Sapphire, and my late grandmother, Ida Mae Owens—thank you. My gratitude to you both is immeasurable."

Message From The Author

For as long as I can remember, I've known I was different. I couldn't name it—only feel how it made me stand out, no matter how much I tried to soften my presence. In 2019, I discovered the Sigma archetype—first on social media, then through deeper study—and that knowledge altered how I see the world, people, and myself. The more I learned, the clearer it became. Sigma's and INFJs—the chosen, the so-called lone wolves, whatever label you prefer—are more than a line on a personality chart. We are not a mistake; we have a purpose—we are the Elect spoken of through the ages. This discovery inspired me to write Refuge of the Mystic Counsel.

This book is, first, Science fiction/fantasy. But it also carries a quieter purpose, to shine a light on our existence.

— Anthony James Owens

Refuge Prelude | The Fall of Petrichore & The Battle of Goa

The sky over Petrichore fractured like glass under strain.

Crimson streaks tore through the upper atmosphere as defense cannons ignited across the horizon, their beams carving frantic arcs into the clouds. Alarm sirens shrieked across the capital; crystal intercoms spat clipped orders as Petrichoren command scrambled to repel the invaders.

"Unidentified vessels breaching altitude—coordinates eighty-nine through one-twenty-two!"
"Deploy dome shield sequence four—now!"

Above the capital, the crystalline dome—once the city's crown—splintered at its apex. Its lattice of light cracked and cascaded downward as the Ikannunaa ships broke through, black and sleek, thrumming with alien energy. The barrier shattered like brittle ice.

"This is your final warning," a desperate voice thundered across the last frequency. "Turn back or we will fire without restraint!"

But the Ikannunaa did not turn back. They descended faster.

Within the Royal Stronghold, Queen Lor moved with purpose. Her bluish robe swept across the spiraling crystal steps as tremors rippled through the citadel. Her guards flanked her, weapons clutched, their armor reflecting the firestorm above.

"They've breached the dome. Restricted airspace is lost," one guard reported.

"Escort me to the chamber. Seal all upper levels," Lor commanded. Her voice carried steady—unyielding, even as the world cracked around her.

Missiles struck. The sky bled fire. Towers folded. The once-proud spires of Petrichore bowed beneath the Ikannunaa barrage.

In the fortified chamber, Queen Lor halted. With urgency, she removed her crown, its crystalline facets gleaming faintly in the flickering light. She pressed it into the hands of a trusted aide, her voice low but commanding.

"Lock this crown deep beneath the castle," she ordered. "They must never get their hands on the Shard of the Heirloom Family. Guard it with your life, for it holds more than legacy—it holds our future."

The aide bowed quickly, clutching the crown to his chest before vanishing into the lower corridors.

Then came the battering.

BOOM.
BOOM.
BOOM.

The bolts screamed as the massive door buckled. With a tortured groan, it wrenched free and collapsed inward, smoke and dust billowing like a shroud.

For a breath—silence.

Through the haze, a silhouette emerged. Tall. Monstrous in its composure. A black military coat, streaked with silver that glinted like fangs.

He advanced with deliberate grace, unbothered by the weapons aimed at him. Pausing, he gave a shallow, mocking bow.

"Clear skies were forecast over Petrichore, Queen Lor," he said, voice smooth as venom. "The clouds have parted—and your reign has ended."

The Queen did not flinch. Her guards tightened their line, though the truth already burned in her eyes.

Petrichore had fallen.

On Earth—before the first light of dawn touched the horizon—the war horns of Satana shattered the stillness.

Across the riverbanks, a horde of warriors surged like a flood of death—faces streaked in war paint, long black dhotis flaring around their legs, steel flashing in the half-light. Their roars carried one promise: conquest.

Goa awoke in chaos. Men scrambled for weapons, women and children fled toward the temple, their cries braided with the clash of steel.

At the forefront stood Leader Parth, his heirloom sword gleaming as though carved from the ancestors' will. Hardened leather and brass armored his frame, but it was his voice that steeled the people.

"Hold the line!" he thundered. "Fight for your homes! Fight for your ancestors!"

The enemy struck.

Steel shrieked against steel. Arrows found flesh. Fires spread like hungry spirits as thatched roofs collapsed in showers of embers. Satana's warriors pressed forward without mercy. Goa's defenders held—but barely.

Through the smoke, Parth met the gaze of General Dagrath, the warlord of Satana. Scarred face, merciless eyes, his sword already slick with blood.

"Goa will burn," Dagrath sneered, locking blades with Parth. "Your people will bow before the sun rises."

Parth's jaw tightened, his strike ringing sparks into the air. "Not while I still breathe."

Yet even as he fought, his men faltered, pressed back toward the temple—Goa's last refuge. Defeat loomed.

Until the wind changed.

Inside the sacred hut, Spiritual Leader Ohm sat cross-legged, white beard falling over his chest, his shawl smelling of sandalwood and turmeric. His disciples chanted in unison, their mantras vibrating through the walls as sacred smoke curled heavenward.

Ohm's fingers traced ancient sigils into the earth. His voice deepened, rising above the chants.

"Our ancestors walk with us. The land has suffered enough. We call upon its spirit to fight."

Ash scattered into the fire. The flames leapt high. Outside, the wind howled as though carrying the voices of the dead.

Parth felt it first. Strength surged into his weary arms, the weight of fatigue falling away. His warriors straightened, eyes alight with fire not their own.

"The gods fight with us!" someone cried.

Swords cut truer. Arrows pierced deeper. The tide turned.

Dagrath's sneer faltered as his men fell in droves. "No! Fight, you cowards!" But fear had already spread. The Satana horde broke ranks, retreating as quickly as they had come, vanishing back across the river.

Goa stood bloodied—but unbroken.

Ohm's chanting ceased. He rose, bones creaking, his disciples silent behind him. At the doorway, the battered warriors of Goa gathered, Parth at their head. His heirloom blade dripped with blood, but his face carried no triumph.

Ohm's gaze met his, voice solemn, threaded with prophecy.

"The battle is won. But the war…" His eyes lifted toward the dark sky, where smoke and embers still swirled. "…the war is far from over."

The smoke curled upward, as if carrying the warning to the stars.

"And now… Our Feature Presentation:
Refuge of the Mystic Counsel – The Red Cloth Rebellion"

Chapter 1 | Arrived And Armed

It was the year 1199—an ordinary day on Earth, or so it seemed, in the remote territory of a tribe that had survived for generations against the sun's relentless cruelty. Their land stretched in vast, arid plains where heat fractured the ground into a mosaic of cracks, and thorny shrubs clung stubbornly to life. The village stood at the heart of it: clay huts hardened by fire and crowned with thatched roofs, rising from the dust as if grown from the earth itself.

Life here followed a rhythm older than memory. Men drove their herds across the plains, women kept smoke-dark homes alive with labor, and children darted about the drying racks, laughing as shirts and skirts snapped in the hot wind. Predictability was their shield, the fragile order that kept despair at bay. Yet beneath that steady cycle, the world waited, coiled for its upheaval.

At midday, the sun blazed mercilessly overhead, but a strange hush gripped the air. Birds fell silent. Even the livestock shivered. Then, without warning, the sky ruptured. Darkness spilled across it as though some unseen hand had torn a wound in the heavens. Clouds, heavy and unnatural, rolled forward like an invading army, blotting out the light.

A wall of gray devoured the horizon. Rain struck—hard, immediate, punishing. Within heartbeats, the village drowned beneath a downpour so fierce the thirsty earth hissed, coughing up steam that thickened into a ghostly mist. Sunlit clarity vanished; in its place rose an otherworldly shroud.

Panic ripped through the settlement. Women snatched clothes from the lines before the storm could claim them, mothers dragged wide-eyed children into the safety of huts, and men froze mid-task, staring skyward. Above them, lightning thrashed inside the clouds—unnatural streaks, jagged and deliberate, unlike anything nature had birthed before. Thunder did not merely crack; it boomed with the weight of something buried deep within the earth itself.

This was no passing storm. The villagers could feel it in their marrow. The air pulsed with a dread they could not name, a harbinger pressing down on them like the hand of a god. Something vast was moving through the fabric of their world, something that would not be turned aside.

And as the storm raged, the tribe stood on the edge of history, about to face the force that would tear apart the ordinary—and replace it with legend.

Then, beyond their wildest dreams—or darkest nightmares—the sky delivered an unimaginable sight. From the storm's boiling heart, immense black shapes broke through the cloud cover above what would one day be called the Bay of Bengal. Their hulking silhouettes cut through the mist like obsidian blades, and from their bellies burst beams of white light, sharp and merciless, slashing the darkness. The plains below glowed in their glare, an eerie stage where no one wished to stand.

Cries erupted across the village. Some fled, stumbling through mud and foliage in blind terror; others pressed themselves into doorways or beneath trees, clutching children and charms. Fear drove them, yet fascination rooted their eyes upward. This was not thunder, not storm, not omen. It was intrusion.

Several dark objects descended in silence, an ominous weight pressing down with them. They touched earth in a clearing of the tribal domain, that would one day be called Goa, India. Towering and alien, the crafts dwarfed huts, trees, and men alike—black monuments set against a world that had known only clay, wood, and stone.

Rain hammered their surfaces, a cold percussion that could not disguise the enormity of their presence. The land itself seemed to recoil. Birds had vanished, insects fell silent, even the wind held its breath. The storm remained, yes—but it no longer belonged to the sky. It belonged to them.

Yet the tribe did not scatter. Warriors stepped forward, painted for war: red, white, and black streaks cutting across faces hardened by resolve. Cloths of orange and yellow clung wetly to their bodies, brass and leather glistened in the downpour, and at their hips swords gleamed faintly in the intruders' unnatural light. Spears and shields were gripped tighter. Shivers coursed their limbs, but none turned away.

The land, lush with ancient trees and alive with unseen spirits, seemed to tense with them—waiting. Mud rose underfoot, the earth reshaping itself into a battlefield where the old ways of survival would stand against something unearthly.

In that suspended moment, every heart beat with one truth: they were not simply defending huts or herds. They stood for their ancestors, their history, the soil that had carried their blood for generations. They stood for existence itself.

And so they waited, rain pounding in unison with their pulse, for the silent giants to make their first move.

Inside the largest craft—the Prominent—at its very core loomed a set of towering metal doors. Frost seemed to cling to their surface, a breath of cold radiating outward as though warning lesser beings to keep away. Beyond those gates stretched the Grand Stratum: a chamber of shadows and silence, vast enough to swallow a cathedral whole.

At its center, two thrones of hammered gold rose high, and upon them sat the Princes of the Ikannunaa Royal Empire. Ata-els and Atsu-els. Their very names rippled like thunder across the fabric of the universe. Identical in form, they were giants of flesh and will—eight feet of hardened sinew and immortal bearing. Golden crowns gleamed on their heads, their light fractured by the dim glow of the chamber's sconces, casting warped reflections on the walls. Their skin bore the look of petrified wood—ancient, weathered, veined with grooves that traced across their bald skulls like the roots of some long-dead tree. Their faces were carved with severity: angular jaws, hollow cheeks, and eyes of living fire, red and merciless.

They were heirs of Nimbbiraa-Six, one of six worlds ruled for millennia by their bloodline, a dynasty so unyielding that entire star systems bent beneath its weight. In their presence, submission was not requested—it was inevitable.

Prince Atsu-els moved first, though only a finger stirred. A servant hurried forward with a glass of thick, tar-black wine. Atsu-els inhaled the fumes as if drawing life from them, then drank deeply, emptying the vessel in one relentless swallow. His lips curved into a smirk, sharp as a blade, as he held the glass aloft for more. The liquid shimmered like oil, brewed from the pits of their homeworld, thickening the malice already burning in his gaze.

"Bokimpa." His voice cut through the silence like a serrated edge.

The servant shuffled forward, a hunched shadow in dark silks, his bony fingers trembling as he bowed.

"Contact General Scorpiondt."

Bokimpa scurried to a gilded console, the glow of its runes casting sickly light across his gaunt face. With a series of deft taps, he opened a channel. Moments later, the air shimmered, and the form of a warrior emerged.

General Scorpiondt stood in holo-projection, his image towering, his expression cold. His scalp gleamed under unseen light, his beard trimmed to military sharpness, a scar carved like a warning across his left brow. He radiated both discipline and threat, a predator clothed in armor.

"You summoned me, Highnesses," he said, voice taut, restrained aggression vibrating beneath every syllable.

Prince Atsu-els leaned forward, his crown flashing briefly in the dim light. "Defiance festers outside our crafts. Quell it. Break them. Show them what it means to stand against Ikannunaa rule."

A smile ghosted across Scorpiondt's lips, more predator than man. "With pleasure."

Beside his brother, Prince Ata-els finally stirred. His voice was low, a hiss that slithered across the chamber's stillness. "And bring me Dr. Von. Alive. His knowledge is the key to what we will build—and to what we will destroy."

The order hung heavy in the chamber, colder than the storm outside. Scorpiondt bowed his head with lethal calm. The transmission faded, leaving only the Princes, their thrones, and the echo of destiny closing its grip around an unsuspecting world.

Rain hammered the earth without mercy, each drop drumming against mud, armor, and flesh, as if the storm itself wanted to drown the world. The tribal fighters stood unmoving, painted faces set in grim defiance. Years of war had carved resolve into their features, yet their silence betrayed the tension thickening in the air.

A sudden siren tore through the storm, a single wail that rattled bone and spirit alike. It faded as quickly as it came, replaced by the whirl of yellow beacons above the crafts' rear hatches. Their beams sliced through mist and rain, casting the battlefield in a shifting, spectral glow.

Metal groaned. The massive doors of the invaders' vessels slid apart, the grinding echo swelling across the plains like gates opening into the underworld.

Inside, rows upon rows of armored soldiers stood waiting—black and white plating polished to a ghostly shine, visors concealing any trace of humanity. Across their chests gleamed the insignia of the Ikannunaa Royal Empire: dominance branded into steel.

From the dark slits of their helmets, they stared outward at a world of mud, paint, and sharpened stone. A clash of eras, of weapons and wills, hung in the air.

Then came the sound. Footsteps—slow, deliberate, weighted with menace—rose from deep within one craft's hollow belly. Each impact reverberated like thunder, announcing something more than a soldier, more than a man.

He emerged—a cyber-enhanced titan, clad in matte black-and-red armor etched with bright lines that pulsed faintly in the stormlight. Upon his arm blazed the mark of the I.R.S—the Ikannunaa Royal Squadron—an elite unit whispered about across the galaxy. His presence bent the air itself, an apex predator stepping into a world unprepared.

He strode to the craft's inner wall, raised a fist, and struck three times. The metallic blows echoed outward, a war drum rolling across mud and rain, declaring the inevitable.

The response was immediate. Engines ignited, hatches flared, and from every surrounding vessel soldiers poured forth in flawless unison. Boots splashed through waterlogged earth, yet their movements carried no chaos—only precision. A wall of armor advanced, their silent order more terrifying than a thousand screams.

The I.R.S operative lifted his wrist, activating the embedded comm on his gauntlet. His voice, filtered and metallic, rasped through the storm:

"Droid! Code 1-7-9-8-4: frontline secured."

The message leapt across distance, delivered straight into the ears of General Scorpiondt. Cold. Efficient. Irrevocable.

The soldier lowered his hand and stepped aside, his task complete. Around him, the storm raged—but the true violence was only about to begin.

Inside the Prominent's shadowed corridors, footsteps rang like verdicts. Heavy, deliberate, they carried the weight of absolute command. A red pulse flickered in the figure's earpiece—frontline secured.

The sealed hatch before him released with a hiss, bolts unlatching like chains cast off. Mist rolled outward, colliding with the storm outside until the very air thickened with dread. For a heartbeat, all sound seemed to retreat. Soldiers straightened. Tribesmen held their breath. Even the storm bent to silence.

And then he emerged.

General Scorpiondt.

Rain struck his black tactical suit in steady rivulets, the Ikannunaa crest glinting gold upon his chest. A precisely armored jumpsuit hung against his towering frame, pistols holstered low at his hips, boots and gloves polished as though the storm dared not mar them. He was a weapon made flesh, simple in attire yet monumental in presence.

Around him, the Ikannunaa soldiers stiffened to attention. Authority radiated from him like heat from a forge—unspoken, undeniable. His scarred brow furrowed as his gaze cut across the battlefield, weighing every figure, every weakness.

Through the haze of rain and steam, another figure stepped forward: Tribe Leader Parth. His red cloth clung to his body, bamboo staff clenched in both hands, eyes aflame with the defiance of a thousand ancestors.

"This land is ours," Parth thundered, pointing his staff toward the General. "These people are mine to protect. I would rather meet my ancestors this day than see them fall to outside tyrants."

Scorpiondt advanced, calm, measured, every stride part of a ritual long rehearsed. The scar above his eye caught a streak of lightning. For a moment, he seemed carved from the storm itself.

A smirk slid across his lips. His voice, low and venomous, cut through the storm. "Your defiance is admirable. But it disrupts our design. Resistance is futility clothed in pride."

Parth stood unyielding. "Then let my pride be the blade that cuts you down."

The smirk hardened. "Then let me hasten your reunion with those you honor."

In a blur, Scorpiondt drew his firearm. A single shot cracked the storm apart. Energy seared through Parth's abdomen, folding him to his knees. Blood mingled with rain, crimson spreading in the mud.

The battlefield froze. Silence again—except for the storm.

Parth's staff clattered to the earth, yet his voice, ragged with pain, rose once more. "Do not yield! For your ancestors… for your children!" His cry was his last gift, a spark thrown into dry grass.

His warriors roared and surged forward, grief and fury twisting into reckless courage. Spears thrust, swords flashed, bamboo and bronze against steel and light. The Ikannunaa answered with merciless precision. Beam gun fire lit the mist, tribal warriors fell, and the plains of Goa drowned in blood and rain.

Scorpiondt watched, unmoved, as his forces tore through resistance. His orders were cold and sharp: "Take the ones who bow. Kill the ones who stand."

The slaughter unfolded as he turned away, rain sheeting down his scarred face. He drew a long breath, inhaling the metallic tang that lingered over the field—iron, smoke, inevitability.

"Conflict," he murmured, savoring the word. "It has its own fragrance."

The storm raged above, but it was his storm now.

Back aboard the Prominent, deep within the towering chamber of the Grand Stratum, a knock reverberated against the massive doors.

"Enter," Prince Atsu-els commanded, his voice echoing across the gilded hall.

The doors swung wide, revealing Dr. Von. He looked almost casual in stark contrast to the chamber's shadowed grandeur: white lab coat draped over a black short-sleeved shirt, gray trousers, and white sneakers that squeaked faintly against the polished floor. A folder of files tucked under his arm betrayed the weight of responsibility, but his eyes—sharp, restless, and tinged with sarcasm—hinted at a mind that refused to bow.

As he stepped forward, Prince Ata-els rose beside his brother, greeting him with a tone warm but dripping with condescension. "Doctor Von," he said smoothly, "we trust you and your daughter are… adjusting?"

Von let out a slow breath, his gaze sliding past them. "We're managing," he said at last, though the hollowness in his voice betrayed the lie.

The twins exchanged a glance, their satisfaction muted but present.

"Excellent," Ata-els continued, his red eyes drifting toward the folder. "Now—the Beta-Gene Fluid Project. We trust its progress is as expected?"

Von's posture stiffened. "Still in research," he admitted. "But we anticipate moving into development within a few Earth months."

Their golden crowns glinted as the brothers nodded in unison. For a moment, the chamber softened. But Von's voice cut the silence again, steadier this time, tinged with quiet defiance.

"But let me be clear: what you've demanded of me—this permanent rewriting of life itself—is not progress. It is mutilation. You're asking me to scar generations unborn. We should not play God."

The temperature in the hall seemed to drop. The faint smiles of the Princes curdled into frowns.

With sudden violence, Atsu-els hurled his chalice of Black Wine to the floor. The thick liquid spread across the golden tiles, dark tendrils splattering at Von's feet.

"How dare you," Ata-els hissed, his voice sharp as a blade. "You are not here to play God. You are here to serve as our biologist. Nothing more."

Atsu-els stepped closer, his smirk now carrying the menace of a noose tightening. "And if you ever speak to us in such a tone again, you and your daughter will share the fate of Petrichore."

Von felt the chill of those words cut deeper than the storm outside, but his face remained stone, masking the turmoil roiling beneath.

Ata-els clapped his hands three times. The sound cracked like a whip through the chamber. From the shadows, two armored guards stepped forward and flanked the scientist.

"Return him to his quarters," Ata-els ordered, dismissive as if waving away an insect.

Von turned to go, shoulders heavy with a burden far larger than himself. He had not taken three steps when Atsu-els's voice rang out, cruel and final.

"Remember, Doctor. The only thing keeping you and your daughter alive is your usefulness. Lose that… and you lose everything."

The great doors boomed shut behind him. Alone in the shadowed corridor, Dr. Von's stride faltered. His mind raced with impossible choices—choices that would decide not only his fate, but Ara's, and perhaps the future of all who still resisted.

Night pressed heavy over the plains, the stars smothered by smoke and drifting embers. Near the hulking shadow of a Servacraft, five Ikannunaa soldiers crouched around the faint blue burn of a ration torch. Their black-and-white armor fractured the light in jagged shards, but their voices — stripped of command and formality — carried the raw weight of men caught between duty and conscience.

One soldier removed his helm, revealing a pale, drawn face lined with scars. He exhaled long and ragged, as though trying to purge the stench of war from his chest.

"Not what I thought it would be," he muttered, staring into the flame. "The orders said rebellion. These were farmers. Shepherds."

Another scoffed, tightening the strap of his gauntlet with a sharp tug. "Farmers or not, resistance is resistance. Better to crush their spirit now than face a tide later."

The youngest, visor still lowered, shifted uneasily. His voice wavered.

"Still… they screamed like us. They bled like us. Don't you ever wonder if—"

He stopped. The unfinished thought hung in the air like smoke.

Silence followed, brittle and dangerous. One of the veterans leaned forward, his tone low and edged.

"Wondering is how men disappear. Remember Ras-Magenta. Remember Petrichore. The General doesn't tolerate doubt. He believes we're chosen. You either believe too… or you die believing nothing."

The torch guttered, its blue flame shrinking. For a moment, the night swallowed their words whole.

Then, with practiced precision, helms locked back into place. Whatever humanity had surfaced was buried again behind steel. One by one, they rose and filed toward a Servacraft, their shadows merging with the war machine that owned them.

Only the youngest lingered. He stared at the torch's fading ember, as if trying to hold its warmth in his chest before the cold took him, too.

The battlefield lay silent, a graveyard of broken bodies and extinguished cries. Smoke curled upward from smoldering grass, the scent of blood and ash carried on the restless wind. Where moments before there had been war cries and clashing steel, now only the whispers of mourning remained.

The survivors moved among the fallen with slow, burdened steps. Brothers, fathers, daughters, and friends bent low, their hands trembling as they touched lifeless faces, preparing them for rites that could not wait. Tradition demanded swiftness—souls had to be guided, honored, and released before the next dawn.

Above them, the heavens churned. Streaks of crimson, violet, and gold tore across the sky, a cosmic tapestry of grief and defiance. The colors clashed fiercely, as though the world itself wept for the dead. In their brilliance was a cruel contrast—vivid life painted over lifeless ground.

Families knelt beside loved ones, whispering farewells through quivering lips. The words carried hope for safe passage into the realm of ancestors, even as their voices cracked under grief. Elders stood in solemn ranks, robes rippling in the wind. Their chants—low, resonant, mournful—rose like a bridge between the living and the departed, each syllable laden with centuries of devotion.

At the center of it all lay the grave of Tribe Leader Parth. His warriors, battered and bloodied, stood guard over him with unflinching eyes. Their grief burned with anger, their sorrow hardened into resolve. Parth's fall had scarred them, yet it had also bound them. His name would not vanish with the storm; it would be carried as a weapon into every battle to come.

The sky's shifting hues mirrored their hearts: turmoil, loss, resilience. The clash of color was the clash within them—life against death, despair against endurance.

Then Spiritual Leader Ohm stepped forward. His arms lifted high, his frail frame silhouetted against the heavens. His voice, worn but steady, carried like thunder across the quiet plain. Ancient words, older than memory, poured from him—words to guide, to sanctify, to grant release.

As his final chant fell away, the heavens softened. The wild sky melted into amber light, washing the field in calm. It was the sign they had prayed for: peace had reached the fallen.

From the rear ranks, another figure emerged—Supreme-Elder Raj. Draped in a robe of deep indigo, lined with threads of gold, he carried himself with an authority that stilled the air. His presence was not mournful but resolute, a reminder that even in ruin, order and vision must remain.

Raj raised his staff, carved from an ancient tree, and drove it into the earth beside Parth's grave. The ground quivered, and the faint outline of a sigil glowed beneath the soil, binding the battlefield as sacred ground. His voice rang out, low yet commanding, echoing in every ear:

"This place shall never be forgotten. By this mark, Parth and all who fell beside him are bound to our lineage. Their sacrifice is not loss—it is covenant. Their blood sown into this earth will birth the defiance needed for the wars yet to come."

The battlefield was no longer a place of carnage but of consecration. Soil and blood had mingled into sacred ground, and the memory of this day would anchor generations to come.

The survivors turned at last, their hearts heavy but their resolve unshaken. They carried with them grief like a brand—and with it, the promise that Parth's sacrifice, and all the others', would forge the path of the future.

The medical bay of a Servacraft reeked of antiseptic and iron, the air heavy with the groans of the wounded and the clipped murmurs of overworked staff. Beds and gurneys filled the chamber, soldiers lined in rows—some stitched, some splinted, all marked by the brutal simplicity of rocks, blades, and desperation.

Among the chaos moved Lieutenant Encrypt. Slim, steady-handed, his presence cut through the disorder like a scalpel. Fair skin, black curls swept high, and the white streak at his right temple marked him as unmistakable even in the crowd. Though a soldier, he carried himself like something more—part healer, part scholar, his mind always at work even as his hands bound wounds.

He knelt by a comrade laid out on a gurney, ankle swollen and twisted. With precise motions, Encrypt wound a stabilizer around the joint, layering specialized cotton infused with regenerative compounds; the strips overlapped neatly under his steady hands.

"How long before I can get back in the field, brother?" the soldier gritted out, jaw tight.

Encrypt's eyes flicked over the injury, his tone matter-of-fact. "Multiple fractures with a sprain. Three days, if you follow the treatment."

The soldier groaned like he'd been shot all over again. "Three days? That's too long. Fighting is all I know."

Encrypt cocked an eyebrow, lips twitching with dry amusement. "And if you rush it, you'll be lucky to limp again in a month. Unless you'd prefer I book you early retirement papers now."

The man's eyes widened, horrified. "A month? Haven forbid. Might as well retire early and collect a pension."

For a moment, laughter rippled between them—small, genuine, a spark of light in a chamber drowning in shadows. The sound was brief, but it lingered, proof that even in war, there was room for wit, for humanity.

Aboard a Servacraft, far from the home they once knew, Dr. Von and his daughter Ara endured lives they had never chosen. In their cabin, Von stood by a rain-speckled viewport, watching storm clouds curl over distant mountains. The alien landscape mirrored the turmoil within him. Flashbacks came unbidden: Petrichore in flames, the chaos of his abduction, everything torn from him in a single day.

It had been only a year ago, yet the memories lived like scars.

That morning had begun as so many others at Sigtrait Laboratory, the biotech pinnacle Von himself had built. He arrived in a crisp shirt and dark jeans, coffee in hand, sunglasses perched carelessly on his face—his effortless charm a shield against the pressure of genius.

"Late again," teased Dr. Cal, his assistant, waving a tablet filled with data. Cal—"Uncle Cal" to Ara—was more family than colleague, eccentric tie askew, hair wild, eyes sharp.

Von smirked, raising his cup. "I am never late. I arrive precisely when I intend to."

Ms. Pan at reception handed him a stack of mail. Von caught it with a distracted nod, then tossed it toward the bin. The envelopes scattered across the marble floor. He didn't break stride. "Hold all my calls, Ms. Pan. Not even Dia gets through—though, knowing my wife, she'll outsmart you anyway."

Cal arched a brow, catching the faint fatigue behind Von's grin. "Breakthroughs wait for no one. And speaking of breakthroughs…" He thrust the tablet into Von's hands. "DNA Thread-Six analysis just came in. You'll want to see this."

Von's eyes lit, scanning the streams of data. "Finally. The thread we've been chasing."

Cal folded his arms. "Try to look less smug, boss, or people might think you planned it."

Von flashed his lopsided grin. "Of course I planned it. I plan everything. I am Dr. Von, Petrichoren genius."

For a brief, fragile moment, life felt normal: the hum of researchers, the promise of discovery, friends bantering in the lab they had built together.

Then Ara's voice crackled through Cal's comm device, bright and teasing from her university. "Uncle Cal! Good morning. Is Dad with you? Mom's been trying to reach him all morning, but—"

Her words cut short. A distant explosion thundered through the line. Another blast followed, louder, drowning her voice. The connection died in static.

Von staggered as if struck. "Ara!" He grabbed the device, trembling, desperate to reconnect. Nothing but silence.

The first explosion ripped through the lab. Sirens screamed, lights flickered, smoke and fire surged through the corridors. The pristine building became an inferno.

"Von, move!" Cal shouted.

They bolted through choking smoke, elevators dead, stairwells crumbling. The lobby lay in ruins, its proud glass doors obliterated, debris and bodies strewn across the floor. Von froze at the sight of Ms. Pan, crushed beneath her desk. His stomach twisted. "What in the grave is happening?"

Explosions echoed closer. Then—footsteps. Heavy. Measured.

Two figures emerged from the smoke—cyber-enhanced soldiers, one in black-and-yellow armor, the other in black-and-red. Their visors were blank, their insignias of the Ikannunaa Empire gleaming. Upon their arms burned the dreaded mark of the I.R.S, the Royal Squadron.

The one in yellow spoke, his voice metallic through the modulator. "Droid! Dr. Von — where is your wife, Professor Dia Von?"

Von's fists clenched. "I don't know—and why is that your concern? People are dying out there! Who are you?"

The red-armored operative stepped forward, his tone flat and commanding. "Droid! Save your questions for him. You're coming with us."

Cal moved, planting himself between them. "He's not going anywhere."

The operative's reply was a gunshot.

Cal staggered, blood blooming across his chest. Von caught him, horror twisting into rage. "Cal! Stay with me!"

Cal's breaths were shallow, his voice a rasp. "Whatever they want from you... make them regret it. Counsel them... about who we are... brother."

Von gripped his hand, tears streaming. "I swear. They will regret this."

The light faded from Cal's eyes. Von roared, snatching a shard of glass, charging at the operative in red. But before the strike landed, a tranquilizer dart pierced his neck. The world spun, darkness swallowing him whole.

When he awoke, he was no longer on Petrichore. The sterile hum of a Servacraft replaced the chaos of fire and ash. Weak, disoriented, he stumbled toward the viewport—only to see his world burning below. Petrichore was a graveyard: cities aflame, skies black with smoke, his people dying by the thousands.

The door hissed open. A man entered, tall, uniform immaculate, insignias of the Ikannunaa glinting in the dim light. His scarred face twisted into a grin that carried no warmth.

"I am him," the man said, arrogance dripping from every syllable. He gestured toward the viewport, to the ruin of Petrichore reflected in his cold eyes.

"Any questions?"

In the present, Ara slipped quietly from her room, a book still open in her hand. The cabin they shared aboard the Servacraft felt more like a refuge than a prison: three small bedrooms arranged around a common room where a modest fire crackled in the hearth. Its glow softened the edges of worn furniture, giving the space a warmth that defied the cold metal hull outside.

Ara's braid, long and thick, brushed her back as she moved toward the center of the room. The fading light of day kissed her fair skin, her casual clothes falling easily against her slim frame. Outspoken by nature, restless in spirit, she carried an energy that contrasted with the stillness around her.

She paused. Her father stood by the rain-speckled window, unmoving, his stare distant. The storm had passed, leaving the world outside painted gold. Trees swayed gently in the breeze, their silhouettes a rhythm of peace that did not reach him.

"Dad?" Ara called softly.

He didn't answer.

"Dad?" Louder this time, worry edging her voice.

Still no response. She closed her book and crossed the room, laying a hand gently on his arm. Her voice dropped to a whisper. "Hello? Dad. Snap out of it. Come back to me."

Von blinked, reality flickering back into his eyes. He turned to her, the haunted distance fading—but not gone.

"Are you all right?" Ara asked, studying him.

"I'm fine," he said, though his voice carried shadows too heavy for the word.

She tilted her head toward the table, where his dinner sat untouched, congealed into something unappetizing. Her brows arched. "I assume you haven't eaten. Shame. The gruel tonight was exquisite—fit for a rat."

Von chuckled, the sound brief but real. "Ah, the critic returns."

Their eyes met, and for a moment the firelight bound them together— father and daughter, survivors tethered by love and loss. Von reached for her hand, his grip steady but weighted with unspoken grief.

"Ara," he said quietly, his gaze holding hers. "Never forget the love your mother had for you. Or the pain of losing her. When the time comes, those memories will give you strength."

Ara's throat tightened. Tears welled as her mind filled with images of her mother—the warmth of her embrace, the comfort of her laughter, the safety of her presence. She nodded, unable to speak, and leaned into the moment, the firelight reflecting the ache and resilience in both their eyes.

Inside one of the few clay huts left standing after the slaughter, Spiritual Leader Ohm sat cross-legged before a fire no larger than a cupped hand. His robe, woven in colors that carried the heritage of his people, pooled around him in folds of red, blue, and brown. A necklace of beads and ancient stones rested heavy against his chest, anchoring him in the duty he bore. Upon his brow, white paint formed a sacred sigil; feathers and gold laced his headdress, crowning him with quiet authority.

His palms lay open on his knees, steady in the smoky air. From a wooden bowl before him, herbs and sacred stones burned, sending tendrils of fragrant smoke curling upward. It was an old scent—earth, ash, memory.

As the smoke thickened, Ohm's spirit drifted beyond the confines of flesh. The world around him dimmed, and the veil parted.

Visions came.

Five hooded figures stood in a perfect circle, their robes flowing like woven light. They radiated an aura that was neither wholly mortal nor wholly divine— halos of silver and gold flickered faintly above them. Power rolled from their forms, serene yet overwhelming, like the tide of creation itself.

One stepped forward. Their face was hidden by brilliance, but their hand rose, beckoning him closer. When they spoke, their voice was both thunder and whisper, echoing deep into the marrow of his soul.

"You are free, Ohm. You are free. Wake up."

The words struck like lightning.

Ohm's eyes flew open. His body jolted upright, lungs dragging in air as though he had been drowning. Sweat streaked his painted brow, his chest heaved, and the small hut seemed to sway around him. The fire flickered wildly, shadows dancing against cracked walls.

His necklace, warmed by his racing heart, pressed into his skin as a reminder of the burden he carried. With shaking hands, he steadied his headdress and tried to calm his breath.

"What was that?" he whispered, his voice raw, half in awe, half in fear.

The vision clung to him—the circle, the halos, the command that rattled him to the bone. Something greater than mortal comprehension had reached across the veil to touch him.

Outside, night spread across the land, swallowing the battlefield in silence. In that silence, Ohm felt the truth: a new dawn was coming. One of trial, one of fragile hope—and one where the will of the divine had begun to stir.

Days bled into weeks, weeks into months, and the tribe's homeland in Goa—once a place of peace and heritage—became unrecognizable. The Ikannunaa Empire spread its shadow across the land, their banners of conquest planted in every corner. Alien structures rose like an infection, vast monoliths clawing at the sky, their presence a blight upon ancestral soil. Built by the calloused hands of the conquered, these towering forms stood as monuments not to progress but to subjugation.

The surrounding tribes resisted, clinging to the land their ancestors had defended for centuries. They fought with valor, with sacrifice that would have stirred the tears of their forebears. But valor was no match for the merciless machine of Ikannunaa conquest. Their resistance broke, crushed beneath a tide of brutal precision.

General Scorpiondt's decree was absolute: no age, no title, no sacred role excused one from servitude. Elders whose wisdom had once guided generations were lashed to blocks of stone, forced to drag them beneath a punishing sun. Children, their voices meant for laughter and learning, strained at crude ropes and splintered boards, their small hands bleeding against alien weight. Warriors and mothers alike bent their backs to build fortresses not their own.

The clay soil—once fertile with crops and traditions—was scarred, hollowed, and desecrated. What had been a canvas of life was reduced to foundations of despair. Each stone laid was more than just construction; it was a fragment of their culture buried, their spirit bound tighter to the yoke.

The Elders' eyes dimmed, their gazes hollow from exhaustion. Children wept in silence when lashes found their skin. And the warriors who had once defended every tree and stream now endured in silence, watching their world become a graveyard of memory.

Yet, in the long shadows of the alien towers, something flickered. A seed buried deep, invisible but alive. In every clenched jaw, every tear unshed, every glance toward the horizon, a quiet defiance endured. The Ikannunaa sought to erase a people—but beneath the weight of stone and sorrow, hope remained. Fragile, yes. But hope nonetheless.

One morning, the sun rose over Goa heavy with dread. Soldiers stormed the village, barking orders as they split the people into two groups: twenty adolescent boys, still more youth than warrior, and nineteen of the tribe's most revered elders.

Their task was brutal and humiliating: to raise a monument for their oppressors—a white stone triangle, vast and cold, meant to glorify the Ikannunaa. Around its base lay enormous rectangular blocks, each one so massive that even many hands together could barely move them.

The soldiers drove the groups forward. The sun blazed mercilessly, turning sweat to mud on their dust-caked skin. Above, black birds circled, their sharp cries ringing like omens.

At the foot of the monument sat Supreme-Elder Raj. The red cloth tied around his right arm marked him as the highest elder, bearer of ancestral wisdom. His long white beard, deep-set eyes, and weathered face carried years of counsel and healing, but today his hands gripped rough rope instead of herbs. Once a master of medicine, he now strained against stone, the ropes burning blisters into his palms.

High on the structure, the boys and elders bound ropes around their waists, preparing to drag one of the massive stones upward. Raj gave the signal, and together they pulled. The stone inched, groaning against gravity. Muscles shook. Breaths came in ragged gasps.

Then—*crack*.

The ropes snapped.

A scream rose as several elders pitched backward, stumbling into the gaping hollow at the structure's peak. Their cries ended in a sickening silence, swallowed by the abyss.

But one did not fall.

Abhay—Raj's younger brother, his opposite in spirit but equal in stature—moved with the reflexes of a seasoned fighter. His blade flashed, severing the rope at his waist. He slammed onto the stone surface, rolled, and rose to his feet. His gray beard clung to his chest, his piercing eyes blazing with fury.

"Lower yourselves—now!" he roared to the boys.

He slashed their ropes before the soldiers could react, freeing them from the death-pull. They collapsed onto the platform, shaken but alive.

Below, Raj sat on the next stone prepared for hoisting, sipping water from a wooden bowl to soothe his parched throat. He did not see the block tumbling from above until a young boy's scream shattered the air.

"Supreme-Elder!"

Raj looked up just as the stone plummeted, ropes flailing like broken wings. Impact thundered through the earth. Dust and fragments exploded outward. When it cleared, there was no movement beneath the ruin. Water and blood seeped together into the soil, a permanent stain, a wound the land itself would remember.

The boy stumbled to the wreckage, choking back sobs as he pulled the elder's limp hand free. Clutched within it was the red cloth. With trembling fingers, he tied it around his own arm.

Tears streaked his cheeks, yet grief hardened into resolve. A vow. A seed of defiance.

When he rose, the child no longer moved like a boy. Something within him had awakened, shaped by anguish into resolve. The red cloth, bright against his skin, was no longer a symbol of loss alone—it was the birthmark of rebellion.

Dr. Von stood frozen at his worksite, soil-sampling tools dangling uselessly from his hands. The tragedy he had just witnessed—the collapse of the stone, the death of Supreme-Elder Raj—hung in the air like ash. But it was the boy, trembling and broken, clutching the red cloth that struck Von deepest. That fabric, bright against the dust, burned into his thoughts like a brand—remembrance, resistance, something larger than either of them.

The boy's grief shifted into rage. His young face, streaked with tears, hardened as he spotted a soldier barking orders, forcing women to drag the bodies of the fallen. With small fists clenched, he marched across the scarred earth, sandals crunching against the earth.

The soldier never looked up.

The boy jabbed him in the back. When the man turned, the child exploded—a storm of punches, wild and desperate, slamming into the soldier's armored abdomen. The blows did little more than irritate, but they carried the weight of loss, of defiance. The soldier staggered back, dropping his device in surprise.

Von's heart lurched. He tossed his equipment aside and sprinted forward.

The soldier recovered, face twisting with fury. He shoved the boy to the ground, hand dropping to the holster at his hip. A beam gun hissed to life, its glow casting a deadly reflection in the boy's wide, terrified eyes.

Von didn't think. He moved.

He stepped between them, his body shielding the boy. "He's just a child," Von said firmly, his voice steady despite the tremor of rage beneath it. "Upset. Confused. He doesn't know what he's doing."

The tension broke with the weight of a new voice.

"Enough."

The word cut the air like a blade.

General Scorpiondt strode into view, the storm itself seeming to bow before his presence. His towering frame and scarred face drew silence from soldier and civilian alike. Even without raising his weapon, his authority was absolute.

The soldier immediately lowered his gun, bowing his head.

Scorpiondt's gaze fixed on the boy, narrowing with cruel disdain. "Stay away from my men," he said coldly, "or you'll meet the same fate as your pitiful elder." His words landed like hammer blows, deliberate and merciless.

Then he turned to Von.

"And you," Scorpiondt sneered. "Remember your place. Every time you interfere, you gamble with more than your own life. Your daughter's safety, Doctor, hangs on your obedience." His lips curled into a smirk. "Why waste yourself protecting this boy… when you couldn't even save your people on Petrichore?"

Von's hands clenched into fists. His jaw tightened, breath sharp through his nose. Guilt flared like acid in his chest, but it fused with something stronger—anger, resolve, a fire that refused to be smothered.

He held Scorpiondt's glare, his own eyes burning.

For the first time since his capture, Von allowed the General to see it—the spark of defiance that no threat could extinguish.

By midday, Ara's cabin flickered with the pale glow of a hologram. Her father's image shimmered in blue light above the console near the door—familiar, weary, yet steady.

"I'll be working late at the lab," Von said, his tone clipped but softening at the end. "The cold box is empty. Order something for dinner, sweetheart. And remember—stay out of trouble."

The transmission cut.

Ara's shoulders sank. She had been hoping for more—just a shared meal, a conversation, a moment that reminded her of home. Instead, silence filled the cabin.

She wandered the small space, fingers trailing absently along the back of the sofa, her braid brushing her shoulder as she thought. The fire crackled gently, but its warmth did little to ease the restless ache. Hours stretched ahead of her, empty.

Her gaze drifted to the door. Outside lay a world she had never touched—alien, dangerous, alive with mystery. The thought stirred something fierce inside her: curiosity, longing, defiance.

Gathering her resolve, she approached the guard posted outside. "I'd like permission to step beyond the Servacraft," she said evenly.

The soldier studied her, then promised to relay her request to his superior. Ara thanked him, sliding the door closed again, her pulse quickening. The mere possibility set her heart racing.

An hour later, drowsiness claimed her. Curled beneath a blanket on the sofa, she drifted into sleep—until a sharp knock startled her awake.

She rubbed her eyes and opened the door. A soldier stood there, taller than most, armored head to toe. His chest plate gleamed with four silver medals, each etched with symbols she did not recognize. The weight of his presence filled the doorway.

"Permission granted, Ms. Von," he said, his voice crisp, professional. "I've been assigned to ensure your safety outside the craft."

Ara blinked against the fading remnants of sleep, then straightened, her tone steady though curiosity tugged at her. "Thank you. Give me a moment to gather a few things."

As the door closed again, she leaned against it for a heartbeat, exhaling. He wasn't like the others—his bearing was sharper, more controlled, his silence heavy with experience. For a fleeting moment, she wondered about his story. Yet she did not dwell on it.

The world beyond the Servacraft was waiting.

The craft loomed dark against the forest's edge, its matte hull stark against the riot of green. When the side door slid open, Ara stepped into daylight for the first time since her captivity began. The soldier assigned to escort her followed close behind, his armored boots crunching on the soil.

The world outside was alive. Alien flowers bloomed in wild profusion, their colors impossibly bright. Air thick with fragrance clung to Ara's skin, and strange birdsong wove through the canopy. For a heartbeat, she forgot the war, the loss, the shadow of the Ikannunaa. Her eyes widened with awe.

Then—something wholly absurd.

A white rabbit hopped across their path, calm as a priest in procession. Between its teeth gleamed a large gold coin, clinking softly as it bounded into the brush.

Ara blinked. The soldier stared. For a long moment, neither spoke.

Finally, Ara let out a soft laugh. "Well… that was odd."

They pressed on, deeper beneath the canopy where sunlight dappled the ground. Ara breathed it in, joy flickering across her face. "I've never seen anything like this. Not even on Petrichore."

From her shoulder bag, she drew gloves, a cutter, and specimen bags, moving through the foliage with careful precision. Snip by snip, she filled her kit, until she froze before a flower the color of living fire. Its crimson petals shimmered with a strange aura.

"Blood Pinnacle," Ara whispered, the name almost a prayer. Memory tugged at her chest: her mother tending flowers back home, their beauty a sacred household ritual. She swallowed hard, snipped a few, and carefully labeled the bag.

The soldier's voice broke the silence. "What do you plan to do with them?"

"Genetic testing," Ara replied, slipping the bag into her satchel. "On Petrichore, the Blood Pinnacle was more than a flower—it was heritage. It mattered to my mother. I need to know if this is the same… or just a cruel resemblance."

He said nothing, but followed as she worked until at last she declared, "I think I've seen enough." They retraced their steps toward the Servacraft, her bag heavy with samples.

As they walked, Ara turned. "What's your name?"

The soldier hesitated. "Why ask?"

"Every uniform I've seen has a nameplate," Ara said, eyeing his chest plate. "Except yours."

A chuckle rumbled from inside his helmet. "I wanted to see if you'd notice." With that, he unstrapped the helmet and lifted it free.

Ara's breath caught. He was young, dark-haired save for a white streak above his right temple. His smile was confident, disarming. His eyes—warm brown, piercing—locked on hers with a steadiness that unsettled her pulse.

"Ledge. Captain Ledge," he said at last, his voice softened now. "It's a pleasure, Ara."

Her cheeks warmed despite herself. "You can just call me Ara."

"Only if you call me Ledge."

They smiled, and walked on. To fill the silence, Ara lifted one of the flowers to the light. "My father once told me my mother noticed him for the first time because of one of these. He wore a single Blood Pinnacle pinned to his coat."

Ledge's expression softened. "I noticed you before you ever held that flower."

Her heart skipped—but faltered at his next question. "Where is your mother? I've only seen your father aboard the Servacraft."

Ara's voice thinned. "I don't know. They took us without her. I can only hope… someday."

Ledge reached as if to touch her shoulder, then pulled back. "I'm sorry. I can't imagine."

Silence followed them back to the cabin. At her door, Ara turned with a small smile. "Thank you—for the company."

"It was my pleasure," Ledge said, though his eyes carried something unspoken. "And remember, if you ever need someone to talk to—or to explore this strange world again—I'll be here."

Ara hesitated, then nodded. "That would be nice."

The door slid closed behind her. Alone in the cabin's familiar glow, Ara pressed the Blood Pinnacle to her chest. Something had shifted. The world outside had called to her—and so had Captain Ledge.

Later that evening, the Prominent blazed with light. Its vast dining hall shimmered like a jewel, the chamber a masterpiece of alien grandeur. Crystalline chandeliers fell from the ceiling like captured stars, casting fractured rainbows over walls draped in tapestries of conquest. Every surface gleamed with the wealth and history of the Ikannunaa Royal Empire, power made architecture.

At long tables, dignitaries from across the stars mingled. Royalty, diplomats, and chancellors of distant systems leaned close, their words cloaked in courtesy but edged with calculation. The twins' reach was evident: to decline their invitation was to risk irrelevance.

Aromatic dishes from countless galaxies filled the tables, plates laden with rare delicacies whose scents mingled into a heady perfume. Tribal servants, their uniforms tailored to disguise servitude as ceremony, carried trays of the famed Black Wine. Its velvet hue gleamed in crystal goblets, loosening tongues, stoking the tension beneath the elegance.

Behind a silken veil, a hidden orchestra played. Strange instruments produced haunting, hypnotic strains that threaded through the air, binding the guests in a collective spell. Yet beneath the revelry, a disquiet hummed—an unspoken understanding that alliances born here could alter the fates of worlds.

Then the music ceased. A hush rippled outward as a figure stepped into the hall's center. He was of the tribe: skin burnished brown beneath the crystalline glow, mustache curled, a red cloth bound proudly about his head. His voice, when it rose, was a river of power and sorrow.

He sang the old ballads: songs of love, loss, and freedom stolen then fought for. His voice swelled with ache and resilience, and soon the tribe's musicians joined him, their rhythms transforming lament into anthem. The hall held its breath as the sound carried, weaving memory and defiance into every note.

High above, on a cliff that overlooked the Prominent's gleaming hull, three figures watched the lights below. Elder Abhay stood tall, Raj's bamboo staff clenched in his fist, fury burning in his eyes. Beside him knelt Spiritual Leader Ohm, robed and solemn, smoke from the herbs at his side drifting into the night. With them stood a young fighter, restless and reverent.

"Do the visions persist, Ohm?" Abhay's voice was steady, urgent.

"They do," Ohm murmured, his eyes fixed on the Prominent's glow. His voice was otherworldly, as if carried by the wind itself.

The fighter stepped closer. "What do you see, Spiritual Leader? What do they reveal?"

Ohm's gaze deepened, distant. "I see five descending from the heavens, robed in darkness yet radiant with light. They do not come as conquerors, but as protectors. Saviors, bound to this world's fate."

The fighter's breath caught. "Who are they?"

Ohm shook his head slowly. "Their faces are veiled. They may be our ancestors, risen to guide us. Or gods, reclaiming what is theirs."

Back in the hall, the song reached its peak—and then shifted. Twenty-five women from the tribe swept in, their entrance a cascade of jewels and fabric. Their costumes shimmered in a thousand hues, catching the crystalline lights at every turn.

The dance began: slow, precise, each gesture telling stories older than the hall itself. Their bodies undulated with resilience and unity, their footwork tracing the memory of survival. Guests leaned forward, some swaying unconsciously to the rhythm, eyes wide at a tradition older than their empires.

Lord Nailatper of Angtroma, famed collector of art and beauty, watched with rapt delight. His laughter rang as he drew a bundle of gold currency from his coat. With a flourish, he tossed it high. The coins glittered as they fell, raining down like stars over the dancers.

The performance ended in a blaze of motion and sound. Applause erupted, thunderous and unrestrained. Guests rose to their feet, their cheers echoing against the vaulted ceiling. The dancers bowed, their faces glowing with pride, and in that moment the hall was alive with awe.

But above, in the silence of the cliffside, Abhay's grip tightened on the bamboo staff. Ohm's voice lingered in his ear like a prophecy: five would come, not to destroy, but to save.

And as the last note of applause faded, the hall—despite its splendor—felt like the stage of something far larger, waiting to unfold.

As the revelry in the grand hall dwindled, three of the Twin Royals' closest allies were escorted into a private lounge hidden deep within the Prominent. The room radiated quiet luxury: crescent velvet seats arranged around a circular wooden table, a fur rug spread beneath, and a gold-and-glass sculpture glittering under the inverted diamond-and-gold chandelier crafted in the shape of a tree. Intricate gray walls gleamed with gold borders, embossed patterns catching the light. Fresh green floral arrangements—rare blooms from distant Nimbbiraa-Three—breathed life into the chamber's polished air.

On the table, plates of jewel-toned pastries and steaming cups of Goa's black coffee awaited. King Nephilesis of Broche Reine Kingdom—heavyset, flushed, and long into his reign—sank deep into the cushions, wine having loosened his voice and dulled his edge. His wife, Queen Angeliqonn, perched elegantly at his side, eyes sharp despite the haze of wine. Opposite them sat Snob the Great, merchant king of entire star routes, his arrogance filling more space than his wealth ever could.

"Tell me," Nephilesis slurred with curiosity. "Why this grand celebration, on a planet you have only just claimed? What is the true occasion?"

Prince Atsu-els's smile was sly. He clapped three times. The door opened, and a server entered—tall, broad-shouldered, the bearing of a once-proud warrior now reduced to servitude. Upon his golden tray rested a single lit candle, five engraved forks, folded handkerchiefs, and five rolled Flat-Paper cigars.

"Better late than never," Queen Angeliqonn quipped, eyeing the smokes with cutting sarcasm.

Each guest plucked a Flat-Paper, lit it from the flame, and drew in the sweet smoke. It thickened the room, softening its edges into haze. Snob exhaled a stream deliberately into the server's face, laughing as the man bowed and turned away without a word. The room roared with boozy amusement at the cruelty, their mirth trailing after the departing servant.

When silence returned, Atsu-els leaned forward. "The truth is simple. This planet is richer than it appears. Its soil is laced with gold particles beyond measure. Enough to stabilize the Ventral Bands of Nimbbiraa-One itself, ensuring our atmosphere for generations."

The weight of the statement sank in, even through the fog of alcohol.

"But," Atsu-els continued, eyes glinting, "we cannot remain here. Politics will draw us back to Nimbbiraa-Three. Extraction is underway, but we will leave behind guardians—five surrogates—to enforce our will for millennia."

His voice darkened. "The Alpha-Gene Fluid Project has begun on Nimbbiraa-Five. The red fluid, when injected, alters the sequence 0-1101-q. Hosts become super-humanoids—faster, stronger, more resilient than anything this world has known."

Prince Ata-els, quieter yet more precise, interjected. "There is also the Beta fluid. Green, not red. Its purpose is control, not strength. The humans of this planet carry... peculiar qualities. Should they rise against us, the Beta fluid will strip their will. Lobotomized cattle, pliant forever."

The air chilled despite the haze of smoke.

King Nephilesis, uneasy, looked down at the folded handkerchiefs. His fingers tightened. Four were white. His, alone, was red.

"Why did he give me this one?" he muttered, suspicion creeping into his tone.

For a moment, the room hung heavy. Then Atsu-els laughed, wine spilling in his throat. "A mistake! Our poor servant, distracted by his own incompetence."

The others joined in, their laughter loud and forced, eager to dissolve the tension. The smoke swirled higher, disguising unease with merriment, while above them the chandelier glittered like a mockery of stars.

In the confines of the laboratory, the hum of machines filled the silence between two weary men. Beeps from monitors punctuated the low thrum of power coursing through alien technology. Among it all, Dr. Von and his closest aide, Dr. Jidohtta, sat with plates of leftovers from the Twin Royals' banquet—a rare indulgence that tasted faintly of both luxury and guilt.

"Tell me something," Jidohtta said at last, eyes narrowing over the rim of his cup. "Why are the Ikannunaa so intent on this fluid project? These humans are no threat. Primitive, fractured. It feels like a waste."

Von leaned back, exhaustion shadowing his features like a wine stain. He toyed with his fork, then answered, voice steady but edged. "Primitive for now. But the Ikannunaa think centuries ahead. Absolute control is the insurance they crave. This fluid ensures genetic sabotage that can't be undone—passed through generations like a curse. One day, humans could evolve into something formidable. Better to chain them early."

Jidohtta frowned, unsettled. "Then why involve you? Surely others could handle this… monstrosity."

Von's eyes lit with the glint of a secret. He leaned forward, lowering his tone. "Because I discovered something no one else has. The Carbon Wall. A hidden barrier within the human genome, sequence 1-0000-x. It resists tampering, shields the code itself. Breaking through it will take time, precision. A year, perhaps more. These people are far more unique than anyone imagined."

The revelation left Jidohtta silent, his mind racing. After a moment, he pressed further. "And the soil testing? What was its real purpose?"

Von's smile was faint, weary, but laced with bitterness. "Gold. The Royals want to strip this planet bare. Their own atmosphere on Nimbbiraa-one is failing. By detonating gold dust bombs into the Ventral Bands, they believe they can stabilize the shield. But one miscalculation... and their world becomes an airless stone."

Jidohtta exhaled sharply, the scale of it pressing down on him. For a while, they said nothing, listening to the sterile hum of machines. At last Von rose, stretching stiff muscles. "Enough. We should call it a night."

But before they reached the door, a faint ringing came from Jidohtta's coat pocket. He froze, then pulled out a small device. His features softened as the hologram flickered to life, projecting the image of a girl no older than eight.

"Hi, sweetie," Jidohtta said, forcing warmth into his voice. "Is your mother home?"

"No, Dad. She's still at work. Grandma's asleep." Her innocent eyes searched his. "Do you know when you're coming back?"

The question pierced him. His throat tightened. "I don't know yet, princess. But when I do, you'll be the first to know."

A silence hung—until her small, certain voice shattered him. "I wish you didn't have to hurt the people on that planet. They don't deserve it."

The words rooted him in place. His fingers shook around the device. His voice came low, broken. "I wish I didn't either. But they've threatened you, and your mother. If I resist, you're the ones who pay. Only a hero stronger than me could stop this. For now... it's the sacrifice I must make." He swallowed hard, forcing steadiness into his tone. "Focus on your studies. Keep Mom safe. That's how you help me."

Her sigh carried a weight far beyond her years. "Alright, Dad… love you."

"Love you more. Always."

The hologram blinked out, leaving the room darker than before.

Jidohtta set the device down with trembling hands, then shoved it away. His shoulders curled inward, face buried in his palms as silent sobs broke free.

Von did not move. He only watched—eyes sharp, expression unreadable. He understood everything. Yet he offered no words of comfort. Only silence, as if already calculating what this grief might one day become.

Morning light streamed through the cabin windows as Dr. Von shuffled into the kitchen, slippers whispering against the floor. His stomach growled, demanding food. He reached for the cabinets—no coffee. With a groan, he settled on tea and a slice of bread, steam rising as he blew across the cup.

Ara padded in moments later, braid falling over her shoulder. She kissed him warmly on the cheek before heading for the cold box.

Her breakfast choice: leftover cake and a bottle of fizzy sweet drink from the banquet.

Von raised his brows, mock disapproval in his tone. "That's not a balanced breakfast, young lady."

Ara grinned, unfazed. "It is today." With her plate in hand, she disappeared back toward her room, leaving him shaking his head, half exasperated, half amused.

He had just lifted his tea when a sharp knock rattled the front door.

Sliding the door open, Von found himself staring at a stranger in a white lab coat, his expression icy and unreadable. Stitched into the fabric were the insignia of the Ikannunaa and another mark Von recognized from Scorpiondt's attire. The man's eyes—slitted, reptilian—swept the cabin with unsettling precision.

"Dr. Serpendt," the visitor introduced himself. "General Scorpiondt has asked me to oversee the project alongside you."

Von hesitated, then stepped aside. He offered tea, and the two men sat across from each other in the standard room.

Serpendt listened with a cryptic smile as Von explained his unease. "The timeline has been shortened. Rushed work at this scale… feels dangerously reckless."

"Reckless?" Serpendt mused, plucking the tea bag from his cup and chewing it like a delicacy. "I would call it… art."

Von stiffened. Art, to him, was creation. This was mutilation. Murder in slow motion.

Before he could respond, Ara reappeared, eyes bright. "Dad—I need to show you something in the office."

The men exchanged a final handshake, Von unsettled by Serpendt's unnerving calm. The reptilian-eyed scientist left as swiftly as he'd come.

Ara led her father to her desk. Sunlight poured across carefully arranged flowers—red, radiant, alive with an otherworldly shimmer.

"The Blood Pinnacle," Ara whispered, her voice trembling with excitement.

Von's brow furrowed. "You left the Servacraft?"

"Permission granted," she said quickly, grinning. "Don't worry. I stayed out of trouble."

She touched the petals reverently. "I found them at the forest's edge. I've studied them, Dad. They're almost identical to the Blood Pinnacle of Petrichore—the same flower Mom loved."

Her smile softened, tinged with memory. "Legends say it counteracts genetic alterations caused by disease. If the properties hold true here…"

Von's breath caught, his eyes glistening. In this alien world where despair pressed at every corner, the flower shone like a miracle.

Together, they stood in silence, gazes locked on the blossoms. The Blood Pinnacle, once a relic of the past, had become something more: a beacon of resistance, a weapon hidden in plain sight.

Father and daughter understood in the same heartbeat. This flower could mean survival.

And from that morning forward, hope no longer seemed like a dream—it felt like a plan.

The morning sun blazed overhead, merciless and unyielding. Around the rising towers of stone, laborers strained beneath its punishing glare. Sweat slicked their skin, dust clung to their bodies, and every muscle burned as they hauled the massive blocks upward. The triangular monuments, symbols of domination, loomed like scars upon the land.

Among the weary workers moved the boy—still young, yet set apart. A strip of red cloth bound tightly around his arm marked him as something more than just another laborer. It was the cloth he had taken from the fallen Supreme-Elder, and with it came the weight of remembrance and the spark of defiance.

Beside him, a young man stumbled, his voice raw with despair. "Why do we break ourselves on these stones, boy? What hope is there? No one comes to help us. We work, we bleed, and still we are nothing but slaves."

The boy paused, chest heaving, eyes shadowed by the sun. He wiped his brow, then turned to face the group of gaunt young men gathered near. Despite his small frame, his voice carried clear, firm, and unshakable.

"I know your despair," he said, the words cutting through the clamor of tools and stone. "But this cloth—" he lifted his arm, letting the red strip catch the light, "—is not only a reminder of death. It is a sign of hope."

The men exchanged uneasy glances, their eyes drawn to him despite themselves.

"When I was nearly killed," the boy continued, "when a soldier's light burned toward me, a man appeared. A man in a long white coat. He shielded me, and in that moment, he whispered words I cannot forget: Our people will rise again, but only if we hold on to hope and belief."

He stepped closer, his young face set with a resolve beyond his years. "Hope gives birth to belief, and belief gives strength to endure. Without one, the other dies. We may not see freedom tomorrow, or the day after, but if we endure—if we resist, even in small ways—then freedom will come."

One of the men muttered, almost scoffing, "Hope and belief? Words cannot shatter chains."

The boy's gaze hardened. "No—but they can keep us alive until we are strong enough to break them. They can remind us that these towers we raise today will one day fall. And when they do, the red cloth will not stand for grief— it will stand for the unity and resilience that carried us through the fire."

A heavy silence followed. The men stared at him, the words settling like seeds in scorched soil. Their doubt did not vanish, but it shifted, leaving room for something new—something fragile, but alive.

The sun still scorched, the stones still crushed, yet when they bent to their labor again, their movements carried a different weight. Not just submission, but defiance. Not just toil, but quiet rebellion.

The red cloth no longer seemed a relic of sorrow. It was a banner—small, tattered, but burning against the light.

And in that moment, among dust and sweat and searing heat, a seed of liberation took root.

The underbelly of the Prominent throbbed with the hum of engines. Deep within its labyrinth, General Scorpiondt entered the training chamber—a place of sweat, steel, and silence.

"Lower the lights," he commanded.

"Lights set to fifty percent," the chamber's synthetic voice responded.

Shadows stretched like blades across the metallic walls. Scorpiondt moved with lethal precision, fists and feet striking in rhythm against a holographic opponent. The projection mirrored his movements, flickering in eerie blue light, but his blows landed with bone-crushing power. Each strike carried decades of refinement—rage distilled into discipline.

His thoughts drifted as he fought. Dr. Von. The capture. The Twin Royals' grand design. Compliance or defiance—it mattered little. Scorpiondt always had contingencies.

After a final flurry, he disengaged. Breathing steady, he crossed to the weapons rack, fingertips grazing steel and plasma alike. His hand paused on a humming energy blade, the weapon vibrating faintly, eager for blood.

Then—knuckles on metal. A sharp knock echoed through the chamber.

"Lights to full," the voice announced. "Training systems offline."

The doors hissed open. A soldier stood at attention: tall, muscular, clad in white and black. His brown eyes flickered with unease, and a streak of white ran like lightning through his black hair.

"Lieutenant Barricade," Scorpiondt said, his tone a mixture of recognition and challenge.

"You asked for me, sir?" Barricade's voice was measured, but a trace of uncertainty edged it.

"That is correct. Step inside."

The doors sealed with a hiss, cutting them off from the world above. Scorpiondt paced, his presence filling the chamber like a storm.

"Tell me," he asked suddenly, "why do all you Grenaivelans carry that white streak through your hair?"

Barricade blinked, caught off guard. "Don't know, sir. I was born with it."

"Hmph." Scorpiondt's grunt was dismissive, yet his eyes lingered, studying. He retrieved a weapon from the rack, turning it idly in his grip. "I've had my eye on you since Grenaivel. You were Keannelden Force, under Captain Ledge. That makes you no ordinary soldier."

Barricade held his silence, jaw tight.

Scorpiondt stepped closer, voice dropping to a dangerous whisper. "I believe you would make an excellent protégé of mine."

The words hung like a snare. Barricade hesitated, the pause almost imperceptible. "Yes, sir." The answer was firm—but not unshaken.

A blade whistled through the air. Barricade's reflexes caught it mid-spin, the weight solid in his palm.

"Catch."

He looked from the weapon to the General. "What do you want me to do with this, sir?"

Scorpiondt unsheathed his own energy blade. Its edges flared alive, the hum filling the chamber with menace. His lips curled into a smirk, predator toying with prey.

"Spar," he said. The word cracked like a whip. "I want to see what Captain Ledge's training left behind."

Barricade exhaled slowly, rolling his shoulders into stance. The blade felt familiar, but the tension pressing in from Scorpiondt's stare was suffocating.

The chamber fell into silence—two warriors locked in a storm of anticipation, blades gleaming in the artificial light.

The test was about to begin.

At the heart of the laboratory, science hummed like a living organism. Screens flickered with cascading data, their pale glow reflecting off steel walls and polished glass. Instruments whispered in clicks and pulses, and assistants moved with careful precision—adjusting calibrations, cross-checking figures, murmuring quietly as though the work itself demanded reverence.

Dr. Serpendt sat forward at a console, the blue light sharpening the reptilian gleam in his eyes. His fingers scrolled through molecular diagnostic files, dense streams of code unraveling across the display. Every line was a puzzle piece, every detail a stepping stone toward something neither of them dared name aloud.

Von approached slowly, his presence as steady as the hum of the machines. His voice broke the silence with practiced calm. "Dr. Serpendt. Tell me—have you studied the Carbon Wall in full, or just skimmed the briefing?"

Serpendt didn't look away from the screen. "The basics," he replied, his tone clipped, deliberate. "Enough to grasp its significance. Enough to know it is... fascinating."

There was an edge beneath the word fascinating—a hunger, almost.

Von inclined his head, watching him carefully. "Then you know this isn't just theory. The Carbon Wall isn't a quirk in the code—it's a safeguard. A barrier stitched into the human genetic chain itself. Break it, and we rewrite more than genes. We rewrite destiny."

Serpendt's lips curled into the faintest smile, his fingers pausing over the keys. "Then let us be artists with sharper brushes."

Von's expression didn't shift, though unease crawled beneath his skin. "Artists paint. We're carving into the marrow of life. Don't mistake this for beauty."

The tension hung sharp between them, a blade suspended in the air. Then, wordlessly, they both returned to their work.

Around them, the assistants resumed their rhythm, the lab swelling with a new urgency. Data scrolled faster, instruments whirred hotter, and the pulse of the room quickened as if the machines themselves sensed the weight of what was at stake.

"We crack this wall," Serpendt said suddenly, his voice slicing through the hum, "or it cracks us. So—no more time wasted."

Von gave a slight nod, settling beside him at the console. The Carbon Wall stretched before them in cascading code—unyielding, enigmatic, alive with secrets. As the hours stretched long, the men pressed deeper into the barrier, every keystroke, every calculation dragging them closer to the edge of discovery.

The Carbon Wall was not merely science. It was defiance. And both men knew—if they broke it, nothing about this planet, or its people, would ever be the same again.

The forest deepened as Ara and Captain Ledge pressed on, sunlight breaking in fractured beams through the canopy. Her satchel was already heavy with specimens, but her questions were heavier still—each one cutting into silence, each one pulling more from him than he had ever offered another.

"I belonged to Petrichore," Ara said softly, her fingers tracing a leaf veined with strange silver light. "I belonged to my parents. Now... I feel as if I don't belong to anyone."

Ledge slowed, his expression tightening. "I belonged to the Grenaivelan military once—rose through the ranks. Then Grenaivel fell. We were given a choice: bend or break." His jaw clenched. "I bent. But I never stopped feeling broken."

Ara met his eyes. "Then perhaps your place isn't in their ranks at all."

For a moment, defiance sparked in him. Then, with a gentler motion, he plucked a flower that shimmered faintly in the gloom and tucked it behind her ear. Ara's lips parted with surprise, then curved into a smile. The forest, just then, seemed almost kind.

But the kindness ended.

The underbrush erupted in a roar, and a beast surged forth—scaled black, claws raking earth, eyes ablaze with primeval fury. Its strike sent Ledge crashing into the ground, his weapon skittering into the ferns. Ara froze, heart hammering, as the monster lunged again.

Ledge grappled its limbs, straining against muscle and malice far greater than his own. He triggered a distress beacon, its shrill cry echoing through the canopy—but the beast only thrashed harder, jaws snapping inches from his throat.

Then—another presence.

A boy stepped into the clearing, bare feet sinking into moss. His arm bore the strip of red cloth. His small frame should have been nothing before the beast's rage, yet calm radiated from him like a tide. He raised his voice—not in a shout, but in a strange, melodic cadence, words rolling like a lullaby older than the trees themselves.

The beast faltered. Its claws lowered. Its breath slowed. For a suspended heartbeat, it bowed to the boy's song.

But the peace shattered.

The mist thickened, and through it came General Scorpiondt. The air bent around him, as though the land itself recoiled at his approach. Black blade in hand, his scar catching the dim light, he was storm given flesh.

The beast roared anew, roused by his presence, and turned on him.

Scorpiondt welcomed it. He moved with merciless precision, his strikes surgical, his blade carving sparks and blood from scale and sinew. Where the boy had soothed, Scorpiondt destroyed. The clash shook the ground until at last he drove his weapon through the beast's chest. Its cry split the air before silence fell like a shroud.

He stood over its corpse, steady and cold. Rain had not touched him, nor mercy.

"Escort her back," he ordered without looking at Ara. His voice was iron. "No more outings."

Ledge pushed himself upright, fury raw in his voice. "General, the boy saved us—"

"Enough." Scorpiondt's gaze silenced him. Then his eyes cut to the boy. Predator met prey. "And you. This was the last time. There will be consequences."

The boy did not flinch. His gaze held steady, fire behind his young eyes. Then, with a final glance at Ara, he slipped into the glowing foliage, vanishing as if swallowed by the forest itself.

Guards appeared to escort Ara and Ledge away. The path back to the Servacraft felt darker now, heavy with what had been witnessed.

But in Ara's mind, only one image remained: the boy with the red cloth, his voice taming the untamable. An enigma. A sign. Perhaps a spark strong enough to endure even the shadow of the Ikannunaa.

Back aboard the Servacraft, Dr. Von paced the cabin, every nerve wired with dread. The sharp echo of Captain Ledge's distress beacon still rang in his head, a sound that confirmed the very fear he lived with daily: Ara had been in danger.

The door slid open. Ara stepped inside, pale but alive, Ledge close behind her. Relief hit Von like a blow. He rushed forward, pulling his daughter into his arms as though he could lock her away from the world itself.

"Thank Rainah," he whispered, his voice raw. He drew back, scanning her face, her arms, her every breath. "What happened?"

Ara's voice shook as she told him—the beast, the boy, the calm, then Scorpiondt's brutal arrival and the killing stroke. Her words spilled out in a mix of fear and anger. "It wasn't my fault, Dad. That boy saved us. He stopped the creature. And Scorpiondt didn't care. He treated me like I was nothing. Like I was in the way."

Von's brow furrowed, his hands curling into fists. "Scorpiondt," he muttered, venom dripping from the name. "He's always where he shouldn't be."

Captain Ledge stood silent by the door, eyes lowered but steady. Von turned to him. "You may have saved her life. For that, I give thanks. But if this happens again—"

"It won't," Ledge cut in, his voice measured, firm. "I miscalculated the risk. That's on me. But she was never unprotected."

Ara's eyes flickered to him, a quiet gratitude beneath her fury.

Von exhaled slowly, tension grinding in his jaw. His gaze returned to his daughter. "Tell me again about the boy."

Ara hesitated, then nodded. "He wore a red cloth on his arm. He was… steady, somehow. Stronger than his years. He faced the beast, and it listened to him." Her throat tightened. "And when Scorpiondt threatened him, he didn't flinch. He just… vanished into the trees."

Von's expression shifted—pain mixed with something sharper. Resolve. That day, a small but defiant spark had been lit, and he knew it.

The cabin settled into silence, but not peace. For each of them carried the weight of what had happened: Ara's brush with death, Ledge's unspoken guilt, and Von's growing certainty that the boy with the red cloth was not chance, but destiny.

The Conqueror I
As told by General Scorpiondt

They call it invasion.

They call it slaughter.

Let them.

The conquered always write poetry when they lack the power to write history.

The year was 1199 by their primitive reckoning. A year of sweat, soil, and the quiet hum of insects who knew not that their sky was about to split open. I remember the way the light died that day—how the sun retreated as if shamed by what was to come. The villagers of Goa looked upward in terror, their spears trembling, their mouths agape. They believed it a storm. Nature flexing her teeth.

But it was I who arrived.

And nature stepped aside.

The Prominent cleaved through the heavens like judgment carved in obsidian. The roar of our engines was the final sermon their ancestors would ever hear. Our crafts landed with precision, not violence. It was their panic that created the chaos, not our presence. They mistook arrival for aggression. How small of them.

I gave them a choice.

I always give them a choice.

But Tribe Leader Parth, that reed of a man dressed in feathers and foolishness, chose defiance. With trembling hands, he raised his staff and summoned the courage of the dead. He believed in spirits. I believed in facts. He spoke of protection; I offered purpose. He warned me to leave. I ended him.

A single shot. That is all it took.

Some say I am merciless. In truth, I am efficient. Where others hesitate, I execute. His blood watered the earth, and his cry ignited a futile spark in the hearts of his people. They charged, painted in mud and desperation. They met the edge of our precision—our steel, our flame, our calculated symmetry of force. And they fell.

The Ikannunaa Empire does not conquer recklessly. We optimize. We bring order to chaos. Structure to savagery. Resistance is not injustice—it is delay.

And delays cost lives.

Let them weep for their fallen. Let their children dig graves with trembling hands. Those who survive shall build. Their tears will mix with mortar. Their songs will echo in our halls.

You see… I am not the villain. I am the architect.

And what of Dr. Von?

Ah, yes. The reluctant genius. Dragged from the embers of Petrichore like a gem buried beneath ash. He mourns a world I dismantled in hours. A feat he has never forgiven me for—and never understood. I took his paradise and showed him the truth of its fragility. He despises me. But his intellect remains… useful. For now.

He forgets that I spared him. I spared his daughter. He thinks that makes him courageous. In truth, it makes him bound—like every other citizen who breathes at my mercy.

Ara.
A curious creature. Sharp-tongued. Unruly. Burdened by sentiment. She ventured into the wilds beyond our vessel, and there—of course—was danger. A beast born of this world's untamed edge, something even my calculations had not anticipated.

Yet it was not her strength nor Ledge's training that saved her.

It was the boy.

That boy.

He appeared like myth, but stood as man. Wielding nothing but calm. A red cloth on his arm, as if he knew its meaning. As if he designed the moment. He subdued the beast—not with force, but with presence. Even I felt it. The way the creature bent to him, for one fleeting second, before I severed its life with steel.

I did what was necessary. Mercy is not a currency I trade in.
He stood there afterward, unshaken. Unafraid.

That is… inconvenient.

I threatened him. I needed to. And yet… he did not waver. I turned my back, but I felt his eyes burn like coals against my spine. Children should not possess that kind of flame.

And yet he does.

It is not the rebellions that worry me. Not the tribes, the rituals, the chants. It is hope.

Hope is the most dangerous weapon ever forged. It is invisible. Infectious. Unquantifiable.

And now it wears a red cloth.

I have already begun the restructuring of Goa. Their temples are scaffolding now. Their soil, foundation for our monuments. Their chants, whispers in work camps. Even their eldest—once wise and sacred—now pull stone beneath the whip.

This is not cruelty. This is legacy.

They call it a massacre. I call it the laying of a cornerstone. They say we have desecrated their dead. I say we have freed them from delusion.

Let them hate me. Let them carve my name into curses.
They will do so with the tools I gave them.

Soon, the Beta-Gene Fluid will reach its full potential. Dr. Von will unlock what lies beneath the Carbon Wall. We will unspool the human spirit strand by strand, reducing it to obedience. I will erase resistance from their very blood.

And yet...

There remains one variable I cannot predict.

The boy with the red cloth.
He is not a soldier. Not a prophet. Not even trained.

But he stood still when I passed.

I have seen warriors flinch under my shadow. He did not. That... intrigues me.

I do not fear him.
But I will remember him.

Because when empires fall—and they always fall—it is not under siege from outside.
It is because something rotted within was left unattended.

I do not intend to rot.
But now... I must keep watch.

The red cloth moves.

And I… am not yet ready to crush it.

Chapter 2 | **Order To Chaos**

A year had passed since the Ikannunaa claimed Earth. Outside, golden morning light bathed alien forests in warmth, but inside the sterile laboratory complex, the world felt cold and unyielding. Screens hummed with endless data streams. Instruments blinked and chimed. Ara bent over a microscope, her mind lost in the alien plant cells dancing beneath the lens.

"Happy birthday, Ara."

The voice startled her. She spun, heart jumping, to find Dr. Serpendt standing a few steps away. His white coat bore the same insignia as General Scorpiondt's—a mark that always put her on edge. His snake-like eyes glinted, unreadable.

"How do you know that?" she asked, guarded.

"Your father told me," Serpendt replied smoothly, a smile curling at his lips. "He made sure the lab knew."

Ara let out a slow breath.
"I don't even know if it makes sense to celebrate a Petrichoren birthday on this alien planet. I'm not sure if I'm still twenty-three, or if I've already turned twenty-four. Different rotations, different years… maybe it isn't even real anymore."

Serpendt moved closer, settling into a chair opposite her. "And yet the moment still exists. Sometimes what matters is not accuracy but ritual."

Her gaze flicked to the insignia on his coat. "You carry the same mark as Scorpiondt. That means you come from the same world."

"From the same world, yes," he said, "but not the same kind. I am Dragunitile. We evolved in perpetual darkness, far beneath the surface. A place where light was a myth."

Ara frowned. "But you see perfectly well here. No signs of sensitivity. What am I missing?"

Serpendt leaned forward, eyes narrowing. "You're missing this—I altered my vision."

Her brows shot up. "Altered it? Why in the grave would you do that?"

A grin spread across his face, sharp as a blade. "So I could witness entropy properly—unfiltered, full-spectrum." He let the words hang like poison in the air.

Ara shook her head. "Do you hear yourself? That's deranged."

Unbothered, Serpendt fished a hard candy from his pocket, unwrapped it with quiet irritation, and slipped it into his mouth.

"I wouldn't take it personally," he said around the sweet. "In fact, I agree with you—pathology clarifies method. It makes for clean work."

A smirk tugged at his lips. "Though I suspect you'd disagree."

"I do," Ara shot back without hesitation.

"Of course you do."

For a moment, his eyes softened—then he began to talk. About his people. Their cold-blooded physiology. Their ruthlessness. Their brilliance. And then, about the day thieves broke into his home, murdered his family, and stole their heirlooms.

"I was grateful," he said flatly.

Ara's stomach turned. "Grateful? How could you say that?"

His gaze darkened. "Because it freed me. I avenged them. Wiped out the entire lower caste who bred such filth. Genocide, they called it. They gave me a life sentence. But I call it balance. Mercy to the strong."

Ara recoiled, disgust sharp in her voice. "That's not balance. That's evil."

Serpendt's eyes flashed irritation before he forced a calm breath. "Perhaps. Or perhaps survival makes villains of us all. Even your father, Ara."

The room chilled.

Before she could respond, he stood. Adjusted his coat. At the door, he turned back. His voice was quiet, but his words cut deep.

"Before you pass judgment on me, I suggest you do the same for your father."

The door hissed shut behind him, leaving Ara alone among the glowing screens and humming machines. His words lingered like smoke, threading doubt into her thoughts.

The meeting had drained him. Dr. Von left the laboratory with his thoughts heavy, the weight of the Beta-Gene Fluid Project gnawing at his chest. When he reached the secondary restroom—an unassuming facility reserved for service staff—he welcomed the brief chance to be alone. The main lab's unit was out of order, and this forgotten corner offered him a rare pocket of silence.

He leaned over the sink, letting the cold water run over his hands. For a moment, the steady flow drowned out the noise of his mind.

Then—voices.

Muffled, faint, but unmistakable, drifting through the air vent above the sink. He froze, turned the faucet off, and listened.

At first, it was static and fragments. Then the tones sharpened into words. His breath caught as he recognized them. General Scorpiondt. Dr. Serpendt. Bokimpa.

Von pressed closer, heart thudding.

"…once the project concludes…" Serpendt's voice, smooth, clinical.

"…eliminate the doctor and his daughter," Scorpiondt finished, his tone devoid of hesitation.

Bokimpa's snicker slithered after. "Neat. Efficient."

Von's stomach lurched. Betrayal pressed in on all sides—the men he worked beside, now conspiring against him and Ara. His mind spun, grasping for reason, but the voices gave him none.

He shifted, too suddenly. The porcelain beneath him was slick from spilled water. His footing slipped, and with a sickening crack, the side of his skull struck the toilet's edge. The world tilted, vision fragmenting into streaks of light before collapsing into black.

Above him, the voices continued, oblivious.

Scorpiondt's final words echoed through the vent, cold and commanding. "Gentlemen, if you'll excuse me—there is entertainment outside expecting my attention."

Footsteps receded. Doors shut. Silence fell.

Von lay unconscious on the cold tile, their secret safe only because fate had knocked him into darkness.

When Dr. Von awoke, the first thing he felt was the dull, throbbing pain at his temple, wrapped in bandages. The sterile white glow of the medical bay swam into focus. Monitors beeped steadily, indifferent to his confusion. Then Ara burst in.

"Dad!" Her voice cracked with relief as she rushed to his side. She embraced him tightly, trembling against him until she was certain he was real, alive.

Von's arms encircled her, his chest tightening with guilt. "I'm still here," he whispered, though the words tasted fragile.

Outside, on the rocky plain, General Scorpiondt was enjoying himself. He leaned against the hull of a Servacraft, arms folded, watching a Petrichoren soldier square off against a towering warrior of Goa. Fists cracked, boots thudded against flesh, blood mixed with spit on the ground.

Scorpiondt smiled. Violence was theater, and he always sat in the front row.

Bokimpa scurried over, bowing low. "General! Forgive the intrusion. Dr. Von has been admitted to the medical bay. He is stable. The Princes request your inspection."

Scorpiondt sighed, almost disappointed. "Just when things were getting good." He drew his sidearm and, without hesitation, shot the Goan warrior through the chest. The body collapsed mid-swing. "Pause pressed," he muttered, holstering the weapon. Then he turned and strode away.

Minutes later, the door to Von's room slid open. Scorpiondt entered with Dr. Serpendt at his side. The attending physician stiffened under their presence, offering a quick report. "Dr. Von's brain shows no damage. remain overnight under observation."

Ara's eyes darted to her father. "What happened?"

Scorpiondt repeated the question, his gaze sharp, suspicious.

Von forced a groan, rubbing his bandaged head. "I don't remember," he lied. "I must have slipped on a wet tile."

His calm tone didn't soothe the General. Suspicion lingered in the air, heavy as a blade. At last Scorpiondt waved a hand. "Clear the room."

When the door hissed shut, Ara leaned in, her stare piercing him. "You're lying."

Von sighed, the fight draining from him. "Yes," he admitted, sitting up. His voice dropped to a whisper. "I overheard them—Scorpiondt, Serpendt, Bokimpa. They plan to kill us once the project is complete."

Ara froze, her heart pounding.

In the corridor, Scorpiondt paced, muttering under his breath. "Von is a pain in my rear."

Dr. Serpendt scoffed. "At least you don't work beside him. I can't stomach that human lover—or his insufferable daughter."

Scorpiondt's face remained unreadable. "Bear with him. Once his part is finished, he's gone."

Serpendt's lips curled into a smirk. "Good. Then I'll take his workload."

"Understood," Scorpiondt replied curtly, watching him stalk away.

A moment later, Lieutenant Barricade approached, nodding with sharp respect. "Afternoon, General."

Scorpiondt returned the gesture. "Afternoon, soldier. Walk with me." Their footsteps echoed down the corridor, conversation swallowed by the ship's hum.

Back inside, Von told Ara everything—the conspiracy, the plan for surrogates forged through the Alpha-Gene Fluid Project.

"They won't obliterate this planet," he explained grimly. "Its resources are too valuable. They'll leave behind surrogates—genetically enhanced infiltrators—to control the layers of human society. From the shadows, they'll govern while making it seem humanity governs itself."

Ara's stomach knotted. "So they won't leave… they'll leave puppets."

Von nodded. "Exactly. That's how they rule worlds without spreading their armies thin. A false freedom—chains you cannot see."

Ara clenched her fists. "We have to stop them."

"We will," Von said, his eyes burning despite the exhaustion dragging at him. "But we must be careful. They are watching us too closely. We must play along until the time is right."

A silence settled over them—thick, dangerous, resolute.

As Ara finally stepped into the corridor, her resolve hardened. She would protect her father. She would fight for this planet.

And she would never forget the boy with the red cloth.

The Grand Stratum was a cathedral of shadows—its vaulted walls inscribed with ancient symbols, its air heavy with the scent of burning oils. Gold stolen from conquered worlds glinted in the dim light, shaped into grotesque forms of beasts and gods long forgotten. At the heart of it sat Prince Atsu-els, pale and gaunt upon his throne of stolen splendor. The carvings of otherworldly creatures writhed in the torchlight, as if alive, reflecting the malice of the one who ruled from above them.

A holographic screen flickered to life before him. The head physician of the Alpha-Gene Fluid Project appeared, his posture stiff, his voice measured but trembling at the edges. Failure before this prince meant death.

"My Prince," the physician began, "the Surrogates of the Mystique Order have received their injections. They are now entering final preparation for their journey to Earth."

Atsu-els leaned forward, shadows swallowing half his face, leaving only the gleam of his eyes and the twisted curl of delight at his lips. "And their provisions?" His voice was silk stretched over steel.

The physician swallowed. "The Gatekeepers have been integrated, my Prince. The data systems are fused to the Surrogates' chips beneath their skin. They are ready to monitor, direct, and, if necessary… correct. Their obedience will be absolute."

For a moment, the chamber held only the hum of the holo-feed. Then Atsu-els's long fingers drummed once against the armrest of his throne. Slow. Deliberate. Predatory.

"Adequate. Proceed."

The physician exhaled relief at the rare acknowledgment. He bowed low. "It is an honor, my Prince."

With a casual flick of Atsu-els's hand, the projection died. Silence reclaimed the chamber.

The prince reclined, lost in the theater of his own design. He pictured the Surrogates descending upon Earth: not as conquerors in open battle, but as phantoms slipping into every layer of society. Their enhancements would make them gods among mortals; their loyalty, shackled by the Gatekeepers, would make them instruments of his will. They would ensure the planet's riches flowed endlessly to his empire—gold, knowledge, bodies—all under the illusion of self-rule.

The thought pleased him. Chaos sown invisibly, resistance strangled in its crib, while the Ikannunaa's name grew into something more than power: inevitability.

"This is not conquest," Atsu-els murmured to the empty chamber. "This is permanence."

He let the words linger in the shadows, savoring them. Soon, Earth would fall without realizing it had already been claimed. And through its downfall, his supremacy would resound across the galaxy like thunder.

Prince Atsu-els, titan of ruin, allowed himself a rare smile. His empire was not coming. It had already begun.

Beneath the pale glow of the moon, silence blanketed the Servacraft. From far beyond the walls, a lone howl split the night—mournful, distant, unrelenting.

Dr. Von stirred restlessly in his bunk, his face betraying the storm beneath his stoic exterior. His brow furrowed, lips twitching as half-formed words slipped out. "Genetic… hero… project…"

His eyes snapped open. He bolted upright, breath ragged, heart hammering as a revelation ignited within him. A surge of clarity burned away the fog of sleep.

"Sigma-Gene Fluid Project," he whispered, the words a vow. He exhaled slowly.

A grin—sharp, dangerous—spread across his face. Slowly, his gaze shifted toward the corner of the room. There, the tiny surveillance lens blinked its steady red light, ever watching. Always watching.

Von met its unblinking stare with calm defiance.

The intercom crackled. A guard's uneasy voice filtered through. "Dr. Von? Is everything all right? I heard you talking."

Von drew in a long breath, masking the fire in his chest. His voice emerged steady, almost casual. "Just a nightmare."

A pause. Then the guard relented. "Understood, sir. Goodnight."

Von leaned back onto the bed, though sleep would not return. His eyes stayed open, fixed on the ceiling, mind alive with blueprints and equations, strategies and secrets.

"Just a nightmare," he murmured again, a shadow of a smile tugging at his lips. "But for them… it will be real."

The howl rose once more, distant yet sharper, as if it answered him. But to Von, it was no longer a cry of despair. It was a herald—a signal of awakening.

The Sigma-Gene Project would rise. Not as a weapon for the Ikannunaa, nor a cage for mankind. No, this was his creation, his rebellion. A hidden seed of resistance.

He would craft the hero this world needed.
One no empire would ever see coming.

Nightfall draped the Servacraft in silence. Ara had drifted into sleep on the standard room sofa, the day's weariness pulling her under. Yet what came to her was no ordinary dream.

She found herself standing in a forest, moonlight pouring through the canopy in soft silver streams. The air was cool, fragrant with earth and wildflowers, each breath sharpening her senses. Mist coiled between the trees, and out of it emerged Captain Ledge.

He was dressed in his uniform, but the severity she had come to expect from him was gone. His eyes, usually hard with discipline, now carried warmth—an unguarded tenderness. With a gentle smile, he extended his hand.

"Ara," he said, voice low, almost reverent. "Come with me."

Her curiosity stirred, and she placed her hand in his. Together they walked, their silence companionable, broken only by rustling leaves and the distant call of nocturnal creatures. The dream forest felt alive, yet safe, as though it had been conjured for this moment alone.

After a time, Ledge turned to her. His voice was steady, earnest.
"Since we met, your strength has marked me. You see truths where others see only shadows. That gift matters, Ara. We'll need it. We'll find what's buried—together
."

Her heart quickened at his words. The certainty in his tone resonated deep within her. She had always sensed their connection, but here, in this dream, it blossomed into something undeniable.

"Yes, Ledge," she replied, her voice firm, filled with resolve. "I will stand by your side. We'll uncover the truth."

A silence followed, thick with unspoken understanding. Then, as if drawn by a force beyond themselves, he leaned close. They kissed, gentle in moonlight. The world dissolved around them, leaving only the two of them, bound by a shared purpose and an intimacy that defied words.

Hand in hand, they walked deeper into the forest. Once a place of mystery and menace, it now felt transformed—alive with possibility, lit by secrets waiting to be revealed.

Ara awoke with a start, heart racing, the dream still vivid in her mind. The memory of his touch, his words, lingered like embers. She knew what it meant. Her bond with Captain Ledge was more than a fleeting connection. It was destiny—an alliance of spirit and strength.

Their journey together had only begun. And she was ready.

The following day, sunlight poured into the Servacraft's medical bay, its sterile glow reflecting off polished walls and gleaming floors. Yet the brightness only sharpened the fury simmering in General Scorpiondt's eyes.

His gaze swept the room like a blade, cutting to the patient bed. A streak of red sauce stained the sheets—trivial carelessness, perhaps, or a message meant to taunt him. Above, the surveillance camera hung gutted from its mount, wires exposed, its shattered lens spitting sparks of fractured light.

And the bed was empty. Dr. Von was gone.

Scorpiondt's jaw flexed, the scar above his eye twitching as anger boiled to the surface. His chest rose and fell with deliberate restraint, but the restraint did not last. He spun toward the door, his voice detonating through the chamber.

"Find Dr. Von. Now."

The command echoed off steel and glass, carrying the weight of promised punishment. Guards scrambled at once, boots hammering against the floor in a staccato rhythm that faded quickly down the corridor.

Alone again, Scorpiondt resumed pacing. Each step landed heavy, reverberating through the empty bay. His gloved fists tightened and loosened at his sides, his breathing low and measured. But beneath the veneer of control, his veins pulsed with molten rage.

The sterile quiet of the medical bay seemed to mock him. Dr. Von had slipped through his fingers. And for that, someone would bleed.

Hours later, the laboratory's double doors parted with a metallic sigh. Dr. Von stepped through, his posture straight, his face unreadable. He carried himself with the quiet confidence of a man entering a lecture hall, not the den of an enemy.

Across the room, General Scorpiondt looked up from his communicator. Fury flickered across his scarred features, his soldiers stiffening at his sides, hands twitching near their weapons. The air thickened, the silence pressing down as though the very ship held its breath.

Von's footsteps echoed, deliberate and unhurried. His calm only deepened the General's rage.

"Dr. Von!" Scorpiondt's roar cracked through the chamber like thunder. He stormed forward, boots pounding against steel. "You were missing. That is unacceptable."

Von did not flinch. His gaze met the General's with measured composure.
"I went for a walk," he said evenly. "To better understand the terrain—and the people who live on it."

A hush followed, sharp enough to cut.

Scorpiondt leaned close, his words dropping into a venomous growl. "You do not leave this craft without my leave, Doctor. Not a step."

Von inclined his head, the weight of the command pressing on him, but his tone remained steady.
"Yes, General."

Scorpiondt's nostrils flared, his voice rising again. "You will remain under guard. This is not leisure. It is control. And you will not dilute it."

From the corner, Dr. Serpendt finally spoke, his voice slick with disdain as he tapped his clipboard. "Decontaminate, Doctor. Field contact brings bio-load."

The jab was petty, designed to sting. Von resisted the urge to roll his eyes, choosing silence over escalation. He knew the walls had ears, and survival meant swallowing words that might one day damn him.

The tension hung, palpable, a taut wire straining between them. Then Von gave a final nod to Scorpiondt, pivoted with quiet dignity, and returned to his workbench.

The storm had not broken, but every man in the room knew it was coming.

Dr. Von sat slouched at the metallic desk in his private office, the hum of the Servacraft's engines a low vibration beneath his chair. The room was dim, sterile, and suffocating, as though the walls themselves pressed against him. A lone soldier stood guard outside his door, silent as stone.

Von stroked his beard, white strands tracing the years of knowledge, loss, and unrelenting duty etched into his life. But tonight the weight of it all pressed heavier than ever.

With sudden resolve, he surged upright, both palms slamming against the desk. His brow tightened as he muttered, his voice low but steady, carrying like a secret oath in the empty room:

"When it's tied around their right, that will be the night we fight."

The words hung, vibrating in the stillness. He smacked the desk once more, sealing the vow. There was no turning back.

He crossed to the glass-paneled closet, where his suits hung like masks for survival. Each one was a carefully chosen façade. But his hand stopped on something more than attire. A striking red tie.

He lingered on it, and the present blurred into memory.

Dia stood before him, her smile warm, her fingers deftly straightening the very same tie before a night at the symphony.

"We'll be late if you keep fussing, Jon," she teased, laughter dancing in her voice. She tugged the knot snug, then leaned in and kissed him. That moment— so simple, so human—anchored him in ways no equation ever could.

Von blinked, the memory cutting deep. The tie in his hand carried her love, her strength. But it carried something else now too.

Unbidden, the image of the boy with the red cloth surged in his mind—the child who had stood defiant against the Ikannunaa, who had worn loss as a banner of resistance. Red upon the arm. A sign of rebellion.

Von's grip tightened. The cloth, the tie—it was all the same thread. A bridge between the personal and the cosmic. Between love lost and resistance not yet born. Between Dia's warmth and the boy's fury.

He looped the tie around his neck, his movements deliberate, reverent. Then he pulled the knot into place, he wasn't just dressing for a meeting. He was donning a symbol—one that whispered of rebellion to come.

When he stepped from his office, stride steady and eyes forward, the red tie gleamed against his chest like a spark. To the Ikannunaa it was meaningless. But to him, it was everything: Dia's memory, the boy's defiance, and the quiet promise that one day, the red would not be a token of subjugation, but the color of freedom.

The conference room aboard the Servacraft gleamed with cold precision—polished steel walls, sterile lighting, and a long black table that seemed more suited for sentencing than science. The air was thick with anticipation as the assembled doctors and assistants whispered among themselves, their voices taut with excitement and fatigue.

When the doors hissed open, silence fell.

Dr. Von entered in an immaculate suit, his stride unhurried, his presence commanding. The red tie at his collar caught the light, drawing every eye to it before he even spoke. He took his place at the head of the table, directly opposite Dr. Serpendt, whose thin smile curved like a blade.

Von cleared his throat. "Ladies and gentlemen, good afternoon. Our project will reach its apex tomorrow."

A ripple of exhilaration moved through the room. Shoulders straightened. Faces lit with pride.

Von gestured, and folders were passed around, each one heavy with charts, equations, and biological reports. "You'll find the details of our progress inside. We are 90% complete. Some aspects remain for refinement, but by tomorrow we will be finished."

The shuffle of papers filled the air until Serpendt's voice cut through. His smile did not touch his cold eyes. "Dr. Von," he said lightly, "I see you have labeled my folder *Sigma-Gene Fluid Project.*"

Von looked up, his face unreadable. "Ah. Noted, Doctor. A clerical error. It will be corrected."

But the room seemed to tighten around them. The 'error' was no error, and both men knew it.

Serpendt's stare lingered, probing, then softened back into feigned civility. "Of course. All is well."

Across the table, Dr. Jidohtta frowned at his notes. "Dr. Von, the data here suggests a later completion. Are you certain the deadline can be met?"

Von nodded, his tone steady. "Yes, Doctor. I'll clarify those details tomorrow. Tonight, you must rest. This final stage will demand clarity." He swept the room with a glance, noticing the fatigue in their eyes. "Doctors, return to your quarters. At sunrise, we reconvene."

Chairs scraped back. The meeting began to dissolve into motion.

"Before we part," Serpendt added smoothly, "let us acknowledge General Scorpiondt's pledge of substantial rewards for your service."

Applause rose, a brittle display of unity. Von joined in with a polite smile, though beneath it his discontent stirred like a coiled serpent.

When the noise faded, he spoke one last time. "Thank you for your diligence. I am confident our princes will be pleased. Over the time we've spent together on this reject—" he faltered, then corrected, "I mean, project—my apologies. Fatigue."

The slip silenced the room for a beat before nervous chuckles and polite farewells resumed.

One by one, they filed past him with handshakes and murmured wishes. When Serpendt's turn came, Von clasped his hand a moment too long.

"I look forward to seeing the return on our investment," Von said, his voice quiet but laced with intent.

Serpendt's smile was tight, brittle. "As do I. It will be… life-changing. Speaking of 'return,' I suggest you take rest, Doctor. You've been… unusual since your disappearance from the medical bay."

Von smiled faintly, his tone disarming. "You're right, Serpendt. I'll heed that advice."

He released the man's hand, turned, and walked toward the doors. A guard fell into step behind him.

The doors sealed shut with a resonant thud, leaving the chamber in silence.

But Von's mind was already far from the Servacraft—beyond the projects, beyond the applause, weaving the first threads of something greater. Something that would shift the balance between science and tyranny.

The door slid open with a soft hiss. Dr. Von stepped into his modest quarters, shoulders still heavy from the weight of the day. On the sofa sat Ara, her posture straight, her gaze fixed on him the moment he entered.

He gave an exaggerated roll of his eyes, as if irritated to find her waiting. She answered with a calm smirk, her expression betraying both amusement and suspicion.

"Well," she said evenly, "it's just you and me now, Dad. Where did you vanish to earlier?"

Von leaned against the doorframe, his tone deliberately light. "What's that, dear?"

Her arms crossed, eyes narrowing. "You heard me."

He chuckled, but the sound rang hollow. "I was mingling with the locals," he said with mock nonchalance.

Ara rose, her finger lifting to point directly at him. "You're lying."

Her voice was sharp, but beneath it lingered warmth—a daughter's rebuke sharpened by intuition. She didn't press him further. Instead, she turned, the red sash tied at her waist swaying as she moved toward her room.

"Goodnight, Dad. There are leftovers in the cold box," she called, vanishing behind the sliding door.

Von stood in the living room, staring after her. His gaze dropped briefly to the red tie still knotted at his collar, the fabric catching the low light. Red. The same red Ara carried unconsciously, the same shade worn defiantly by the boy in the forest.

"My daughter," he whispered, his voice thick with conviction. "Your mother would be proud. You've become extraordinary."

The tie. The cloth. The color of love, of defiance, of rebellion. Symbols were stitching themselves together, and Von knew his duty with clarity. He would ensure Ara's future—one worth living for, one worth fighting for.

His jaw set. The rebellion had already begun.

Night draped the Servacrafts in an uneasy stillness—until an explosion shattered the silence.

The blast ripped through the cabin walls with a thunderous crack, hurling Ara from her bed onto the cold floor. The room quaked as a second explosion followed, rattling the fragile sense of safety they had built within these metallic confines. Dazed, ears ringing, Ara blinked against the haze until her father's figure loomed in the doorway. His face was set like stone, lit by the dim emergency glow.

"Get up!" Von barked, urgency biting every syllable. "Grab what you need. We have to go!"

Still disoriented, Ara pressed a hand to her temple. "What's happening?"

"No time for explanations!" His tone was sharp, uncompromising. "Move!"

Her heart pounded as adrenaline burned away the fog. She scrambled to her feet, hastily stuffing a backpack with essentials—her hands trembling so hard she nearly dropped it. When she emerged into the living room, Von was already at the door, a heavy bag slung over his shoulder, ready to move.

In an uncharacteristic moment, he pulled her into a tight embrace. "I love you, Ara," he said, voice low but fierce.

"What's going on?" she whispered, fear clawing at her chest.

Von's gaze burned with urgency and something heavier—resolve. "Just stay close to us."

"Us?" Ara echoed, confusion etched into her face.

Von didn't answer. He drew a steadying breath, then slid the cabin door open.

The corridor beyond was no longer serene. Sirens blared in the distance. Shouts, hurried footsteps, and the high-pitched whine of charging weapons filled the air. Smoke hung in the passages, dim light strobed against the walls, and the Servacraft's once-orderly halls now felt like the veins of a beast under attack.

Von urged Ara forward. Together they navigated the chaos, their footsteps quick against the metal floor. Every corner seemed alive with shadows, every echo a possible threat.

Then, from a junction ahead, three soldiers appeared. At their head strode Captain Ledge, his sharp eyes scanning the corridor with predatory focus. On either side, Lieutenant Barricade—broad and unyielding—and Lieutenant Encrypt—calm, precise—flanked him.

Without hesitation, the trio closed in around Von and Ara, forming a protective phalanx. Ledge's voice cut through the din, steady and commanding.

"Stay tight. We're moving you to safety."

Ara fell in beside them, breath quick, pulse thrumming. The small party pressed forward, moving as one through the labyrinthine corridors. The clash of rebellion swelled around them—gunfire cracking, steel ringing, the cries of men locked in mortal struggle echoing off the walls.

When they burst into the grand hall, the sight that met them stole the breath from their lungs.

Once a place of order and command, the hall had been transformed into a battlefield. Smoke curled from ruptured conduits; flames licked the walls, their glow illuminating chaos. Rebels in red bands swarmed against Scorpiondt's armored loyalists. The air reeked of scorched metal and blood. Sparks rained from overhead girders, casting wild light across overturned machinery and shattered stone.

This was no skirmish. It was war.

"Cut through!" Ledge ordered, tightening his grip on his blade.

Encrypt surged forward, firing with precision. Barricade hammered the enemy lines, his massive frame breaking their formation. Von shielded Ara as best he could, but in the swirl of fire and steel, safety was an illusion.

A beam seared across their flank. Ara cried out as it struck her arm, pain searing through muscle and bone. She staggered, nearly collapsing, but Barricade threw himself in front of her, intercepting the next barrage.

"Stay low!" he roared, steady as a wall.

Captain Ledge was at her side in an instant. His eyes flicked to her wound, then to the red cloth bound around his own arm. Without hesitation, he tore it free and tied it tightly around her wound.

Ara winced, her breath sharp, but when she met his gaze, she found no pity there—only fire. She nodded once, her fear hardening into resolve.

Ledge rose, weapon ready. "We move. Now."

Together they pressed toward the rear exit, the chaos behind them fading into a haze of smoke and flame. The rebels fought on, their reddish armbands glowing like embers against the black tide of loyalist armor. Every step forward felt earned in blood.

And then—the noise shifted.

The clash of battle dulled, fighters on both sides pausing, their attention drawn to the rear hatch. Shadows bent strangely in the firelight, pooling around a lone silhouette.

A towering figure stood framed in smoke and sparks, blocking their only escape. Broad-shouldered, unmoving, his weapon glinted with lethal promise.

No name was spoken. No words were needed.

The path to freedom had just become a gauntlet.

General Scorpiondt stood in the rear hatch, clad in his dark uniform, exuding menace like a living shadow. His I.R.S operatives and most loyal enforcers flanked him in tight formation, weapons raised with mechanical precision.

The clang of armored boots sealed the hall behind them. The only exit was gone, swallowed by his presence.

"Not a step further."

His voice was a calm, calculated hiss—authority wrapped in threat.

His gaze landed on Lieutenant Barricade. Disappointment sharpened his expression. "Barricade," he drawled, disdain dripping from every syllable. "How disappointing—you will pay dearly for this betrayal."

He tilted his head, feigning regret before his voice sank into a growl. "Your punishment will be severe."

But Barricade didn't flinch. His fists tightened, his jaw locked, and his eyes burned with defiance. "Do what you have to."

Scorpiondt's nostrils flared. A slow breath hissed through his teeth as his stare shifted to Dr. Von.

"And you." His voice was no longer mocking—it thundered, vibrating through the metal chamber. "Did I not make myself clear? You do not leave this craft unless I permit it."

Von stood his ground, unarmed, unshaken.

The General sneered. "I should have known you were scheming the moment you vanished from the medical bay. Mingling with locals. Testing my patience."

Tension gripped the hall. The storm outside mirrored the silence within, every eye locked on the two men.

Von broke it. "You planned to kill me and my daughter after the project's completion, didn't you?"

Scorpiondt's lips curved into a predator's smile. "Then consider your contract concluded, Doctor."

He raised his weapon—then froze when Von's measured voice cut in, low and deliberate.

"Perhaps," Von said, his tone steady as steel, "you should worry more about the men behind you than the ones in front of you."

The General's finger hovered on the trigger. A flicker of doubt passed through his eyes. Slowly, he turned.

From the shadows poured a tide of rebels, more than a hundred, reddish cloths tied to their arms like banners of defiance. Weapons raised, their faces shone with grim resolve. The General's enforcers, who only moments before flanked him, now lay crumpled on the floor, weapons scattered, their bodies still.

Von allowed a faint smile. "Brute force collapses without position. You were outmaneuvered, General. It's the quiet moves that win the board."

The rebels tightened their circle. One stepped forward, voice like a blade: "Stand down."

For the first time in years, uncertainty cracked Scorpiondt's mask. His eyes swept the room, calculating, trapped.

His sneer returned, brittle with defiance. "Dawn is generous," he spat — an Ikannunaa curse, promising death before morning.

From the back of the rebel line emerged Elder Abhay, leaning on his gnarled bamboo staff. His presence commanded silence.

"Step aside, General," Abhay said, his voice steady as stone. "It is the least thing you can do, after taking my brother's life."

The weight of unity pressed in from every side—rebels, tribesmen, even children, their red cloths fluttering like flames. Among them, a boy no older than ten stood at the front, his small hands gripping a weapon too large for him, yet his stare fearless.

Outside the craft, hundreds more had gathered: the tribe of Goa, the warriors of Santana, even General Dagrath himself—all bound by the same scarlet mark. And at their feet, almost absurd in its stillness, a white rabbit sat, unmoved, gold coin clenched in its teeth.

The sight was unshakable: a reckoning had arrived.

Dr. Von stepped forward, deliberate, unhurried, his red tie gleaming faintly in the chaos.

"This is not rebellion born of chaos," he said, his voice clear and cutting. "It is unity. And unity is the weapon you refused to fear."

Scorpiondt's jaw tightened, his chest rising and falling with suppressed fury. His hand shot out, gripping Von's shoulder as he tried to pass.

"The ground beneath you has crumbled, Doctor," he growled. "I will bury you and your daughter so deep the earth itself won't remember your names."

Von calmly removed the hand, meeting his gaze without flinching.

"We'll see who digs first. Goodnight, General."

And with that, he stepped past him, Ara at his side, disappearing into the forest's dark embrace.

The Conqueror II
As told by General Scorpiondt

There is a myth the conquered like to believe—
That order is fragile. That rebellion is noble. That defiance is destiny.

I do not indulge such fictions.

Order is not a gift. It is not a right.
Order is imposed.

And for a time, we imposed it well.

The second year of our presence upon this primitive rock should have been the consolidation phase: compliance cemented, memory erased, dissent sterilized at the root. We had infiltrated their soil, their science, their myths. Their warriors had been broken. Their temples, repurposed. Their elders, silenced. The Servacrafts hovered like gods above the forests they once prayed to.

And yet…

Even in the tightest grip, something small can squirm through your fingers.

It began with Dr. Von—a man I once considered intelligent. Strategic, even. A rare Petrichoren whose brain did not dissolve into superstition and tears when his world collapsed beneath my boots. I offered him purpose. He mistook it for chains.

He wandered.
He listened.
And in doing so, he remembered the sound of his own defiance.

He will say I betrayed him.
No. I made no promises. I gave him time, tools, and a laboratory. He gave me suspicion, secrecy… and eventually, rebellion.

He claims he overheard our plans—mine, Serpendt's, and that twitching fool Bokimpa. Perhaps he did. Or perhaps he conjured fantasies to justify his own treason. Either way, the outcome remains unchanged.

He should have stayed unconscious on that lavatory floor.

But let us not blame him alone.

Ara, the daughter. Sentimental, impulsive. She absorbs ideals like a sponge and leaks them wherever she walks. There is danger in that softness—danger I overlooked. I thought her a weakness. I see now she was a weapon. Von's real weapon.

And then there is Captain Ledge.
The blade I trained. The one I thought sharp enough to cut only what I pointed him at. I was wrong.

He aligned with Von. Hid Ara's explorations. Helped their escape.

Worse still…
He believed in something.

A commander can deal with liars, even with traitors. But believers? Believers must be eradicated. For they do not kneel when broken. They rise when shattered.

Still, not all failures were mine.

Lieutenant Barricade—a soldier whose strength I once considered unyielding—stood against me in the final corridor. There, surrounded by rebels with red cloths tied like bloody oaths around their arms, he dared to stare me down. He said nothing. But his silence roared.

I could have killed him.
I should have.

But I miscalculated the moment.

The rebels emerged from behind me. They had infiltrated the very arteries of my Servacraft. Disguised. Coordinated. Their timing... exquisite.

And then came Elder Abhay.
That relic of ritual and bamboo wisdom. He spoke like he had summoned the sun to rise with his words alone. Even my I.R.S operatives hesitated. That is the true poison of culture—it makes martyrs of the weak and gods of the stubborn.

I was flanked.
Outmaneuvered.
The corridor that had once been mine became a tomb for my authority.

And there...
There stood the boy again.
The red cloth still wrapped around his small arm like a prophecy.
That boy. That cursed boy. Always there. Always watching.

No matter how I twist the narrative, no matter how many bodies I leave in my wake...
He does not flinch.

He was at the rear. He was at the front.
In dreams. In forests. In fire. In smoke.
He is always there.

And Dr. Von? He passed me in that final moment. Calm. Dignified. Smirking like the teacher who'd corrected the unruly student. He said I'd been outmaneuvered. That the board had shifted.

No, Doctor.
The board has only begun to bleed.

You think your red tie is rebellion?
That your daughter's flower is a flame?
That the Sigma-Gene Project is a salvation?

Let me remind you—
I built the parameters in which you rebel.
I crafted the very thresholds you now believe you've surpassed.
Your fire burns within a chamber of my design.

And yet…
A strange thing happens to a man standing amid the ashes of his own order.

He begins to feel cold.

Even I—General Scorpiondt—must acknowledge the obvious:

I underestimated belief.

I dismissed symbolism.
I thought red cloth was cotton.
I see now that it is memory, rage, and prophecy… soaked in the blood of
those who refused to bow.

You have shifted the wind, Doctor.
But I am the storm.

You are no longer a pawn.
You are now a threat.

And I do not lose to threats.
I erase them.

Chapter 3 | **Fugitives With Guidance**

The rebel crew pressed through the dense forest, swallowed by towering ancient trees that seemed older than memory itself. Moonlight pierced the canopy in shattered beams, scattering fleeting patterns across the damp earth. The air smelled of soil, moss, and living things, rich and heavy with anticipation. Every step felt guided by something beyond them, as though the land itself held its breath.

At the front, Elder Abhay walked with deliberate certainty, his gnarled staff striking the ground like a heartbeat, keeping rhythm with their weary march.

From the shadows, a figure emerged, breaking the stillness with a sharp, drum-like crack. Front Warrior Khalfani strode forward, his towering frame radiating raw strength. Dirt and streaks of paint scarred his body, testaments to countless battles fought and survived. He wore only a brown loincloth and headband, his muscles corded like the bows of the trees around them, his gaze fierce enough to pierce stone. At his waist hung a knife, and across his back a bow and quiver rested—tools of survival and judgment.

Behind him, thirty-three warriors fanned out in disciplined formation. Their stares were sharp as blades, their faces illuminated by shafts of silver light. Like the forest itself, they were weathered, scarred, unyielding—rooted in purpose.

Abhay and Khalfani shared a silent nod, the weight of shared history passing between them. Then Khalfani stepped forward, extending a massive hand toward Dr. Von. His grip was firm, his stare cutting straight to the man's center.

"My friend," Khalfani said, his voice a low rumble of distant thunder, "your freedom cost blood. It will cost more."

His words carried no judgment, only truth.

Von held his gaze, his voice steady. "Front Warrior, I'm grateful. I don't plan for failure. A small margin is all I need."

For a moment, Khalfani's expression softened, acknowledging both burden and resolve. "I'm sure it does," he replied quietly.

Abhay faded back into the night then, swallowed by the forest, leaving the two leaders to carry the moment forward.

The journey pressed on, each mile heavier than the last. When the moon reached its peak, Khalfani raised a hand and gave the order to halt. "Eat. Drink. Be strong by dawn."

They made camp under the stars. Fire crackled, casting shifting light over tired faces. Ara sat beside her father, her voice carrying both frustration and longing. "Where are we going, Dad?"

Von's smile was secretive, but his tone was soft. "You will know soon enough, Ara."

Though she frowned, trust anchored her anger, especially with Captain Ledge seated nearby, a quiet pillar of reassurance.

On the far side of the fire, Encrypt and Barricade leaned close, whispering in low tones, their words weaving tactical patterns for the days to come. Around them, Khalfani's warriors stood watch, silhouettes carved against the night.

One by one, the rebels settled into uneasy rest. But Von remained awake, his eyes on the stars, mind turning like the gears of a great unseen machine. Plans built themselves in the darkness, urgent and restless, shaping paths that could not yet be spoken.

At dawn, the ground around the Servacrafts lay desecrated. Where Dr. Von, Ara, and their companions had once stood, now only silence reigned. Bodies of rebels and the Indigenous tribe of Goa littered the scarred earth, a grotesque testament to the night's violence. Blood mingled with the dust, dark and wet, soaking into the soil as if the land itself mourned.

Among the dead, one soldier still clung to life. His body was broken, his breaths ragged, each inhale rattling through shattered ribs. He twitched against the weight of his wounds, crawling no further than an inch before collapsing again.

Heavy boots struck the ground, deliberate and unhurried, General Scorpiondt emerged through the smoke, the dawn casting his broad frame into long, jagged shadows. The air stank of scorched metal and blood, yet he breathed it in as though it were incense. His scarred lip curled into something like satisfaction. The battlefield was quiet—precisely as he had intended.

A groan broke the stillness. His eyes snapped to the source: the dying soldier, defiant even in futility. Scorpiondt approached, each step landing with the weight of inevitability.

He stopped over the writhing figure, then placed his boot on the soldier's chest. The man's ribs creaked under the pressure, his eyes bulging with fear and pain.

Scorpiondt tilted his head, studying him like an insect under glass.

Pathetic.

With a slow, deliberate motion, he drew his energy gun. The weapon's core pulsed with lethal light, its hum swelling into the silence. He lowered it until the muzzle hovered inches above the man's face.

"Your resistance," Scorpiondt said evenly, "was always futile."

The shot split the morning. A flash of white seared across the battlefield, and the soldier's body convulsed once before going limp, his stare fixed in death.

Smoke curled from the barrel as Scorpiondt holstered his weapon. He glanced at the corpse with nothing more than a sneer. "He wouldn't have seen dawn," he muttered, wiping his beard with the back of his gloved hand.

Without another look at the fallen, the General turned toward the looming Servacraft. His mind was already moving beyond the dead—calculating, advancing, shaping the next phase of his ruthless campaign.

Behind him, the dawn spread its light across the battlefield, illuminating rows of lifeless bodies. The shadows of the Servacrafts stretched long across them, claiming even the morning as its own.

Prince Atsu-els sat slouched on his throne, the dim flicker of surveillance monitors painting long, uneven shadows across the chamber's gilded walls. His stare lingered on the shifting images—rebels cut down, tribesmen falling in waves around the Servacrafts and The Prominent. Each scene was a grim reminder of both their strength and their vulnerability.

The silence fractured with a sharp chime from the communication console. Bokimpa, hunched at his station, bony fingers twitching like talons, tapped the glowing interface. At once, a holographic projection shimmered to life, casting an austere radiance into the chamber.

King Atan-els appeared.

The patriarch of their bloodline radiated authority as if born of stone and fire. His aged face bore a texture like ancient bark, furrows etched deep across his skin. Veins crawled over his bald crown like the roots of a dying forest, while his tall golden crown gleamed cold and merciless. A chiseled jawline, hollowed cheeks, and jutting bones gave him the appearance of a ruler carved rather than born. But it was his eyes—piercing, ember-red—that commanded fear, burning unyielding against his pale, cracked complexion.

"My son." His voice was stern, cold iron wrapped in command. "Word of an insurrection has reached me. Where is Ata?"

Atsu-els straightened at once, tone clipped. "With General Scorpiondt. The revolt is under control as we speak."

The King's exhale was heavy with disappointment. "Tighten your ranks. Sloppiness invites revolt."

"Yes, Father," Atsu-els said, swallowing his resentment.

"Was Dr. Von found?"

The younger prince's jaw tensed. "No. The humans aided his escape. He could be anywhere, hidden in these forests."

King Atan-els's stare darkened further, his voice laced with disdain. "Does the project stall?"

"No, Father," Atsu-els replied quickly. "Dr. Serpendt claims he can finish the work himself. There will be some delay, but not ruin."

The King scoffed, a sound sharp as breaking bone. "Forget Von. The planet itself will kill him—and his human pets."

He leaned back slightly, already withdrawing from the matter. "Keep me informed of further developments. I have greater matters to address. Good night, son."

The holographic projection cut off, the King's form collapsing into nothingness.

Once more, the chamber was silent. Atsu-els sat rigid in his throne, the echo of his father's words pressing like a weight on his chest. The monitors flickered on, indifferent, replaying scenes of carnage as though mocking his failure.

The forest hushed around them, as though the towering trees themselves were holding their breath. Every step stirred whispers in the underbrush, subtle tremors that set Khalfani's instincts aflame. His hand brushed the bow at his side, body taut with readiness.

Captain Ledge caught the same current in the air and motioned sharply to his soldiers. "Stay sharp," he ordered, his voice low, clipped, precise.

The rustling deepened, joined by guttural syllables of a tongue unfamiliar to most. Khalfani raised a hand, steadying his warriors with a calm but firm voice.

"These might be the Drifters."

Lieutenant Encrypt, curiosity as keen as his blade, leaned closer. "Who are the Drifters?"

Khalfani's stare did not leave the shadows. "Renegades," he answered. "Outcasts who severed ties with their tribes after unforgivable acts. They survive alone, dangerous and desperate—hunters of men as much as beasts."

Before Encrypt could respond, a shrill, blood-curdling cry ripped the silence apart. The undergrowth exploded.

The Drifters surged from the gloom, eyes ablaze with wild hostility. Their bodies were painted in ash and streaked with mud, their crude weapons raised high.

Chaos erupted.

Captain Ledge's soldiers snapped their beam rifles to bear, volleys of white-hot energy tearing through the dark. The air lit with searing flashes, the smell of ozone mingling with the sharp tang of earth. The Drifters answered with arrows whistling through the trees and blades flashing in the pale moonlight.

The battle was brutal—a clash of desperate ferocity against disciplined force. Drifters lunged with reckless abandon, heedless of their own lives. Ledge moved like a steel wall, cutting down attackers with precision strikes. Encrypt's blasts curved with uncanny accuracy, every shot deliberate. Khalfani loosed arrows that struck like lightning, each finding its mark.

And yet, the price was steep.

When the frenzy broke and the last Drifter lay crumpled beneath the boughs, silence returned—heavier, darker than before. Five of Khalfani's warriors did not rise. Their bodies lay still beneath the canopy, faces calm now, as though the forest itself had claimed them.

A hush fell over the survivors. Together they dug shallow graves, the damp earth clinging to their hands. A prayer was murmured, brief but potent, rising like smoke into the trees. The flickering firelight caught Khalfani's face as he straightened, his eyes shadowed with grief but lit with unyielding resolve.

"Von," he said, voice low but ironclad, "sacrifices will continue. Let us get back on the path. We have a long road before we meet the Karibegoan."

The group pressed forward, their steps weighted by loss. Above, the branches whispered in the wind, carrying with them unspoken grief and the hard-edged determination of those who endured.

The forest closed around them again, vast and ancient, as if testing their resolve with every mile.

Ara could no longer contain the question burning in her chest. She turned to Captain Ledge, her voice steady though hushed.

"What's his play, Ledge?"

Ledge's eyes swept the horizon, his jaw tight with thought. "Ara, trust him. He's the sharpest mind we have. If anyone can turn the tide, it's him."

Her shoulders eased, but doubt still flickered behind her stare. Ledge, sensing her unease, pivoted the conversation.

"How are the red flowers coming along?"

At once, the scientist in her stirred. Her eyes gleamed with purpose.

"I've been studying them. One drop of nectar neutralized key compounds of the Beta fluid in vitro. Even the petals are effective—if ingested."

Ledge frowned. "So why not gather more?"

Ara sighed. "They're difficult to cultivate. Slow to mature. The nectar from one flower can only treat a single person. But the petals… each bloom has thirty-three."

The number hung in the air like a prophecy.

Ledge exhaled, realizing the magnitude. "I haven't seen a single flower since we left. Seeds are impossible to find. And returning to Goa? Suicide."

Ara's lips curved into a sly smile. "Good thing I came prepared. When I gathered those samples, I pocketed a handful of seeds."

Ledge shook his head, torn between admiration and relief. "You always think ahead, don't you?"

"Someone has to," she said, smirking.

Even Lieutenant Barricade broke the silence with a grumble.

"I forgot my lucky trigger glove."

Ledge glanced back. "That explains the shot that nearly clipped my ear."

Encrypt chuckled. "I knew his aim wasn't luck."

Barricade glared at them both before pounding his fist into his palm. "It's not about luck. That glove's been with me since my first mission—stitched black leather, fitted just right to my hand. It saved me once when a beam rifle jammed, gave me the grip I needed to clear it before the enemy closed in. Been wearing it ever since."

Ledge raised an eyebrow, smirking. "So what you're saying is… without it, you're just clumsy."

Barricade snorted but didn't deny it. "I'll get it back—when we return."

The banter carried them a little further down the winding path, but Front Warrior Khalfani soon slowed, his grave expression cutting through their mirth.

"Von," he asked quietly, "do you believe the outsiders will hunt for you here?"

Von shook his head, unreadable. "No. They see me as harmless. A scientist bound to their leash. But they're wrong. When the time comes, I won't wait for them to come to me. I'll go after them."

Khalfani studied him, then nodded. "Then you'll need all the strength you can summon."

Later that morning, the group reached two towering boulders standing side by side like sentinels of stone. The natural gateway cast long shadows across the earth, its presence heavy with meaning. Khalfani halted there, his warriors forming a silent line behind him.

"Here," he intoned, voice resonant with finality. "Our paths now must part."

Von extended his hand. Khalfani clasped it, the grip firm, a meeting of equals.

"You are the chosen ones," the Front Warrior said. "A greater spirit watches over you. Let that spirit guide your counsel. Wherever you come from, know this—you will always find refuge here. This world is yours now. Its hope must rise through you. The hero must come from you."

His words sank deep, echoing in their hearts like a vow.

Without another word, Khalfani and his warriors slipped into the wilderness, vanishing into the forest's dense embrace until only silence and memory remained.

Von, Ara, Ledge, Encrypt, and Barricade lingered at the divide, the weight of Khalfani's blessing heavy on their shoulders.

Then, with resolve hardening their steps, they turned and pressed forward— into the unknown.

The rebels stood in the clearing where two great boulders loomed side by side, their rough surfaces catching the sunlight. The forest was alive with birdsong and the chatter of unseen creatures, but tension threaded through the group like a taut wire.

Ara, arms folded, let her impatience spill. "So, Dad, what's next? Do we stand here until these massive stones roll over us?"

Von, steady as ever, answered without flinching. "Don't be silly, Ara. He's only running late."

Her eyes narrowed. "Who's he?"

"Our last Guide," Von said simply.

A rustle and panting breath carried through the trees. "Hold on, hold on— I'm coming! I know I'm late!"

Lieutenant Barricade shifted eagerly, cracking his knuckles. "Want me to give these rocks a push, Doc? Maybe speed things up."

Encrypt shot him a sidelong glance. "No. Landmarks. Not puzzles."

Von raised a hand, stilling them. From between the sunlit boulders emerged a cloaked figure, short and stout, a black hood pulled over his head, brown loafers scuffed from long use. He bent forward, catching his breath.

"Sorry I'm late," the newcomer said, voice muffled by the hood. "My wife asked for an iced coffee and an egg-and-cheese from the stand. As for me, I went with a soda and a whole-wheat beef-and-cheese—trying to cut back on carbs."

He shrugged, then tipped back his hood. Sunlight glinted on black dreadlocks streaked at the tips, and a single red marble dangled from his ear on a gold chain. His face broke into a wide grin.

"Anyway—I'm Mentor. The Guide. Your guide."

Encrypt arched a brow. "Mentor and Guide. Isn't that redundant?"

Mentor grinned wider. "I didn't choose my name. 'Mentor' was my mother's idea. 'Guide'—well, that's what I've become. Any more questions? No? Good. Now—which one of you is Dr. Von?"

Von stepped forward. Mentor gave him a long once-over, then chuckled. "Well, look at you—famous and still acting humble."

He pulled a bundle from his pack, five black hooded coats identical to his own. "Wear these. Hide your faces. Besides," he added with a smirk, "you're fugitives now. I considered orange for that full-on prison look—complete with mugshots—but black is just more flattering."

Ara rolled her eyes but couldn't suppress a smile. The moment cut the heaviness in half.

And so, under the clear light of day, they took on their new disguises. The forest stretched wide and endless ahead, but with Mentor's easy stride leading the way, they stepped into the third phase of their journey—not merely running, but preparing for what destiny would demand.

That night, camp was lit by a restless fire, its smoke curling toward a sky freckled with stars. Mentor dug into his pack, produced several glass bottles, and flashed a grin.

"Hope you brought your own drinks—because I don't share."

The group chuckled, grateful for even a shred of levity.

Nearby, Captain Ledge carefully unwrapped Ara's injured arm. She winced but held still as he cleaned and bound the wound with quiet precision. The firelight traced the lines of focus on his face.

Ara broke the silence. "So, Ledge… does your name mean anything special?"

He kept working, his voice calm but sure. "It does. "It means 'courage.'"

Ara smiled faintly. "Well, that fits. Cute and courageous, Captain."

Ledge glanced at her—long enough to let the compliment hang—before leaning back against a tree. His eyes lingered on hers with something unreadable. Then his voice cut back to business.

"So tell me, Ara. How did the I.R.S capture you? I already know the story of your father's laboratory. But you—what happened on Petrichore?"

Ara pressed her back against the rough bark, inhaled, and let the memory drag her under.

The sun poured through the spires of Petrichore University, gilding marble paths in soft gold. The air smelled of damp stone after morning rain. Students crowded the courtyard, voices mingling with the hum of hovercrafts overhead.

Ara jogged across the open square, tablet pressed to her ear. "Uncle Cal, good morning! Is Dad with you? Mom's been trying to reach him, but he's ignoring her again."

She smirked—she already knew the answer.

Cal barely had a second to respond before the first blast.

BOOM.

The ground heaved. A shockwave slammed the courtyard. Fire and smoke tore through the east wing of the university. Screams erupted as students scattered.

Ara froze, her heart hammering. "What was that?" she gasped into the tablet.

BOOM.

Closer this time. The lecture hall disintegrated in fire. Glass and stone shards rained down. Alarms wailed. Her call dissolved into static. Cal's voice warped, broke—then silence.

Ara's tablet slipped from her grasp. It hit the ground, lifeless.

She stumbled forward through smoke and chaos, dodging debris. The air was thick, choking, hot.

"Ara!"

Tes—her closest friend—burst through the haze, auburn hair plastered to her face, eyes wild. "We have to go!" She grabbed Ara's arm and pulled toward the gardens.

They didn't make it.

The third explosion hit like the end of the world.

The blast flung them both. Ara crashed hard onto stone, ribs burning. Ears ringing, she blinked through dust. Tes lay near a shattered fountain, clutching her ankle, blood streaking her arm—but alive.

Relief was short.

A boot pinned Ara's wrist. A gloved hand yanked her upright. Black-and-white armor filled her vision, visor cold and faceless.

"Droid! Target acquired."

Panic surged. Ara twisted, drove her knee into the soldier's midsection. He staggered. She tore free and ran—lungs searing, eyes stinging with smoke.

Bolts of energy ripped past her. Heat licked her skin. The courtyard was a warzone.

Then came the sting—sharp, burning. Her shoulder seized; her legs buckled.

A tranquilizer.

"No…" The word broke in her throat. Vision smeared. Breath stuttered.

Darkness consumed her before she hit the ground.

The campfire hissed. Ara's eyes flickered back to the present, her voice trailing into silence.

No one spoke. The crackle of the fire filled the space her story left behind.

Captain Ledge finally nodded, quiet but resolute. "You survived what would've broken most. That's why you're still here."

Ara met his stare, the memory still burning behind her eyes. She said nothing—but the way her hand brushed the red cloth on her arm spoke louder than words.

Ara exhaled slowly, her fingers tightening against the bark. The memory clung like smoke, as if she were still back there—Petrichore burning, Tes's voice breaking through the chaos, only to be swallowed forever.

But Petrichore was gone.

The place where she had grown, where she had dreamed, where she had last clasped her friend's hand—nothing more than a drifting grave in the abyss.

There was no going back.

She forced herself to lift her head. Captain Ledge's gaze met hers, steady and unyielding. He did not look away. There was no pity in his expression, only a steadiness—an anchor holding her in place when the weight of memory threatened to pull her under.

"You went through it," he said, his tone calm, carved from certainty. "But you're here. That means you still have the chance to carry forward—to find peace in what comes next."

Ara swallowed hard, her chest tightening around the words she had carried like a stone.

"I never saw Tes again," she admitted. Saying it out loud made it final. No searching, no calls unanswered, no faint hope of reunion. Tes was gone with Petrichore.

Ledge inclined his head, the firelight tracing the line of his jaw. "I know." His voice softened. "But closure doesn't only come from finding someone. It comes from carrying them—honoring them in the way you live. Whatever happened, Ara… she'd want you to keep moving."

Her throat closed, tears pressing against her eyes. She looked down at the red cloth tied around her arm, the fabric catching the fire's glow. For a moment, she imagined Tes's hand tying it there, steadying her grip, reminding her she was not alone.

Ara blinked. And for the first time since losing everything, she almost believed him.

Nearby, Dr. Von and Guide Mentor sat apart from the others, the firelight painting their faces in shifting amber.

"How far are we from your home?" Von asked, his voice low but steady.

"Tomorrow," Mentor replied, poking at the embers with a stick. "By then, we'll be under Indigo's stealth dome. Safer ground awaits. And the sooner we find Fin—the white rabbit—the better. He still owes me a gold coin I lent him."

Von chuckled, shaking his head. "Let's hope we do. The faster we reach Indigo, the sooner we can begin the transformation… and the training."

Mentor's expression softened, his usual humor tempered with something more sincere. "Wasn't sure we'd get this far, but here we are. You're all right, brother."

From his pack, he pulled his last bottle of beer and handed it over, raising his empty hand in a toast. "To peace throughout the universe."

The glass clinked lightly, and for a rare moment, there was quiet hope between them.

As the fire cracked and the stars burned bright above, Mentor stretched, his grin returning. "Well then, rebels… time to hit the pillow."

"More like hitting the log," Barricade muttered from his bedroll, earning a snort from Encrypt.

One by one, they settled in. Wrapped in cloaks and firelight, the rebels let exhaustion claim them, their dreams lit by both the shadow of danger and the promise of what lay ahead.

The morning sun poured gold through the canopy, stirring the forest awake. Birds darted between branches, and the scent of damp earth hung in the air. Lieutenant Barricade, who rarely claimed the role of early riser, was the first to stir. As he pushed himself upright and stretched, he caught sight of something that made him blink twice.

Perched on a thick branch above camp, their Karibegoan guide was slumped like a rag doll. Mentor's snores rattled through the leaves, and at the base of the tree lay a small graveyard of empty beer bottles glinting in the light.

"Unbelievable," Barricade muttered, rousing the others with a low growl.

When the group's eyes followed his pointing finger, Encrypt smirked. He stooped, flicked a pebble with practiced precision, and struck the guide square in the shoulder.

Mentor jolted awake, rubbing his eyes and muttering, "This sun's burning my eyes out, man. Somebody pull down a banana-leaf shade, please."

Before he could adjust, the branch cracked with a sharp snap. Mentor tumbled in a tangle of limbs, bottles, and leaves, landing flat in the dirt. He rolled once, then popped upright with a yawn, brushing himself off as if this was a perfectly ordinary way to start the day.

"Morning, rebels," he greeted with a grin. "What's up?"

At her father's side, Ara tilted her head toward Von and whispered, "So this is the one we're supposed to follow? Haven't you and Mom always told me to stay away from bad influences?"

Von hid a smile, his eyes twinkling. "He may be rough around the edges, but he knows the terrain better than anyone."

Ara smirked. "Looks more like he knows the inside of a liquor cabinet."

Captain Ledge chuckled, resting a hand on her shoulder. "Be nice. Drunk or sober, we need him. He's the only one who can guide us to Indigo."

Barricade stepped forward, folding his massive arms. "Speaking of which—when are you leading us to breakfast, before I mistake you for breakfast?"

Mentor threw back his head and laughed, unbothered. "Big man, if it's between me and a wild boar, I'd prefer you eat the boar. But since I'd rather not end up on your menu, let's get moving. My home isn't far—and I promise, it'll be worth the walk."

With that, the rebels doused the last of the fire, shouldered their packs, and followed their eccentric guide deeper into the wilderness, the forest swallowing their laughter as quickly as it had taken their doubts.

The towering trees closed around them as they pressed deeper into the wilderness, the canopy weaving shifting mosaics of shadow and light across their path. Despite his rumpled appearance and lingering smell of ale, Mentor walked with a surprising confidence, each step sure and unhesitating—as though the forest itself bent to guide him. With every mile, the rebels found their faith in him growing, even if they would never admit it aloud.

The calm shattered in an instant.

Brush exploded outward as a colossal winged, horned beast surged from the undergrowth, its eyes burning like molten ore. Twisted horns spiraled like the roots of ancient trees, and its hide—gray and ridged like weathered stone—looked impervious to blade or beam. The earth trembled beneath its bulk, the air thick with the stench of raw menace.

Captain Ledge's voice cut through the panic, sharp and steady. "Company. And it's not here to parley."

Barricade stepped forward on instinct, his massive frame braced, beam gun clenched tight. His usual humor was gone, replaced by the grim focus of a soldier born for impact. Encrypt, meanwhile, narrowed his eyes, his sharp mind dissecting the beast's movements, desperate for some hint of weakness.

Von leaned in toward Ledge, his voice low, urgent. "We need a plan—fast."

The beast roared and lowered its head to charge.

But Mentor? He simply tilted his head, a sly grin tugging at the corners of his mouth, as though this was no more threatening than a stray goat in the market square.

"That's just Sauruvex," he said casually, waving a hand. "Ugly as ever, but manageable once I have a word with him. Step aside, rebels."

Before anyone could argue, Mentor thrust his palm forward. The air vibrated, and a sudden swirl of emerald energy coiled, twisting into a shimmering wall of force.

"No-Esca-Pe: Wall Brace!" he bellowed.

The beast slammed into the barrier with an earth-shaking crack. Sparks cascaded where horn met magic, the forest lighting up as though under a storm. The ground quaked with every lunge, but the wall did not yield. Mentor's eyes glowed brighter, his grin widening as he fed more power into the shield, shoulders rolling like a man half-amused by his own spectacle.

Ara's breath caught, her wide eyes darting to Ledge. "Did you know he could do this?"

Ledge's jaw tightened, though his lips curved faintly. "I had a suspicion."

Encrypt let out a low whistle. "Well. Resident sorcerer noted."

Even Von's stoic mask cracked, his voice quiet but edged with admiration. "Impressive."

Sauruvex thrashed one last time against the impenetrable wall before retreating into the trees, snarling in frustration.

Mentor dusted off his hands and winked. "Told you—nothing to fear. Now, my rebel crew, let's keep moving. Home's just ahead."

The forest grew quiet again, but not the same quiet as before. Now it thrummed with possibility, as if the woods themselves acknowledged the strange power walking among them.

The group pressed on through the enchanted woods, the beast still snarling faintly behind Mentor's shimmering barrier. Its futility only strengthened their faith in him. With such power on their side, the rebels felt, perhaps for the first time, that survival was more than a fleeting hope.

Dr. Von and Lieutenant Encrypt drifted into step together, their voices hushed beneath the rustle of leaves overhead. The doctor's tone carried the weariness of confession.

"The night we escaped," Von said quietly, "the project was already 90% complete."

Encrypt's brow tightened. "So it ends there? Humanity will remain unaltered?"

Von shook his head, his eyes shadowed. "No. Our escape only delayed them. Months, perhaps. But eventually, they'll finish what I began."

Encrypt's jaw tightened. "But why? The Ikannunaa are already untouchable. What threat do humans pose?"

Von's gaze swept the horizon, distant, mournful. "The project isn't for the Ikannunaa. It's for their Surrogates."

"Surrogates?" Encrypt pressed.

Von nodded grimly. "Humanoids drawn from other star systems, near identical to us. Altered through the Alpha-Gene Fluid. They'll be left behind to manage Earth once the Twin Royals depart—agents in plain sight, keeping humanity chained while making it appear humanity governs itself."

The revelation silenced them both, the weight of inevitability pressing down as heavily as the branches above.

Ara, eager to break the tension, turned toward Barricade. "So, big guy, remind me—your name again?"

"Lieutenant Barricade, ma'am," he replied with mock formality, flashing a grin.

Captain Ledge raised an eyebrow at her, his tone teasing. "And what do they call you?"

Ara smirked. "For the thousandth time, just Ara."

"Ara," Ledge repeated, letting the name linger. "Beautiful name. I'll remember it."

Her retort came swift. "It would be in your best interest, Captain."

Barricade laughed, shaking his head. "She's going to keep us on our toes."

Ledge's answering smile was softer, but his eyes agreed. Ara's fire would carry them farther than most weapons could.

Then the air shifted. A savory aroma curled through the trees—rich, spiced, and irresistible. Stomachs growled as the group slowed, heads turning to trace its source.

Mentor stopped mid-stride, inhaling deeply. His eyes lit with recognition, a smile tugging across his face.

"I'd recognize that smell anywhere," he said with a laugh. "That's my wife's cooking. And judging by the spice in the air, she definitely went heavy on the chili powder again."

The scent tugged him forward like a tether, his voice warming. "Come now. Follow the aroma. It'll take us home... and to the wooden table."

The rebels exchanged glances, fatigue momentarily forgotten. The promise of food, shelter, and laughter rose before them like a vision. Together, they pressed on through the trees, guided by the fragrance of spice and the unshakable hope of refuge.

The Conqueror III
As told by General Scorpiondt

There is a moment in warfare more dangerous than the first shot.

It is the moment after blood has been spilled.

When silence returns and the smoke clears... and you realize you underestimated the enemy.

I do not often miscalculate.

But this—this insurrection cloaked in whispers and foliage, in tribes and red cloth—this proved to be a more persistent infection than expected.

The rebels fled, of course. They always do. Cowards flee. But what I failed to account for—what my algorithm could not compute—was the forest's loyalty to them. It did not conceal them by chance. It welcomed them.

Even the land itself seems eager to betray me.

Their escape was not graceful. It was frantic, primal. Von, Ara, that treasonous Captain Ledge, and the other two—Barricade and Encrypt—all guided by a parade of warriors and mystics more myth than military. They made contact with a forgotten titan named Khalfani—some backwater warlord wrapped in dirt and conviction.

He greeted Von like a brother. How tragic.

Allies rooted in sentiment rarely survive the winter.

And yet—Khalfani's intervention bought them time. That... was my first oversight. He fed them, sheltered them, even offered his warriors as tribute to their cause. For what? A story? A legend? A scientist?

Idiocy.

But idiocy backed by loyalty becomes something worse:

Momentum.

They rested. Regrouped. Wove bonds around firelight and foolishness. Ara and Ledge even dared to exchange glances thick with juvenile longing—as if love is armor. As if memory will make them bulletproof.

Let them have their romances.

The forest took five of Khalfani's best when the Drifters attacked. Drifters—renegades, castoffs, the type of filth even wildlands reject. Their assault was a gift I would have paid for—watching the rebels bleed would have been a comfort. And yet they survived that, too.

More importantly... they adapted.

Ara studied the Blood Pinnacle—that flower I had once dismissed as decorative nuisance. She now theorizes it can undo my Beta-Gene fluid. Foolish? Perhaps. But her success rate is statistically annoying. She is becoming a scientist in her own right. That makes her dangerous.

Even the brute—Barricade—is not to be taken lightly. Beneath that slab of muscle is a man who follows cause with terrifying resolve. He left me, not because he feared me, but because he no longer believed I could win.

That is what stings.

And then there is Mentor.

Ah, yes. The cloaked clown. Their newest guide. A drunk, a rambler, a man who claims to speak to rabbits and builds walls from air.

On paper, he is useless.

In practice? He stalled a Sauruvex, a creature bred in the flesh pits of our early colonies, using nothing but light and laughter. He radiates unpredictability. That makes him lethal. I do not like variables I cannot trace to origin.

He called the rebels fugitives and dressed them as such—hoods and cloaks, a gang of shadows slipping through my grip. It is a clever strategy. Dress the revolution in the garb of anonymity. Strip away name and rank until only cause remains.

It is what I would have done.

They move now toward Indigo, that pocket of obscurity I had long since filed under irrelevant. But I see the game now. It is not refuge they seek. It is transformation.

They are building something inside those woods.

Something I cannot yet calculate.

And I do not like when my enemies grow invisible.

The Twin Princes are restless. Atsu-els simpers and scratches at failure while his brother plots in silence. The King breathes fire from his throne, blaming me for cracks forming in what should have been an unshakable dominion.

They blame me.

Let them.

They forget—I do not answer to their bloodline. I answer to outcome.

Let them keep their crowns and rituals. I command machines of fate. They require men like me—monsters who do not flinch when the world must be remade.

Still... I will admit a truth, buried and bitter.

Von escaped because I gave him too much time.

Ara thrives because I gave her too little credit.

Ledge betrayed me because I trusted him to believe only in war.

That ends now.

The rebels believe they have found hope.

But hope is only a signal flare.

And every flare gives away a position.

Let them run.

Let them train.

Let them bloom their red flowers in hidden gardens and hold hands beneath shooting stars.

When I return—when I bring the full weight of engineered obedience and the next generation of Surrogates—no forest, no wall of magic, no rabbit prophet or mystical cloak will save them.

I will burn Indigo until the soil itself begs for surrender.

And I will salt the Earth where Von's rebellion tried to take root.

Because I am not chasing fugitives.

I am correcting an equation.

And this time, I will leave no margin for error.

Chapter 4 | **Birth Of Mystics**

At last, the rebels reached Guide Mentor's home, and a collective sigh of relief passed through their ranks. The journey had been long and perilous, every mile fraught with shadows and unseen threats, but here—at the edge of the Karibegoan's domain—stood respite.

The cottage rose from the wild like something remembered from an older age. Weathered wood bore the scars of time, yet remained unbroken. Ivy curled along its walls in stubborn embrace, while the sagging thatch roof whispered of decades endured. The scent of damp earth mingled with aged timber, and from the stone chimney a thin plume of smoke twisted upward, carrying with it the faint perfume of burning wood. Candlelight glowed warmly behind shuttered windows, beckoning them in. Amid the vast and merciless wilderness, this place radiated a promise of shelter, of comfort—perhaps even of hope.

Lieutenant Barricade, never one to linger in reverence, grinned and broke the quiet.

"Last one to the table owes me dessert!" he bellowed, and with a burst of energy, launched himself forward.

His heavy strides carried him halfway across the clearing before—*THUD!*

He slammed headlong into something unseen, rebounding off the invisible barrier and sprawling onto the earth with a grunt that knocked the wind from his lungs.

For a beat the rebels froze. Then laughter erupted—raw, startled, cathartic. The sound spilled into the clearing, their first true laughter since the march had begun.

Lieutenant Encrypt stepped forward, eyes wide, pointing at the empty space before them. "Did he just—?"

Mentor groaned theatrically, pinching the bridge of his nose. "Lord, the fool ran straight into the dome."

He lifted his hand, fingers glowing with a faint inner light. The air rippled, then parted, revealing a seam of brilliance that spread into a doorway of shimmering energy. The unseen wall dissolved like mist, granting them passage.

With a flick of his wrist, Mentor gestured them through.

Barricade climbed to his feet, brushing dirt from his uniform with exaggerated dignity. He strode past the others, chin high, muttering, "I saw it coming."

The rebels exchanged smirks, their laughter trailing after him as they followed Mentor inside. And for the first time in weeks, the wilderness seemed to release them—if only for a little while.

As they reached the entrance, Mentor paused, his hand on the latch, and turned with the air of a man who had led many through both wilderness and war.

"Wipe your feet before you step inside," he said, voice stern yet courteous. even in chaos, rituals mattered.

He fumbled with a ring of old keys, fingers rough from years of guiding. With a sharp click, the door creaked open, releasing a tired groan that echoed down the hall.

The rebels expected warmth. Instead, disarray met them.

A thick soot clung to the beams. Cracks ran jagged through plaster. Cobwebs shrouded the corners like forgotten curtains. Papers, scrolls, and odd artifacts littered the floor, as though a storm had swept through and left behind nothing but chaos.

Still, they obeyed. Each wiped their boots dutifully before stepping in.

Ara, unable to resist, muttered to her father, "What's the point of wiping our feet?"

"Ara Von," Dr. Von said, full name clipped with quiet authority. That was enough. She pursed her lips and fell silent.

At Mentor's insistence, they gathered around a rough-hewn wooden table. Lieutenant Barricade eyed a chair, wary but resigned. He lowered himself into it.

Creak.

Groan.

SNAP.

The chair gave way, collapsing in a spray of splinters. Barricade landed on the floor with a thud that rattled the table.

Before laughter could fully erupt, a back door burst open.

A woman strode in—small in stature but commanding in presence. Miraj.

Her dreadlocks, twisted high into a bun, glittered with shells. A multicolored scarf framed her face, large hoops swinging from her ears. Beads glistened against her dashiki, each step of her brown loafers firm and sure.

Her hands planted on her hips, her eyes flashing like lightning.

"What is going on in here? My house cannot look like this! Who broke it up?" The Karibegoan patois rolled like thunder, authority laced with the rhythm of lived command.

Flustered, Barricade scrambled upright. "My apologies," he muttered, cheeks flushed red.

Miraj huffed. "I'm still paying for those chairs, you know."

The tension might have lingered, but Barricade dug into a pocket of his armor and produced a gold coin. He held it out. Miraj snatched it, bit it with sharp teeth, and slipped it into her apron. A sly wink softened her glare.

"That will do."

Mentor, ever the mediator, clapped his hands together. "All right, my people—drinks on the house!"

Laughter bubbled up, filling the crooked little home with warmth.

Ara, smirking, leaned close enough for only her father to hear. "Why not? Everything's already on this house."

Dr. Von's stare cut across the table, sharp as a blade. She looked away, biting back her grin, satisfied she'd pressed just far enough.

As if on cue, Miraj reemerged with bowls of steaming stew and loaves of baked bread. The savory aroma filled the cottage, pushing aside the soot and dust with something older, deeper—home. Tin cups clinked as drinks were poured, and soon the room hummed with talk, with laughter, with the fragile relief of survivors allowed, for a fleeting moment, to feel human again.

Then, with a mischievous grin, Mentor slammed both palms against the wooden table, beating out a steady rhythm. The cups rattled, the spoons chimed against bowls, and the pulse of it seemed to crawl under everyone's skin. One by one, shoulders loosened, heads began to nod, and feet tapped along to the beat.

Miraj, watching from the hearth with folded arms, arched a brow. Amusement softened her fiery stare.

"Go on, dear," she said, her tone teasing but warm. "Show them what you can do."

Mentor's grin widened. He pushed back from his chair, rose with a flourish, and let the rhythm take hold. His hips began to spiral in wide, exaggerated circles. He rolled his shoulders, let his arms sway like branches in the wind, then threw them overhead, snapping them side to side with wild abandon.

The room erupted. Laughter mingled with the clapping beat, and soon every rebel found themselves drawn into the dance. Even Von cracked a rare smile as Ara spun in a mock twirl, her red cloth fluttering like a banner. Barricade stomped his boots in time, Encrypt snapped his fingers with mechanical precision, and Captain Ledge—stoic as ever—allowed himself the ghost of a smirk as he moved just enough to prove he hadn't been left behind.

The cottage became a swirl of bodies, music born from nothing but wood and spirit. For a time, the weight of war fell away. They were not fugitives. They were not soldiers. They were simply alive.

When exhaustion finally won, they collapsed back into chairs and onto the floor, flushed with laughter and weariness. The fire burned low. Outside, the black sky reclaimed its silence, punctured only by the unfamiliar constellations that glittered above Earth's horizon.

Mentor, still standing at the table's center, raised one hand. His smile lingered, but his tone cut through the haze of drink and revelry with quiet authority.

"Enough for tonight," he said. "Rest well. Tomorrow at dawn, you begin your training in the mystic arts."

With a sweep of his arm toward the back of the cottage, Mentor's tone softened. "Rooms are ready. Barricade, Encrypt, and Captain Ledge—you'll share the one on the left. Von and Ara, yours is to the right."

He clapped his hands once, the sharp sound echoing in the cozy space. "No arguments. Beds are simple, but softer than dirt. Make use of them while you can."

Barricade muttered something about preferring a battlefield to a bedmate who snores, earning a playful elbow from Encrypt. Ara rolled her eyes but hid a smile as she followed her father toward their quarters.

The words settled like embers into the room—warm, but dangerous with promise.

They drifted into sleep with full bellies, sore muscles, and laughter still clinging to their chests. Yet under it all lay a new weight—purpose. Whatever awaited at sunrise, they would face it together.

The hearth burned low, shadows climbing the cottage walls like silent witnesses. Outside, the forest hushed itself, as though listening.

Mentor sat alone by the window, staff resting across his knees, his usual brightness stripped away. Moonlight silvered his face, and for once, no smile touched it.

"Three of you," he murmured. "Just three. Thought maybe that number would be small enough to keep safe."

His gaze lingered on the glass, but the forest beyond wasn't what he saw. He saw Earth — a village far from Indigo, where clay ovens smoked and river reeds whispered in the breeze. He remembered dirt paths winding through huts, the rhythm of drums pulsing through the night, and three young faces lifted toward him, burning with questions and hunger for more.

They hadn't been warriors. Not scholars, either. Just spirited souls who had listened when he spoke of hidden strength. He had trained them in secret, away from the eyes of Guides who would never have understood. Earth was not meant to be touched that way. But Mentor had believed. He had believed the world itself was calling them.

The memory shifted. Flames licking the sky. Screams cut short. His three pupils falling, one by one, their courage snuffed out before it could even rise.

Mentor's eyes shut tight. His hand tightened on the staff until the wood groaned.

"No one saw. No one knows," he whispered. "That mistake belongs to me alone."

Leaning back, he let the moon carve a hard line across his face. "Not again. Not this time. If I fail once more, then it won't just be three that vanish."

Upstairs, Barricade's snore rumbled like distant thunder. Encrypt turned in his sleep, muttering fractured phrases of thought. Ara breathed steady, dreamless — her spirit already bearing a weight she did not yet understand.

The cottage slept with the sound of beginnings. Mentor sat awake in the dark, haunted by the memory of endings.

The morning sun slanted through the shutters, spilling gold across the cottage floor. Its warmth did nothing to soften the pounding in their skulls. Groans echoed through the room as each rebel slowly dragged themselves upright, the price of last night's revelry now exacted in full.

Somehow, during the night, their plans for separate quarters had collapsed along with their discipline. One by one, drawn by the lingering warmth of the fire and the comfort of proximity, they had abandoned their beds and drifted back into the shared room by the kitchen. Von had slumped into a chair, cloak still wrapped tight. Ara had curled up by the hearth, red cloth draped over her like a banner. Barricade stretched across half a bench, while Encrypt and Ledge had claimed corners of the floor, their boots still on. The cottage bore witness to their retreat, bowls and cups scattered like relics of their laughter.

Lieutenant Barricade was the first to break the silence, clutching his stomach as if it might revolt against him.

"Hey, Mentor," he rasped, his voice like gravel. "We could skip training this morning, yeah? And where'd my appetite go? You think it's coming back?"

Mentor, leaning against the doorway with a carved staff in hand, rolled his eyes. "For the sake of dinner later, I hope not. The last thing I need is to see you devour my whole pantry like some wild hog."

Encrypt groaned, massaging his temples. "Feels like my head's been scrambled by a magnet."

"More like cracked open by a hammer," Captain Ledge muttered, rubbing his own.

Then Ara, far too chipper for someone who had kept pace with them last night, stretched with mock elegance and asked, "Hey, magic man—"

"It's Mentor, young lady," he cut in, brow arched.

"That's what I said!" she countered with a grin. "Anyway, those beers were good. Got any Black Wine around here?"

Mentor sucked his teeth, staring at her as though she'd sprouted horns. "What? Girl, are you serious? Black Wine at this hour? I already know you're going to be the one to give me grey hair. I know it."

Barricade barked a laugh, wincing immediately after. "Let's see how much fun she is when the sobering part hits."

Mentor only smirked, tapping a foot against the floor. "Well, lucky for all of you, I have a cure. An unusual remedy, but trust me—it works."

Dr. Von, curiosity always outweighing caution, leaned forward. "What remedy?"

"The Elamamgis fruit," Mentor declared, his grin widening. "Sweet, tangy, good for breakfast—and strong enough to wash out that headache living in your skulls."

Encrypt smirked despite himself. "Explains your liver's longevity."

"My liver is older than some empires." Mentor shot back with a chuckle. Then he waved them toward the rear of the cottage. "But I'm not a vendor to carry fruit straight to your plate. Go wash up, change into the robes Miraj laid out, and meet me out back. I promise—after breakfast, training begins in earnest."

The group exchanged wary glances, half-dreading the promise, half-hungry for the cure. With weary groans and muttered complaints, they began preparing for the day, each step carrying them closer to the strange, mystical path Mentor had set before them.

At the grove of Elamamgis trees, the rebels stood transformed. Gone were their travel-worn clothes. In their place: crisp white dashikis with a black Karibegoan insignia stitched over the chest, loose-fitting trousers, and brown loafers. The uniformity bound them together—no longer scattered fugitives, but a unit.

They tore into the golden-orange fruit with gusto. Sweet juice ran down their chins, smearing shirts and fingers, but none of them cared. Every bite dissolved the throb of their hangovers, replacing it with warmth that coursed through their veins like a gentle fire. For the first time in days, they felt alive.

Barricade leaned back against a trunk, wiping his mouth with the back of his massive hand. A satisfied grin split his face.

"Five stars for the fruit, little guy. I'll post a five-star review."

The group burst into laughter. Even Ara, cheeks sticky with juice, managed a genuine laugh that made her look almost carefree.

Mentor, however, only smirked. He was dressed differently now: a multicolored dashiki tight to the shoulders, loose orange pants, a strand of carved wooden beads at his neck, and a gold medallion engraved with curling inscriptions resting on his chest. A tiny red marble dangled from his ear on a chain, catching the morning sun, while a worn bracelet clinked softly at his wrist.

"Glad you enjoyed it," Mentor said, voice warm but eyes sharp. Then his tone snapped like a whip. "But the fun time is done. We have pressing matters."

Barricade licked the last of the juice from his thumb. "Like what?"

"The training, you big muscle-head!" Mentor barked, stamping his foot for emphasis. "Now get your bloated bellies off the ground, wipe your hands, and report to my underground room. This fruit cures your hangovers, yes—but it also fuels your bodies. No excuse now. It is time."

Laughter faded. One by one, the rebels straightened, their expressions sobering as Mentor's words settled. What had been a feast became a summons, a reminder that the real work—the transformation, the fight ahead—was only beginning.

The back door creaked shut behind them, the cool morning air trailing in as they stepped across the threshold. The back entrance had led them in, but now they stood clustered by the open door to the underground room. The stairwell gaped below, candlelight flickering faintly from the chamber beneath.

Barricade leaned against the table beside the stairwell, arms crossed, shoulders filling the space like a barricade in flesh and bone. His gaze swept the others, sharp and unflinching. "You heard Mentor," he said flatly. "We don't have time for games. Learn fast, or die faster."

Encrypt smirked, lounging in a chair with calculated carelessness, flicking a strand of hair from his face. "Die faster? That's inspiring. If death's the point, why waste time training at all? Let's just hurl ourselves off a cliff and hope mystic wings sprout on the way down."

Barricade pushed off the table, the heat in his voice rising. "Mock all you want. Some of us actually take this seriously."

"And some of us," Encrypt fired back, "know that seriousness doesn't make you smart. You can't muscle your way into being a Mystic."

Von's hand rose, voice calm but edged. "Enough. Strength without thought is reckless. Wit without discipline is useless. We need both, not bickering."

Ledge, sitting nearest the stairwell with his elbows resting on his knees, broke his silence. His tone was clipped, measured. "Von's right. If we can't hold the line together, we won't last a breath against Scorpiondt's hounds. I won't spend my strength protecting those too busy proving a point to fight as one."

The words struck. Barricade's nostrils flared, Encrypt's smirk faltered. Tension coiled in the air, stretched tight as a drawn bow.

Then Ara stood, hair catching the candlelight. One word cut through it all. "Enough."

Her eyes moved deliberately from one to the next. "We've all lost something. Don't lose each other before the real fight even begins."

For a moment, silence reigned — until a voice thundered up the stairwell.

"Knock it off, all of you! If you've got so much fire, save it for the enemy. Get down here now; training does not wait for quarreling children!"

The command snapped the tension like a whip. Without another word, the rebels exchanged glances and filed toward the stairwell, their footsteps echoing down into the chamber below where Mentor awaited.

Heavy with dust and incense, pressing against their lungs until each breath felt measured. For a moment, no one could even see their own hands. Then— flick. A candle flared to life, its dim flame shivering in the gloom. Mentor stood there, his face half-shadowed, his expression sharper than any they had seen before.

He lit more candles one by one, casting the chamber into a wavering amber glow. The space revealed itself: shelves stacked with ancient leather-bound tomes, glass bottles filled with liquids that shimmered unnaturally, bowls of strange powders that caught the light like ground starlight.

Mentor's voice cut through the silence. "What you are about to learn is hidden knowledge—forbidden. My ancestors carried it in secret, passed down only through our bloodline. But tradition will kill us under these circumstances. And so—I share it with you."

He motioned for them to sit in a circle, two feet apart, their bodies forming a perfect ring. "Hold out your hands." His tone was calm but commanding.

"Each of you will receive one solitary star seed. Do not eat it until I give the word."

Captain Ledge turned the seed in his palm, a flicker of recognition in his stare. "These look familiar."

"Familiar," Mentor confirmed, "because they come from the same fruits you just devoured for breakfast."

Ara squinted at hers, unable to hold back. "So... you're going to make us eat something you scooped off the ground?"

Von's head snapped toward her, his voice clipped. "Ara Von."

She bit her lip and looked down, though a smirk lingered.

Encrypt's curiosity sharpened his features. "What's the purpose of consuming these seeds?"

Mentor's reply was steady, solemn. "They will put you in a trance for thirty-three Earth days. It's the only way your body can endure what comes next."

Von's brows furrowed as he pieced it together aloud. "A transformation... a rebirth. These seeds are the threshold. They'll realign our energy signatures to match a mystic Karibegoan's."

Mentor's eyes gleamed. "Correct. But the seeds are only the beginning. Now—keep silent. Keep still. I will manifest the Fetal Orb."

He spread his hands and began to chant in the flowing cadence of Majeskrit.

"Tra-Ns-Fus-E: Orb Incubate."

The ground shivered. A low hum vibrated through the chamber. The candles flickered wildly, then guttered out all at once, plunging them into total darkness.

And then—light. A small orb appeared in the center of the circle, pulsing like a living heart. It grew, layer upon layer of radiance folding over them until the chamber was gone. They now sat within the Orb itself, suspended in its soft white glow, the air thrumming with power.

"Now," Mentor's voice echoed gently inside the Orb, "consume the seeds."

One by one, they obeyed. The bitter taste of the star seeds lingered only a moment before their consciousness began to slip. The glow wrapped tighter, like a womb, and each rebel sank into a trance deeper than sleep, their bodies slack but their souls pulled elsewhere.

Mentor watched them, his face unreadable. He whispered as the Orb sealed shut:

"See you in thirty-three days."

The heavy door closed behind him with a thud. Alone in the candlelit hall above, Mentor exhaled. Never before had off-worlders entered the Fetal Orb. Never before had anyone attempted to force transformation this way.

The fate of his people—and of Earth itself—now hung in the balance.

Thirty-Three Days In Incubation.

From the depths of the underground chamber, Mentor emerged, the flickering candlelight casting wavering shadows against the rugged stone walls as he ascended the creaking wooden steps. The scent of aged wood and faint traces of dried herbs clung to the cottage like ghosts of old rituals.

He sank into the rough-hewn table, fingers brushing its scarred surface as his gaze drifted toward the small, grime-streaked window. The heavy beams above groaned with the slow shift of dusk, while outside, the rhythmic hum of Indigo birds stitched their haunting song into the silence.

Through the dull glass, he caught Miraj's reflection—her face half-hidden, her stare sharp and unblinking. Curiosity mingled with concern in her eyes. The candle between them flared, stretching their shadows long across the walls, as though the very cottage leaned in to eavesdrop.

"Did that go okay? Did it go all right?" she asked at last, her voice soft but probing, a whisper carrying more weight than the words themselves.

Mentor leaned back, exhaling. A half-smile curved his lips, but it did little to disguise the heaviness in his shoulders.

"Yeah, it started off just like we planned." His tone was casual, but he let the end trail off, unfinished. Miraj knew him too well—the pause was the truth, the silence louder than his grin.

She folded her arms, waiting.

To deflect, he straightened, a sparkle of mischief creeping back into his eyes. "So, what kind of enchanting feast did you conjure up in the kitchen this afternoon?"

Miraj arched an eyebrow. Her voice dropped to a hushed, sarcastic lilt. "A stuffed white rabbit."

Mentor's eyes went wide, his face lighting with mock delight. "Ah! Finally! I told you he owed me money! Let's eat the debt!" He laughed, a burst of levity pushing against the lingering shadows.

But Miraj shook her head slowly, smirk tugging at her lips. "Not an edible rabbit, my love—one stuffed with cotton. I'm not cooking tonight. I have to travel tomorrow to replace the chair your big friend broke."

Mentor blinked, then frowned theatrically. "Wait… so what exactly are we going to eat?"

Right on cue, his stomach growled, loud enough to make Miraj's smirk widen into a grin.

"Whatever your Guide salary can conjure up."

Their stares locked, the duel wordless but sharp. Mentor sighed, throwing his hands up in mock surrender, though the grin never left his face.

"Fine, fine. I will fetch something. But don't blame me if I come back with something… strange."

Miraj tilted her head, earrings glinting in the candlelight. "Stranger than you? That is something I would like to see."

Mentor paused mid-stride, pretending to weigh her words with great seriousness, then smirked. "Careful now. Indigo always finds ways to surprise—even me."

He winked, then pushed through the door. The last flare of candlelight caught his silhouette, stretching him tall and thin before the sunlight swallowed him whole. Outside, the faint buzz of Indigo's market lights glimmered in the distance, calling him toward beer, street food... and the secrets he kept tucked behind every grin.

The air wrapped around Mentor like a cloak, carrying the scent of warm earth and the promise of rain. Above, the sky stretched in a wide, clear blue, sunlight glinting through drifting clouds. The towering trees leaned close, their leaves whispering as the light filtered down in shifting gold.

He stepped forward—then stopped.

There, perched just beyond the bend, sat a white rabbit.

It seemed almost to shimmer in the sunlight, its fur bright against the dappled shade. Between its small paws it clutched an orange carrot, nibbling with calm indifference. The sight was almost absurdly ordinary—yet in the stillness of the forest, it felt uncanny.

The rabbit stilled, ears twitching. Mentor's gaze met its bright eyes, and for a breath, neither moved. Recognition sparked—half memory, half omen.

Mentor squinted, tilting his head.

"I see you've got coin for a carrot," he muttered, his voice half-chiding, half-amused. "But not for this Karibegoan, eh?"

The rabbit blinked once, as if weighing the jab, then in a flash of white fur it spun and darted into the undergrowth. Its cotton tail vanished into the green, the brush swallowing the sound.

Mentor sucked his teeth, shaking his head. "You'd better run, Fin." he called after it, though the forest gave no reply.

For a moment, he lingered, staring into the light where the rabbit had fled. Then a low chuckle broke free, and he tugged his coat tighter.

Still, as he turned toward the path, the image clung to him—white against the green, small but unyielding. A reminder, perhaps, that omens could appear even under the brightest sun.

Indigo's market unfurled like a living tapestry beneath the burnished afternoon sun. Colorful canopies rippled in the warm breeze, and glass jars filled with trapped fireflies shimmered faintly beside the light, more decoration now than necessity. Stalls spilled into narrow dirt paths, overflowing with fruits that gleamed as though polished by daylight, bundles of herbs bound in red twine, and meats roasting on spits that hissed when the fat struck the coals.

The air was a heady cocktail of spice, smoke, and fermented root beer. Every step pulled Mentor deeper into its rhythm—the calls of vendors, the clatter of coins, the laughter of children darting between stalls.

"Ah, Indigo," Mentor muttered with a grin, patting his pocket. "Let's see what a Guide wallet can buy today."

He stopped at a grill, where a stout man basted skewers of glowing fish. The flesh shimmered faintly blue, sizzling in a marinade that smelled equal parts heavenly and hazardous.

"Two skewers," Mentor ordered.

"Two coins," the vendor countered.

Mentor slipped him one. "One coin now, one coin after I confirm that this fish doesn't make me glow like a lantern."

The vendor snorted but handed them over. Mentor bit into one, chewed thoughtfully, then raised his brows. "Not bad. It glows on the grill, not in the gut. Approved."

Further down, a spice stall run by an old woman with cataract-clouded eyes beckoned him. She held up a pouch and whispered, "Powder for courage. Powder for forgetting. Both cost the same price."

Mentor cocked his head. "Lady, I already have enough courage and forgetting to last me three lifetimes. Do you have anything for indigestion?"

She cackled and tossed him a bundle of dried leaves. "Chew three. Four if the rabbit stew comes back to haunt you."

Mentor tipped her a coin and moved on.

It was then that a cluster of cloaked figures caught his attention. The Monks of Mercy—rarely seen outside their shrines—spoke in hushed tones beneath a fluttering awning. Most of their words were swallowed by the noise of the market, but one cut through the air like a blade:

"Surrogates."

Mentor froze mid-step. He slid behind a rack of hanging scarves, pretending to weigh the merits of a gaudy blue one while listening.

"The visions say they will move soon," one monk rasped. "They've already been injected. The Gatekeepers tether them."

Another answered, "I see the same. If they reach Earth, the tribes are finished. Not even Indigo's dome can hold."

Mentor's grin faltered, the humor draining from his eyes. He draped the scarf over his shoulder, muttering under his breath, "So, di game is moving faster than Von thinks…"

Shaking it off, he ambled toward the beer stand. The vendor filled a clay jug with frothy brew, foam spilling over the rim. Mentor took a long pull, wiped his mouth, and forced his grin back.

"Food, beer, and little whispers of doom," he said. "That's what I call a balanced diet."

With skewers in one hand and ale in the other, he left the market. His steps were light, his whistle jaunty—but his mind weighed heavy. He had heard enough to know the Monks of Mercy weren't trading rumors. They were naming inevitabilities.

And below his home, wrapped in the steady glow of the Fetal Orb, the rebels slept. When they woke, the world outside would already be shifting against them.

Day Ten

As the sun dipped below the horizon, Indigo's marketplace softened into an amber haze. Lanterns swayed between poles, fireflies trapped in crystal jars flickered like captive stars, and the chatter of merchants faded into the hush of evening. Children darted through the cobblestone lanes, their laughter thinning as stalls shuttered for the night.

Miraj moved easily through the crowd, her scarf catching the lantern light. At her side walked Mojo and Miracle—sisters in spirit if not in blood. Together, they slipped into the corner of the square, where a crooked wooden sign swung above a village bakery. The scent of spiced bread and smoke clung to the air.

They claimed a table outside, steam rising from chipped mugs of clove tea. A tray of warm buns sat between them, their buttery fragrance cutting through the chill. For a time, they were just three women in the lamplight, their laughter swelling and falling like waves—gestures wide, stories exaggerated, as if recounting battles rather than the tangled dramas of daily life.

Then Miracle, slim and radiant in the glow, quieted the night with a single name.

"The Humming Black Trunk."

The words struck the table like a stone in water. Their laughter broke. Even the market's fading chatter seemed to recede, as though the name itself commanded silence.

Miraj leaned in, her sharp eyes scanning the street. Her voice dropped low, carrying a weight meant only for trusted ears.

"The time has come. We must act before the stars shift. Mentor find five—five who can face what others cannot. But before dem rise, before dem can fight di Ikannunaa, he and I will send them to recover the trunk."

Mojo shifted in her chair, her dashiki glowing with its stitched colors, her triangular green earrings catching firelight. Her broad shoulders stiffened. "And if he frees himself…?" Her voice was more growl than question. "Then none of us are safe. Not Indigo. Not anywhere." Her hands twitched, then she half-joked through the tension: "If he ever crosses me—I'd give him a right, then a left, then another right, and an uppercut for dessert." She shadow-boxed the air, her movements more defiance than comedy.

Miracle gave a sharp laugh, though unease softened it. "Mojo, sit yourself down. All that swinging won't mean nothing if he breaks loose. He'd overpower us all."

The truth hung heavy, chilling the steam from their tea.

Miracle's voice dropped again. "Does Mentor still hold the energy signature device?"

Miraj shook her head, a flicker of frustration tightening her jaw. "We've searched. It's gone. If only it came with a tracker built into itself."

Silence followed. Then Mojo exhaled sharply and leaned forward, her voice steady, stripped of its humor. "Then take my husband's. You and Mentor will need it more than we ever will."

Her words fell with the weight of finality.

Miracle broke the heaviness with her familiar grin, blinking her left eye in its signature wink. "If there's anything else you need, let me know. I'm Miracle. I can make it happen."

The three women sat in that fragile space between camaraderie and conspiracy, their laughter gone but their bond unbroken. Above them, the lanterns swayed, casting long shadows that made the quiet promise of their mission feel both sacred—and perilous.

Day Twenty

The cottage had traded its usual hush for the clatter of dice, the scrape of game pieces, and the belly laughs of three old friends. With Miraj away visiting her mother, Mentor's home became a stage for competition and teasing, the wooden table littered with pint glasses and crumbs from half-eaten bread rolls.

Maestro—the Piper—leaned back, his long dreadlocks sweeping the floor as he lifted his flute to his lips, playing a triumphant trill at Mentor's latest loss. His multicolor dashiki shimmered in the firelight, the shells at his neck clinking when he chuckled.

Then his laughter caught.

A faint glow bled up through the floorboards. Not firelight. Not candlelight. Something older, stranger.

"Mentor," Maestro drawled, half-teasing, half-uneasy. "You left a candle burning in your room again, didn't you?"

Mentor didn't look down. He smirked, slid a game piece across the board. "Nope. That's no candle."

Maestro leaned forward, suspicion sharpening his tone. "Then what in the daylight am I seeing?"

The game fell silent. Even the fire seemed to hush. Mentor set his piece down, folded his arms, his gaze grave now.

"Brothers," he said, voice low. that light? A Majeskrit-manifested Fetal Orb. Inside it—five beings chosen to stand against the Ikannunaa."

The room shifted. Laughter dissolved into the weight of his words.

Guardian Mythic, bare-chested save for his beaded bracelet, fingers brushing the hilt of his sword, tilted his head. His bandana shadowed his eyes, but the glow caught them like coals.

"Tell me plainly," he said, steady but heavy. Mentor— do you think those five could help retrieve the Humming Black Trunk?"

Mentor's grin faded. The easy humor was gone. He met both their stares, the Orb's glow flickering in his pupils.

"That's why they're in the Orb," he said, his voice heavy with intent. "They already know of Scorpiondt. They already know of the Ikannunaa. But the Trunk—" his tone dropped lower, almost a whisper, "—the Trunk is what still stays hidden from them. For now."

Silence stretched. Mythic's grip tightened on his blade.

Mentor eyed the sword and asked softly, "Guardian, why you still carry it everywhere you go? The war of Ras-Magenta ended with your brothers."

Mythic's jaw flexed. "Ended for them, not for me. I should have died with my kin. Instead, I walk alone. This blade reminds me who I lost. Every swing is their memory."

Maestro's voice gentled, flute lowered to his lap. "They wouldn't mind you carrying' the sword, brother. But the guilt? No… no they wouldn't."

Mentor's stare lingered. "Or maybe you survived for another purpose still waiting."

The words hung like smoke. The game was forgotten. Beneath their feet, the Fetal Orb pulsed once, twice, like a heartbeat   reminding them all that tonight's laughter sat atop something far greater, and far more dangerous.

Day Thirty-Three

The moment of reckoning was nigh. The rebel crew, prepared to be unshackled and unleash their mystic powers, were on the cusp of action. But a sudden anomaly disrupted the harmony—the Fetal Orb pulsated, its glow intensifying beyond reason, its energy spiraling out of control.

Miraj awoke with a start, a cold sweat beading on her forehead as she sensed the disturbance. She slipped out of bed and hurried into the shared room, her bare feet whispering against the floorboards. Through the cracks she saw it: the Orb below, its light far too bright, its pulse erratic and dangerous. Panic seized her chest.

She rushed to Mentor, shaking him hard. "Something's wrong," she cried, her voice trembling.

Mentor groaned, half-asleep. "What's wrong, girl?" His words were thick with sleep.

"The Fetal Orb," she pressed, her eyes wide. "It glows too bright—it beats too fast. This isn't right."

Mentor shot upright, the haze of sleep gone in an instant. He yanked on his coat, heart hammering, and together they stumbled down toward the underground chamber. The cottage itself seemed to quake with the Orb's surging energy—papers fluttering, shelves rattling, walls groaning as though alive.

But before they reached the chamber, the Orb tore free of its cradle. It lifted, defying gravity, blazing with white brilliance. With a violent shudder it phased through stone and timber, soaring upward until it burst through the cottage roof. Mentor and Miraj staggered back, shielding their eyes as the Orb streaked into the night sky like a rising sun.

It climbed higher and higher, until—

A detonation. A blinding flash split the heavens. The Orb erupted mid-air, raining sparks and shimmering embers across the treetops. The light scattered like dying stars, and then there was nothing. Only silence, and the whisper of the wind.

Miraj stood in stunned disbelief, her breath caught in her throat. Mentor fell to his knees in the grass, clutching his head as the enormity struck him.

"What have I done?" he rasped, tears stinging his eyes. "I killed the one chance this world had for freedom."

He stayed there, muttering, the morning wind tugging at his coat. "All gone… all gone."

Miraj turned away, too shaken to answer. She disappeared back into the cottage, leaving him kneeling alone beneath the paling night sky.

And then—whispers. Low, melodic, impossible. Chants that seemed to float on the air, circling him like unseen spirits. Mentor stiffened, his pulse quickening.

"Who's there?" he demanded, twisting left and right. His voice echoed through the trees, but no answer came.

A tap landed on his shoulder.

Mentor spun, his heart lodging in his throat—

—and there he was.

Mystic Von.

Not the man who had eaten with them, laughed with them, hidden his fear behind sharp wit—but something changed, something ascended. His clothing hung in tatters, but from every tear blazed rivulets of white-hot energy. Embers of light drifted from his skin. His veins glowed like living circuits of fire. His eyes burned with an unearthly calm.

"That," Mystic Von said, his tone steady as if discussing the weather, "was a close call."

Mentor staggered backward, nearly tripping over himself. "Von… no. You should be dead. The Orb—it detonated!"

Von's smile was faint, sly. "Dead? Please. I rerouted the Orb's channels, aligned them with our alien aura. Without that correction, the transformation would've failed. This way, it completed."

Mentor shook his head, stunned. "But you swallowed the seed. I watched you!"

Von chuckled, shaking his head. "I didn't. I spat it out the moment you turned your back. Couldn't let chance decide the outcome."

For a moment, Mentor just stared, then let out a harsh laugh. Relief and disbelief tangled in his voice. "Lord, you're dangerous, man."

Von's grin faded, replaced with steel. "Clean up the cottage. No one can suspect the Orb misfired."

Mentor swallowed, then asked the question burning in his chest. "And the others? The girl—her father—Encrypt, Barricade, Ledge?"

Von's gaze drifted toward the dark forest. His voice was calm, but it carried weight. "They're out there. Scattered in the undergrowth. Mystics don't vanish—they return."

The words rolled like prophecy, leaving Mentor frozen. Above them, the stars still glimmered faintly, as though watching.

The dawn had not yet broken, but a new order already had.

After getting cleaned up, Mystic Von joined Mentor and Miraj at the wooden table, the three of them sitting in the dim light of the cottage. They acknowledged the gravity of the situation, the weight of what had just transpired pressing down on them, but they also knew they had to focus on the path forward. Mystic Von had a genetic project in mind that could grant them an advantage against General Scorpiondt. But before they could delve into the details, a knock at the front door and pulsating energy signatures interrupted their conversation.

With eager anticipation, Miraj swung open the door, revealing the mystic heroes Mystic Ara, Mystic Encrypt, Mystic Barricade, and Mystic Ledge, their bright-white energy embers glowing in tattered clothing and illuminated energy coursing through their glowing veins. Mystic Von smiled at the sight of them, but Mystic Ara, his daughter, stepped forward. Her expression was one of irritation rather than joy.

Mystic Ara didn't bother with a hug. She tapped her father's forehead. "You left us unconscious in the bush. Wild monsters eat unconscious things," she scolded, her frustration clear.

"But you weren't," Mystic Von retorted, his tone calm and unbothered by her anger.

"That's not the point," she huffed, frustration reaching exhaustion. "You know what? Never mind. I am starving and drained. Where is the food, for Rainah's sake? Because all we have had in the last thirty-three days was one dirty fruit seed!" She stormed into the kitchen, ransacking the shelves with mounting desperation.

Miraj raised her brows, her hands planting firmly on her hips. "Girl, my cupboard can't take that kind of raid! You tore down my kitchen like you're still dreaming."

Mystic Encrypt leaned against the doorframe, smirking despite the fatigue in his veins. "Thirty-three days inside a glowing Orb, and the first thing she does is raid the pantry. Legendary."

Mystic Barricade, still brushing twigs and dirt from his massive shoulders, muttered, "Don't laugh. I'd eat a stone if Miraj served it with salt."

"Salt too expensive to waste on stone," Miraj snapped, swatting his arm with a ladle before moving toward the hearth.

Mystic Ledge sank into a chair, his glowing veins pulsing faintly in rhythm with the candlelight. "She's not wrong," he admitted. "One fruit seed in thirty-three days isn't exactly a feast."

Mentor leaned back in his chair, mug in hand, a grin tugging at his lips. "You glow like gods but complain like beggars. Lucky for you, stew's on. And no rabbit this time." He winked, earning a rare chuckle from Von.

Ara paused her frantic search, eyes narrowing at her father. "You planned this, didn't you? Leaving us to wake in the dirt, starving."

Von folded his hands on the table, his face unreadable, his voice measured. "Discomfort sharpens gratitude, Ara. You endured the Orb, you survived the seed. Now you rise as Mystics. Hunger reminds you of the cost of that gift."

Ara groaned and flopped into a chair. "Spare me the lecture, Dad. Just pass the stew."

Miraj shook her head but ladled out bowls, sliding bread onto the table as well. "Eat, all of you. But Mark my words—lick every crumb from my shelves again, and tomorrow you'll train on an empty belly."

For the first time since their transformation, laughter—tired, hungry, and human—spilled through the cottage, the sound wrapping around them like a promise of the unity they would need in the trials to come.

Later That Night

Deep within the cottage's underground room, Mystic Von seized the perfect moment while the others above slumbered, their breaths steady and peaceful. This was his clandestine laboratory—a sanctuary carved out of secrecy, lit only by the wavering glow of scattered candles. Dust clung to the stone walls; cobwebs stretched between wooden beams like forgotten signatures of time. The air carried the musk of aged parchment and the faint metallic tang of well-worn instruments. Shelves sagged beneath old tomes, bottles of strange powders, and delicate apparatuses. Here, time itself seemed suspended.

For hours, Von worked, his hands moving with surgical precision. He poured over cracked notebooks and brittle scrolls, scribbling fresh annotations until the table became a sea of cluttered parchment. Candles guttered low as he studied samples under their strained light, his every movement a mixture of scientist and sorcerer. Each discarded page drifted to the floor, forming a paper trail of his relentless thought.

He paced between the workbench and the shelves, restless, driven by a singular weight—the Sigma-Gene Fluid Project. The problem consumed him. The puzzle of its design loomed like a riddle from the stars, one he alone could solve. His mind hummed with possibility, yet his weary pacing betrayed the stakes: this was no theory. This was survival.

At last, exhaustion claimed him. His head fell against the scarred wooden table, his body surrendering to the pull of sleep even as his mind refused to quiet. Dreams consumed him, blurred and violent, a kaleidoscope of symbols and shadows.

Suddenly, clarity struck.

He stood in a sterile medical room—not here, not now, but in some future place. The sterile hum of Yonkers, New York, pressed against his ears, impossibly vivid. A pregnant woman lay at the center, sweat beading her brow, her breaths heaving with effort. He knew her name though he'd never met her: Mrs. Courthall. At her side, a man named Robert clasped her hand, whispering strength.

Von was there too—not as the fugitive mystic-scientist of Indigo, but as her doctor. His voice guided her through the final push, words of calm woven through the sterile light. And then—life.

A newborn boy cried into the world, his small form lifted into the arms of his parents. Their voices rang with joy, naming him aloud:

"Stephan Courthall."

But the dream shifted. The child did not lie helpless in blankets. He stood at the foot of the medical bed, impossibly poised, his stare piercing through Von as if centuries separated them. Moonlight-silver eyes, too wise, too knowing, burned into him. In that silent glare lay something prophetic—accusation, warning, promise. Von felt stripped bare, as though the boy peered into the very marrow of his secrets.

The name echoed in his ears as the dream fractured into shards of white light.

Von awoke with a violent start, sweat dampening his collar. His pulse hammered. The dream clung to him like a mark he could not shake.

"Stephan Courthall…" he whispered into the candlelit shadows.

Was the vision bound to the Sigma-Gene Fluid? A thread of destiny woven into his own forbidden project? He could not yet say. But one thing was certain—his work had crossed from science into prophecy.

And the stakes of his journey had just multiplied.

The Conqueror IV
As told by General Scorpiondt

There is an ancient Karibegoan proverb that says: "A man who sleeps in the mouth of the forest will either wake transformed… or not at all."

It is an elegant deception—this belief in transformation. Change, they think, is the solution. That by drinking from rivers of mysticism and singing with the trees, they can rewrite what they are.

But no forest can cleanse what is bound in the blood.

Not theirs. Not mine.

I've studied the mutations. I've ordered the engineering. I've watched entire civilizations rise and collapse under the illusion of evolution. So when I learned that Dr. Von had disappeared into the wild, escorted by that cloaked jester they call Mentor, I did not worry. I laughed. Quietly.

Because I know what becomes of mystics.

They die.

And yet…

Something flickered in the dark.

My surveillance had lost them beyond the Karibegoan perimeter. That land—Indigo, they call it—defies logic. Its electromagnetic irregularities render our sensors dull. Its terrain folds over itself like memory resisting recall. And in the center of that overgrown fairy tale… sat a cottage.

How quaint.

The rebels reached it. Alive, weary, and still audacious.

Barricade fell through an invisible dome like a child testing glass.

They laughed. They always laugh before they break.

The walls welcomed them.

The cottage, I'm told, nearly collapsed from joy.

They ate. Drank. Danced.

Celebrated their fugitive status as if defiance were a crown.

And then, in the belly of that ancient hovel, they performed the unthinkable.

They transformed.

Mentor—a fool cloaked in riddles and rum—summoned an Orb, a relic from Karibegoan mysticism known only through rumor and rebel whisper. He fed them seeds. Put them into a trance. Thirty-three days, encased in that womb of light, suspended between biology and blasphemy.

Had it worked as intended, perhaps I wouldn't be speaking of it now.

But the Fetal Orb… malfunctioned.

Ah, yes. This is the part where fiction might call it divine error.

But I know better.

It was Von.

Of course it was Von.

While the others surrendered to the seed, he spat his out like a spoiled olive. While the others dreamed of power, he rewired the Orb's channeling grid. He didn't undergo transformation.

He directed it.

A man pretending to be a pawn so he could rig the board.

I should have executed him in Goa.

And now... now he walks among them not as a doctor, but as something far more dangerous:

A Mystic who remembers who he was before the mask.

I've reviewed the scattered reports. The aftermath. The embers in the trees.

The Fetal Orb did not explode—it birthed.

From it emerged five glowing silhouettes.

The girl, Ara—his daughter, full of anger and inconvenient promise.

The twins of force and calculation—Barricade and Encrypt.

Ledge, ever loyal until he wasn't.

And Von… always Von.

They did not crawl. They did not stumble.

They returned, bright-veined and weaponized by belief.

And yet, what disturbed me most was not their survival.

It was their laughter.

After all they endured, after rewriting their very cells, after rebirth through ancient power…

they laughed.

Like children around a hearth. Like gods playing human.

It sickens me.

Let me explain what they do not understand.

Mysticism is not strength.

It is instability wearing a necklace of light.

It is the whimpering science of tribes too frightened to codify their power.

The Mystics do not control what they are becoming.

They channel it blindly, desperately, clinging to ritual like armor.

They believe transformation makes them chosen.

No.

I choose.

I craft loyalty in laboratories, sculpt obedience into bone.

The Alpha-Gene Fluid bends flesh.

The Surrogates obey.

My soldiers do not dream. They execute.

And still…

I feel the air shift.

There was a moment—brief, but unforgettable—when I stood at the rim of the scorched battleground the rebels had fled. The forest beyond glared at me, as if it had grown eyes in my absence.

I remember the silence.

And I remember what I felt:

They had changed.

Not just in form, but in consequence.

The game had altered beneath me.

Von now plays a deeper game. His daughter grows into her wrath. Barricade has found purpose. Encrypt... understanding. And Ledge—he is what worries me most. For in his silence, I suspect calculation.

And that damned Guide, Mentor... he is no clown. He is a keystone. One I now intend to remove.

Let them believe they are safe within their dome.

Let them sip their stew and chant their songs.

Let them train and dream and prophesy.

Because when I return to Indigo…
I will not come with warnings.

I will bring silence.
I will bury their belief in the same earth they think shields them.

The Mystic Counsel will not rise.
Not while I draw breath.

They have awoken as something new.

But I am not what I was either.

I am what follows transformation.

I am the corrective force.

The consequence.

The final shape of order.

Let them glow.

Light is easiest to erase in darkness.

Chapter 5 | Time Well Spent

Before dawn, with the world hushed and the air holding a faint chill, Mystic Ara moved quietly into the garden behind the cottage. She held a small pouch of thirty-three Blood Pinnacle flower seeds—each one glimmering faintly under the pale starlight, as though holding a fragment of Petrichore's memory within.

Miraj joined her, wooden pole in hand, her movements steady and practiced. Together, they worked in silence. The pole struck the soil in a steady rhythm, opening shallow hollows for each seed. Ara followed, placing a seed in each hollow and brushing earth over it with reverent care. The two women moved in harmony, the quiet task feeling less like labor and more like ritual.

With each buried seed, Ara whispered a thought to herself: For Petrichore. For my mother. For tomorrow's sake.

When the last seed was set, they watered the row, the soil darkening and drinking deeply. For a fleeting moment, the patch seemed to shimmer in the early half-light, as though acknowledging the weight of what had been entrusted to it.

Ara stood back, wiping the soil from her hands onto her robe. Her brow glistened with sweat, but her heart felt lighter. She exchanged a glance with Miraj—a silent acknowledgment that something larger had just been set into motion.

"Thirty-three," Miraj murmured, lowering the pole. "A sacred number. Let us hope they rise."

Ara nodded, her lips pressing into a determined line. With that, she turned toward the cottage, where the faint warmth of the hearth was just beginning to stir. She pushed through the door, already planning breakfast, the smell of firewood and the promise of bread waiting to meet her companions as the first light of day crept over Indigo's horizon.

The first rays of dawn crept into Mystic Von's underground abode, slipping like golden threads through the cracks in the warped floorboards above. He stirred, the shift in light mingling with something else—an unsettling presence. A sensation of being watched pressed against his senses, sharp and insistent. His breath caught.

From the far corner came a faint hum, low and resonant, a sound more felt than heard. His head turned sharply, eyes narrowing into the dim. But as quickly as it had come, the sound faded, leaving behind only silence and the restless echo of his own heartbeat.

The morning light thickened, spilling across stone walls in radiant streaks, grounding him in the present. He let its warmth soak into him, steadying his pulse, though the lingering chill of that unseen stare refused to fade.

Then another presence rose—a far more tangible one. The tantalizing aroma of breakfast slipped down the creaking stairs, curling through the underground air like a beckoning hand. Spiced, savory, unmistakably alive, it wrapped itself around him, tugging him upward with the quiet promise of hearth and company.

Drawn by curiosity, Mystic Von followed the savory trail up the stairs with a scholar's focus. But instead of answers to his questions, he found a spectacle.

The kitchen—usually a modest realm of bread, roots, and herbs—had been transformed into a storm of chaos. At its center stood his daughter, Mystic Ara, embers of newfound energy glowing faintly in her veins. She had claimed dominion over breakfast, wielding her mystic gifts with the bravado of a master chef—and the precision of a thunderstorm.

Eggs spun in orbit, Elamamgis fruit pulsed like floating lanterns, and corn flour exploded in radiant puffs that clung to everything like ash from some holy fire. Yolk streaked the walls, the air thick with flour fog, and a frying pan clattered across the counter like a cymbal. Even Mystic Von and their Karibegoan Guide, Mentor, found themselves spattered, accidental canvases in Ara's culinary chaos.

Miraj, long-suffering mistress of both mystic discipline and household order, finally intervened. With a single, sharp manifestation—*"Qui-Et: Chaos Still"*—the room froze. Eggs dropped like stones, fruit plopped to the floor, and the flour haze dissipated in a slow, pitiful drizzle.

Mystic Ara, shoulders slumped, gave a sheepish sigh. "Well… breakfast is served—sort of."

Mystic Von arched a brow, sarcasm sharpened to a blade. "How 'bout we serve her a mop, a bucket, and a bar of soap, eh mystic chef?"

Mentor, shaking his head with that eternal half-smile, let out a deep hum of amusement. He had guided warriors through death, spirits through shadow, and yet, nothing tested his patience quite like Ara at the stove. Still, he knew these small catastrophes were part of the greater journey—a life where discovery, laughter, and a daily whirlwind of breakfast ingredients were the new order of things.

Mystic Ledge, Mystic Encrypt, and Mystic Barricade wandered through the Karibegoan community in the quiet predawn hours, the roads hushed beneath the blush of first light. The calm around them stood in sharp contrast to the turmoil within—each man carrying the ghost of Grenaivel: days before the Ikannunaa invasion, when laughter and life still thrived.

It was Barricade who broke the silence. His deep voice carried a mischievous edge as he launched into a childhood tale from the orphanage. With a grin, he described how he had once cracked the digital lock on the Food Containment Room—a vault of rare treats in their otherwise meager existence. With the gusto of a king at a banquet, young Barricade had scooped cold cream with his bare hands until his belly swelled like a drum.

Ledge and Encrypt erupted with laughter, the mental image of the hulking soldier as a gluttonous boy too vivid to resist.

"Were there consequences?" Ledge asked, fighting back a grin.

Barricade smirked. "Caretaker dropped me into the punishment chute. Problem was, my stomach wouldn't fit. I got stuck halfway down, and the whole orphanage came running to laugh at me."

Their laughter rang through the waking streets, shattering the stillness of dawn.

Not to be outdone, Ledge recounted his teenage years at Compass Square, where he led a team of clumsy giants in a Push Ball match. Quick thinking and relentless legs carried them to a last-second win, a triumph that earned him a reputation far beyond his years.

Then Encrypt, ever the quiet one, offered the infamous "Fire Core" story. Calmly, he described stabilizing a malfunctioning energy core, cooling it before it could destroy an entire Grenaivel city.

Barricade gave him a sideways look. "An unsung hero," he teased.

Encrypt only shrugged, a faint smile tugging at his lips. "I was there. That was enough."

Their easy banter cut short when something unusual appeared on the path ahead: a massive stone, oddly placed, unlike any of the natural rocks around it. Ledge raised a hand, signaling for silence. His eyes narrowed with focus.

He stepped forward, palm outstretched. The stone trembled, then lifted from the ground, suspended in the air. Sweat gathered at his brow, his body straining as he forced it higher. Encrypt and Barricade watched, awed by the raw force spilling out of him.

"Higher!" came a voice from down the path.

Two Karibegoans approached, their dreadlocks catching the morning light. Maestro's voice carried encouragement, while Guardian Mythic clapped his hands in rhythm.

"Push through it, boy! Project—don't yank! Think pressure outward, not just lift, my man!"

Ledge roared with effort, raising the stone a little higher before his strength gave out. It crashed back to the earth as he dropped to one knee, chest heaving.

The Karibegoans applauded.

"We are friends of Mentor," Maestro introduced warmly. "My name is Maestro—they call me the Piper. This one here is Guardian Mythic. We've been waiting on you a long time."

Their eyes gleamed—not just with recognition of power, but with the certainty of destiny.

As they helped Ledge to his feet, Maestro leaned closer, lowering his voice. "Your strength is going to matter in the days ahead. But strength alone is not enough. There are other things to learn… things Mentor hasn't told you yet."

"What things?" Encrypt pressed, his brow furrowed.

Maestro only smiled. "Ask him about the Humming Black Trunk, alright?."

Confusion flickered across the three Mystics' faces, but Maestro offered no more.

Their walk continued, no longer weighed down by memories but pulled forward by mystery. What had begun as reminiscing now carried the charge of prophecy.

As the Grenaivelan Mystics strode down the path, Mythic and Maestro exchanged a look.

"Those men," Mythic said quietly, "they've grown far more powerful—even beyond Mentor. But the one they call Ledge… his core aura is still sleeping, I can feel it."

Maestro's brow furrowed. "Meaning he doesn't even know he's stronger than all of them."

"Correct," Mythic replied gravely. "And the only other soul with the sight to feel that hidden power… is that mystic monster—Mal-Monger himself."

Maestro's expression darkened. "Then we're going to keep a quiet eye on him. For his sake—and for our own."

After the morning's chaotic kitchen misadventures, the group gathered around the rustic wooden table in Mentor's cottage. Firelight flickered warmly from the hearth, the smell of cooked food filling the air. Despite the morning's disasters, Mystic Ara had managed to conjure a full spread—steaming bowls, fresh bread, and platters that glowed faintly with her new mystic touch.

Mystic Barricade, curiosity winning over caution, poked at the food on his plate before digging in. "Looks great," he said, his deep voice hopeful.

Ara grinned, tilting her head proudly. "Oh, just a little something infused with belief in magic. Eat up before it gets cold—you'll need your strength."

Miraj eyed her own serving suspiciously, then quipped dryly, "I'll pass on the food—a cup of water to wash down the wooden plate, please?" Her sarcasm drew chuckles from the table and a sharp side-eye from Ara.

Barricade, however, seemed delighted. He devoured every bite, scraping his spoon across the bowl and even licking it clean. Ara beamed as he leaned back, satisfied.

"He'll eat anything you put in front of him," Mystic Encrypt muttered with a smirk.

Barricade turned toward him with mock menace, eyes gleaming. "You're in front of me too, Encrypt. Watch out." His playful glare earned laughter all around.

Ara, feigning indignation, wagged a finger at Encrypt. "At least Barricade has discerning taste," she shot back before turning to Mystic Ledge, who was idly stirring his food without taking a bite.

"When are you going to stop drawing lines in your porridge and actually eat, Ledge?" she teased.

Ledge smirked, lifting a spoonful but not tasting it. "Ara, what exactly did you put in this? Beyond the magic and charm."

Ara began ticking off on her fingers. "Salt, pepper, onions, diced mushrooms, whatever I could find in the garden…"

At the word "mushrooms," Mentor froze, brows knitting. "Mushrooms? Girl, where exactly did you find them?"

Ara waved it off. "Out back. Beautiful little green mushrooms, growing in clusters. There were plenty!"

The room went still. Miraj leaned forward, her voice firm but kind. "Ara, my darling, those mushrooms are poisonous. That's why you see plenty."

Ara's eyes widened, her confidence collapsing into horror. Around the table, plates were hastily pushed away.

All except Barricade's—already scraped clean.

The hulking Mystic glanced around, patting his stomach with exaggerated dread. "Oh no. Is this it? The end of the road for me?"

Mentor folded his arms, lips twitching. "No, big man. But you might wish it were. Those mushrooms got… a rather violent purging effect."

Barricade frowned. "Purging?"

"Grab the wiping paper, lock the outhouse, and play loud music," Mentor advised with a sage nod. "Trust me."

Barricade's eyes went wide. Without another word, he bolted from his chair and thundered toward the door, one hand on his stomach, the other clutching his backside.

The cottage erupted in laughter.

Ara, cheeks flushed crimson, snatched up a rag and stormed toward the kitchen. "Ungrateful heroes and their delicate stomachs," she muttered under her breath.

Her frustration only fueled the others' laughter, their mirth echoing off the cottage walls long after she'd vanished behind the doorway.

Later that evening, as the sun dipped beneath the horizon and bled the sky in shades of blue and gold, Mystic Von and his daughter, Mystic Ara, sat just outside the cottage. The stars unveiled themselves one by one, quiet witnesses to their moment of peace after a long and chaotic day.

Ara's shoulders slumped. Though laughter had carried through the cottage walls earlier, the weight of her mistake still pressed on her chest. Poor Barricade was still barricaded in the outhouse.

She drew a deep breath. "Dad… I'm sorry. For the mess. For Barricade. For all of it."

Von's lips curved in a knowing chuckle, his gaze soft. "My daughter, I know why you tried. Cooking for us—it reminded you of your mother."

His tone grew wistful, eyes fixed on a memory only he could see. "I remember the first meal she ever made me. Our second date, back at my parents' house. I brewed black tea because the market had no coffee, and I set the table with red flowers she loved. She cooked a dish so good, I knew right then—she was the one."

Ara's eyes glistened, but her mouth quirked with a playful grin. "Tea on a date? No wine? No bubbly?"

Von raised a brow. "Who's telling this story, Ara?" he teased, before softening again. "Every year after, she proved me right. Every anniversary, every meal, every moment… she was the one."

Ara's throat tightened. "She was tough," she whispered, "but humble too."

Von reached for her shoulder, his stare unwavering. "And so are you. That apple never strayed far from the tree."

Ara blinked through her tears, resolve sharpening her features. "I'll seek justice for her."

His hand squeezed her shoulder, steady and warm. "Whatever comes, she'd be proud of you."

The moment hung heavy—until the underbrush rustled.

A small white rabbit hopped into view, moonlight gleaming on its fur. It stopped, lifted a paw, and clearly waved.

Ara blinked. "That… rabbit looks familiar."

Von squinted, recognition dawning. "Fin. Mentor's debtor. The one who still owes him a gold coin."

The rabbit rolled its eyes, flicked its ears, and bolted into the forest.

Ara stared, speechless. Von only sighed, muttering, "Figures."

The cottage door creaked open. Mystic Ledge stepped out, his presence grounding the moment back to the here and now. The three exchanged quiet greetings before Von excused himself, retreating to his underground lab with the same determination that never seemed to leave him.

As Mystic Von disappeared into the cottage, Ara and Ledge lingered outside beneath the spill of moonlight. The night air carried a hush, the forest swaying like an audience to their silence.

Ledge finally spoke, his voice thoughtful. "A former Grenaivel captain turned mystic hero. Who could have ever imagined?"

Ara's gaze softened, though her words carried an edge of reflection. "I guess you never know your true destiny… until the one you thought was written fades away."

Ledge smiled at that, a spark of playfulness glinting in his eyes. From behind his back, he revealed a single Blood Pinnacle flower, its petals glowing faintly as though holding the memory of fire.

"Speaking of destiny," he teased, "I may or may not have 'borrowed' this from one of your research bags."

Ara raised a brow, taking the flower, humor dancing in her eyes. "Borrowed, huh? Bold move. And here I thought I was the only handful." Her grin turned sly. "By the way, I did some digging. Turns out you were once captain of the great Keannelden Force—before the Ikannunaa's overthrow. Impressive. Someone tucked it away in the Armed Empires Database. I was curious."

Ledge chuckled, shaking his head. "Of course you were. You're a Von."

Their laughter faded into stillness, leaving only the hum of insects and the glow of the Blood Pinnacle between them. The air seemed to bend closer, charged with something unsaid.

Ara spoke first, her voice steady though her heart raced. "I think I'm captivated… Captain."

Ledge's answer was quiet but sure. "And I admire you, Miss Von."

"Once again—it's just Ara." Her eyes narrowed, mock-annoyed.

"I know," Ledge said, his grin warm, his stare unflinching.

And then—without planning, without hesitation—they leaned together. Their lips met in a kiss lit by moonlight and mystic embers. The Blood Pinnacle in Ara's hand flared with a crimson glow, mirroring the red cloth that marked rebellion, as though binding their moment to something far larger than themselves.

It was more than affection—it was vow, omen, and spark. Love and destiny entwined, the universe pausing to bear witness.

Inside the cottage, laughter and the clink of tin cups spilled into the night air, weaving with the rustle of leaves outside. Candlelight flickered across worn wooden beams, throwing a golden glow over Mystic Barricade, Mentor, and Miraj as they shared drink and story.

Miraj, flushed with warmth from the beer, tilted her head toward Barricade. "Boy, you've got quite the appetite," she teased. "Your mother must have been an amazing cook."

The words landed heavier than intended. Barricade's laughter stilled; his stare sank to the tabletop. Silence wrapped the room. Realizing her slip, Miraj softened, leaning in. "Forgive me. I never meant to touch a wound, alright?."

Barricade exhaled, finishing the last swallow from his tin cup before speaking. "There was no mother's kitchen," he admitted, voice low and steady. "Raised in an orphanage. My size made me the easy mark—every day, every hour. They'd pile on me, fists, words... anything to cut me down." He paused, knuckles whitening around the cup. "But they never broke me."

Mentor leaned forward, his tone half-serious, half-reassuring. "And look who's sitting here now. A mystic. A giant that stands for something greater than himself."

Barricade gave a quiet nod. Miraj reached out, patting his back with a motherly firmness, and the heaviness of the moment lifted.

Then Mentor's eyes narrowed toward the last tin cup of beer on the table. Barricade noticed at the same time. Their gazes locked, mischievous grins sparking like flint.

The cup trembled, sliding an inch toward Mentor—then jerked back toward Barricade. Energy embers spiraled from both men's hands, the wooden table rattling under the tug-of-war.

Mentor planted his other palm against his forearm, teeth gritted. The cup crept within reach—until Barricade let out a primal growl, his aura blazing brighter, raw and unrefined. The tin cup shot into his hand like iron to a magnet.

Mentor blinked, incredulous, before bursting into laughter. "Rainah's breath—what in the Orb did Von do to you?"

Miraj smirked, arms crossed. "Whatever he wanted, I guess."

Barricade raised the cup triumphantly—then surprised them both with a grin. "Split it?" He offered the tin toward Mentor.

Mentor chuckled, shaking his head as he accepted. "A big man with an even bigger heart."

The three clinked what little beer remained and drank, their laughter echoing long into the night. Whatever storms lay ahead, for this moment they were bound by warmth, humor, and the strange new powers awakening within them.

In Goa, a Servacraft's corridor thrummed with engine pulse and fluorescent hum. Five shadows advanced in lockstep, boots whispering over polished deck. At point, the operative in red armor set the cadence—visor blank, gait predatory. Behind him came his counterparts: white, yellow, green, and blue. Together they moved like a spear honed to a single edge.

They halted at double sliding doors. Beyond lay the recreation hall: cards slapped on a table, a sparring match drawing chuckles, the easy sound of soldiers at rest.

The doors parted with a hiss.

Laughter died. Cards froze mid-slap. In the threshold stood the Ikannunaa Royal Squadron—the I.R.S—a wall of color-shot black plating and predatory calm. The room stiffened as one, every trooper snapping to attention as if pulled by invisible wire. No salute. No words. Their presence demanded silence.

The red operative entered first. The others flowed after him, their stride measured, seamless. They neither glanced left nor right. Servos whispered, armor gleamed, and the temperature seemed to drop as they passed. At the far end, another set of doors slid open. The five disappeared into shadow. Steel closed behind them.

Only then did the hall exhale—a ragged, collective breath.

"Storm and stars," someone muttered. "That kit... no seams. Silent actuators. That plating's not in any quartermaster's ledger."

At the card table, a corporal half-smiled, eyes far away. "They're more than their armor," he said. "I've seen what rides inside it."

A few heads turned. "You've served with the Squadron?"

"Babelmound," the corporal answered, gaze locked on the sealed doors. "Tallest skylines you'll ever see. Thirty-three of us tapped for a run after the local government cut itself from the Empire—without King Atan-els's blessing. Command sent the I.R.S to... correct the math."

His voice dropped. "The Special Security Forces tried to decapitate them the second we hit atmosphere. They didn't last a minute. I watched the red lead tear their vanguard apart like paper while the others boxed flanks and shut down comms. We weren't led—we were carried through a war we couldn't even name."

Silence. Reverent.

"Whole thing ended before our boots cooled," he finished. "Fast. Clean. Final."

A private blew out a low whistle. "One day," he said, grinning, "we'll march beside them."

Around the room, nods followed. Quiet "yeahs." That kind of hope soldiers tuck away like a coin between teeth.

Down-corridor, the Servacraft shuddered with a change in heading. In the rec hall, cards shuffled, gloves laced, chatter resumed—softer now, edged with awe, as if the very air still remembered the legends that had passed through.

Back in Indigo, the cottage's underground room was low-lit, the air thick with wax and parchment. Flickering candlelight carved long shadows across the walls, stretching over a sea of Von's scattered papers. The place looked less like a laboratory and more like the mind of a genius tipped onto a table.

Mystic Von and Mystic Encrypt bent over the chaos, their night consumed by the Sigma-Gene Fluid project.

Encrypt, sifting through the mess, realized that Von had already carried the work far beyond its foundations. "You've practically finished this thing," he murmured, suspicion edging his curiosity.

Von smirked, brushing ash from a candle wick. "Notes from the Beta-Gene project. Think of it as a roadmap—when you know where the dead ends are, you skip them."

Encrypt studied him, then gave a short laugh. "You're always one step ahead, Von. Even ahead of the Universe."

Von waved off the compliment. "Don't sell yourself short. You've carried plenty of the weight here."

For a rare moment, Encrypt allowed himself honesty. "I once wanted to be a doctor in the Grenaivel military," he admitted, voice softened by memory. "But my parents had other plans. They wanted a captain—someone like Ledge."

Von leaned back, eyes catching the candlelight. "Dreams don't expire, Encrypt. You're standing in a lab with me—consider this your residency. Learn everything you can. Time's on your side."

Encrypt nodded, resolute. "Yes, doctor." They clasped hands, the gesture firm, lit by the wavering glow.

Von's gaze sharpened. "Tell me—what do you actually know about General Scorpiondt's origin?"

Encrypt hesitated, then spoke carefully. "Among soldiers, there are whispers. Before he became the Empire's General, he was Lord Scorpiondt—

ruler of Tusilbarrh. Diplomatic, shrewd. He wanted to merge his clan with the Ikannunaa. His family forbade it."

Von arched a brow. "And?"

Encrypt's tone dropped into shadow. "They plotted to remove him. Assassination. They thought his loyalty to the Empire made him unfit to rule. But he found out. Struck first. Burned his royal garments, swore allegiance to the Empire, and cut down his bloodline. Tusilbarrh fell. Scorpiondt rose."

Von's jaw set, eyes steely. "Then perhaps we finish what his family couldn't."

The thought hung heavy, before Von shifted to the matter at hand. "The Sigma-Gene Fluid won't stabilize without ultra-heated gold under pressure. That's your puzzle for tonight."

Encrypt leaned closer. "How did you handle it during the Beta project?"

Von grinned. "We used a machine called the Applimacx. It applied phantom pressure to all forms of metal, including gold. That can't be achieved without the machine—but I'm certain we'll figure something out."

Encrypt frowned, then glanced at a bowl of snacks Von offered. He waved it back with a flick of his mystic energy. The gesture froze him mid-motion.

"Wait," Encrypt whispered, eyes sparking. "That's it. We could use our powers directly—generate the pressure ourselves."

Von's grin widened. "Only thing we're missing now is the gold."

He slipped a coin from his pocket, tossing it onto the table.

Encrypt cocked a brow. "That's Barricade's coin. The one meant for Miraj?"

Von shrugged. "Saving the world outranks buying new furniture."

Encrypt chuckled, then exhaled, his aura igniting in drifting embers. Together they lifted the coin, suspended it between their palms.

"On three," Encrypt commanded.

"One. Two. Three."

They pushed.

The coin trembled, heat shimmering from its edges. Smoke curled into the air.

"More, Von!" Encrypt urged.

Energy flared. The cottage shook. And then—

The coin detonated in a flash of brilliance, searing light flooding through the floorboards, as though the earth itself bore witness.

A step had been taken. A dangerous, vital step toward unlocking the mysteries of the Sigma-Gene Fluid.

The Conqueror V
As told by General Scorpiondt

They buried seeds, as if flora could rival fire.

Petrichore's remnants—those fragile little flowers—are all that child has left of her mother, her home, her delusions. She thinks that by planting them in foreign soil, they might remember the scent of extinction and choose instead to bloom. Foolish. Legacy is not a root you water—it is a weapon you sharpen. Let the girl plant her hope. It will wither all the same.

They laugh now, the newly born Mystics. They jest, they spar, they flirt with one another beneath starlit skies as though war has passed them by. As though the Empire didn't raze Grenaivel, didn't gut Petrichore, didn't break the lineages they cling to like sentimental artifacts.

Ah, but I forget—they are still in that precious stage of ignorance. The false dawn of rebellion. Where power is a novelty, and laughter masks the tremor beneath the skin.

I watched them train. From afar, yes, but even distance cannot obscure imbalance. The girl—Ara—has power, yes, but no discipline. She cooks with chaos and poisons her companions with ignorance. Barricade, the brute, swallows poison with a smile and declares victory for surviving his own stupidity. How quaint.

Miraj remains the only one among them with any semblance of order. Her command could serve a far more deserving cause than this sad, stitched-together rebellion. But I digress.

Then there's Ledge. Quiet. Too quiet. He lifted the stone. Not with grace, nor full control, but with a fire that disturbs the shadows. I felt it across the ether—the echo of something ancient, perhaps even forbidden. The Karibegoans noticed it too. Maestro and Mythic, those cultural fossils still playing prophet on a land they barely protect, whispered of him. They sense what I suspect.

He doesn't know yet. But I do.

That boy will become a problem.

Mentor should never have trained him. And yet… perhaps it is better this way. Let him ripen. Let him believe in destiny. When the time comes, I'll harvest him myself—bone, blade, and all.

As for the others—Encrypt, Von… clever minds wasted on a cause destined to devour itself. Von toys now with Sigma-Gene Fluid. Amusing. The fool actually believes he can replicate what took me decades and a thousand minds to perfect. His daughter calls him genius; I call him naive.

They've reached a breakthrough, or so they think. A coin, a pulse, a flicker of light in a basement. Children playing with fission, calling it revelation.

Encrypt's loyalty to Von is touching. Touching and exploitable. Every great rebellion is sabotaged not by force, but by fractured belief. I have time. They, on the other hand, burn theirs for sport.

The boy, Barricade—he revealed his past over cheap beer. Orphaned. Mocked. Bruised. I know this story. So many rebels are made from rejection. They find power not to change the world, but to avenge the one that ignored them. I've seen it before. I broke it before. I will again.

Their camaraderie is growing. So is their confidence.

I allow this.

Let them feel safe. Let them bond. Let them kiss beneath the moons like their cause is more than myth and mushroom. Ara and Ledge—how poetic. Red cloth and rebel lips. But love is not armor. It is fracture.

A time will come when she must choose between her father and her flame.

I have already chosen for her.

Meanwhile, the I.R.S. remains flawless. My elite—my hammers in the forge of civilization—moved through the Servacraft like ghosts made of glass and death. The soldiers aboard saw them and remembered silence. This is discipline. This is unity. Five weapons, no chatter, no ego, no chaos.

No heart.

Exactly as they should be.

They whisper legends about us. Let them. Legends are the bait for the brave. The brave make excellent examples.

And so, the Mystics dine. They dream. They dance in the cottage under the illusion of time well spent.

But time is not a gift.

It is a ruse.

And I am the one who ends it.

—General Scorpiondt

High Commander of the Ikannunaa Empire

Last Lord of Tusilbarrh

Scribe of Final Truths

Chapter 6 | **Lost Then Found**

Eleven months had passed since their arrival on the land of refuge. Mystics Von and Encrypt walked side by side beneath the amber wash of a sinking sun, their boots pressing softly into the forested earth. The alien landscape stretched around them—towering trunks with silver-veined leaves, soft-winged dusk moths drifting lazily in the twilight, and the low, resonant calls of unseen creatures rolling across the distance like drums of the earth itself. The cool air smelled of moss and spicewood, carrying the faint rustle of leaves as the wind stirred.

Their conversation, as always, turned toward the looming shadow of unfinished work.

"By your estimates," Encrypt asked, his tone edged with restless curiosity, "how far along do you think they've gotten with the Beta-Gene Fluid project?"

Von slowed his pace, the golden light catching the sharp lines of his face. "My best guess," he said, voice even, "93% completed… and climbing."

Encrypt's chest tightened, resignation leaking through his sigh. "So there's no stopping this, is there?"

Von shook his head. His answer was measured, but its weight pressed hard between them. "Not now. Not as we are. And in our current condition, we're in no position to intervene."

The silence that followed carried the gravity of inevitability. Yet Encrypt—ever the soldier, ever searching for levity when despair pressed too near—lifted a brow and let a crooked smile play across his lips.

"In that case," he said, "we'd better head toward the marketplace. The cottage is fresh out of beer again."

Von chuckled, the brief humor loosening the tension. "It always seems to vanish faster than wisdom, doesn't it."

Turning the corner, they stepped into Indigo's bustling marketplace. Night gathered as the paths flared to life with glowing clay lanterns strung overhead, their warm light dancing over the crowd. The air thrummed with life—meats sizzling on spits, fragrant clouds of spiced smoke curling into the night, merchants shouting over one another as they pitched wares of shimmering textiles, golden grains, and fruits that glowed faintly under the lanternlight.

Drummers pounded stretched-hide drums, their beats weaving with the laughter of children who darted barefoot through the lanes. But laughter stilled when the young ones spotted Von and Encrypt. A hush rippled through them. Wide eyes, whispers. One boy with bright gray eyes and thick dreadlocks stepped forward, curiosity etched across his small face.

The murmurs spread beyond the children now. Some traders bowed their heads in reverence; others exchanged glances heavy with recognition, lips whispering the words that carried like a quiet tide—

"Mystic heroes."

Encrypt tilted his head, smirking at the attention. "Word travels fast around here."

Von's gaze swept the crowd, his expression unreadable. "Indeed," he said. "And perhaps too fast. We'd be wise to walk with quieter steps."

While Encrypt busied himself refilling the two metal gallon containers— Mentor's daily request—at a bustling brew stand, Von lingered near the counter, striking up small talk with the vendor. The man was short and wiry, a Karibegoan with eyes that shimmered like twin moons, their glow catching the lanternlight whenever he smiled. Their exchange was easy, mundane, almost comforting—until a shadow fell across the stall.

A woman approached. Her presence was both commanding and gentle, a balance that made heads turn without her ever raising her voice. She introduced herself simply:

"Miracle—friend of Miraj."

Her stare was steady, threaded with quiet intensity as it swept across Von and Encrypt. "I've heard much about you," she said, her tone carrying both respect and gravity. "We've kept our distance—less attention, fewer eyes. Especially while preparing for the standoff against the Ikannunaa Empire."

Von inclined his head, acknowledging both her candor and her caution. "That explains the isolation," he said. "It makes sense now."

But Miracle's expression darkened. She stepped closer, her voice lowering to a near whisper. "Then allow me to ask what Mentor and Miraj should have asked you themselves. The Humming Black Trunk—have you retrieved it yet? Do you know where it lies?"

Von froze, his composure bending just slightly as his eyes flicked toward Encrypt.

"What trunk?" he asked, his curiosity sharpening into something more guarded.

Encrypt's brow furrowed. "Mythic mentioned it," he admitted, his voice edged with unease. "I assumed Mentor and Miraj would've briefed us. If Miracle's right, this trunk… it's not optional. It's critical. Von, she says it must be returned to our Guide."

Miracle's gaze bore into them both, unwavering. "It hums to be found…
and obeyed." The words hung in the air like a chill.

At that moment, the vendor set the heavy gallon cans onto the counter with
a metallic thud. Von gripped the handles automatically, but his mind was already
elsewhere, racing with questions.

What was the Trunk? Why had Mentor and Miraj kept silent? And why did
Miracle speak of it as though it were alive?

As they left the stall and the noise of the marketplace swallowed them again,
one truth pressed harder than the weight of the cans in Von's hands:

Their mission here was far from over.

The night wrapped the cottage in firelit warmth, laughter and clinking tin
cups softening the edges of a long day. Ara eyed Mentor over the rim of her
drink.

"You never touch anything but that cheap beer, do you."

Mentor smirked. "That's right. Cheapest brew Indigo's got. If you don't like
it, get a job—stock the good stuff yourself."

Before Ara could jab back, Miraj cut them off with a sharp, "Eat your
food."

Down the table, Barricade reached toward Encrypt. "Pass me the biscuit?"

Encrypt slid the plate across, smug. Barricade shook his head. "Not those—yours."

Encrypt raised an eyebrow. "And why would I give you mine?"

"Because it's the only one baked with coffee beans," Barricade explained, grave as a judge. "Plain biscuits are worthless. Coffee's rare."

Encrypt grinned. "All the more reason it's staying right where it is."

Barricade leaned in, lowering his voice. "Remember that time I saved your life?"

Encrypt leaned back. "Nope. Don't recall."

"I'll trade you these greens."

"Still no."

The back-and-forth drew chuckles around the table until Von set down his fork with a deliberate clink. The shift was immediate. The room stilled. The fire popped.

"At what point," he asked, gaze drilling into Mentor, "were you going to tell us about the Humming Black Trunk?"

Mentor's easy smirk faded. His stare lowered, then rose again, slower this time. The candlelight flickered across his face as he spoke.

"Some truths are not served over supper. The Trunk isn't a relic; it's a prism in a prison."

Ara leaned forward, eyes sharp. "So… what's in it?"

Mentor's voice dropped, almost a whisper, as if the very walls might betray him. "Not what. Who." He hesitated. "A Guide—once of our kind, but darker. Too dark. His name…" Mentor's words faltered, then came out strained, "…is Mal-Monger."

The name itself seemed to thrum in the air. The fire snapped louder, shadows stretching thin. Even Miraj's steady hands paused.

Mentor's voice tightened as he spoke.

"He conquered Ras-Magenta—our first home before we ever set foot on Earth. Our Guardians, our Guides, our Monks… all of them poured their lives into sealing him away. Mal-Monger sought to imprison our people within his Trunk, to lock us in silence for eternity. But we turned his weapon against him. Even then, it was not enough. The Trunk was his to begin with—we merely forced him to taste his own creation."

Ara's voice broke the hush. "How did it end up here?"

"I was chosen to carry it," Mentor admitted, shame pulling at his tone. "I opened a portal to move it from Ras-Magenta to Earth, but something went wrong. I lost control. It re-formed on the tallest northern peak—the Northern Ice Ring. The cold there is no place for the fragile physiology of a Karibegoan. I could not reclaim it."

Encrypt's eyes narrowed. "Then how can you be sure it still rests there?"

Miraj placed a device in Mentor's hand. Its faint pulse glowed between his fingers.

"We trace it," Mentor said simply. "Its energy sings like a heartbeat—a hum that never stops."

Ledge's skepticism surfaced. "Hums? You mean... it makes noise?"

Mentor's eyes flickered. His answer was almost a confession.

"The hum isn't 'sound.' It's him—pressing, reaching, sensing auras beyond the seal. When you hear it... you know he is listening back."

A chill swept the table. The warmth of the fire seemed thinner now, its crackle swallowed by silence.

Von rose, his voice firm, each word like iron. "Then at dawn, we set out. Bundle your cloaks, sharpen your resolve, and say your prayers. Tomorrow we climb to the Northern Ice Ring."

The flames guttered as though bowing to the weight of the vow. Around them, even the shadows seemed to lean in, listening.

The rising sun bathed the forest in gold, its light breaking through the canopy in shifting beams. Towering trees swayed gently, their branches scattering dappled shadows over the mossy ground. Inside the cottage, anticipation thrummed like a second heartbeat. Heavy black hooded overcoats, snug red wool scarves, and sturdy boots—garments Miraj and her friends had stitched through the long night—waited by the door, ready for the frigid mission ahead.

Outside, Mentor tuned the Tracer with steady hands, the device vibrating as it locked onto the distant pulse of the Humming Black Trunk. His eyes tightened with the weight of the reading before passing it to Mystic Von.

Von studied the glow, his brow furrowed. "The signature's too distant. On foot, we'd risk starvation—or hypothermia—long before we reached it."

Mentor nodded grimly. "I never wanted you all to face this trek." Regret laced his voice, but it didn't linger. His fingers traced ancient signs, his words a measured cadence in the Majeskrit tongue.

"Op-End-Oor: Portal Key."

The air tore open, shimmering like liquid glass. A gust of icy wind burst through, carrying the breath of the northern peaks.

The Mystics emerged from the cottage bundled tight against the cold, their scarves snapping in the sudden gale. Von's voice cut through the frost: "Mystics, move. I've work waiting when we return."

Ara, unable to resist, quipped, "Ladies first, gentlemen." Her eyes sparkled with mischief.

With mock gallantry, Ledge swept his arm. "After you."

From behind his scarf, Mentor muttered, "If only she acted like one."

Ara shot him a glare over her shoulder. "I heard that."

Barricade's chuckle rumbled, muffled by wool, while Encrypt's eyes lingered on the portal's rim, studying its rippling edge. "When we return, Mentor, you'll teach me how you formed this. The words. The craft."

Mentor nodded, pride flickering in his gaze. "By the book, man—every line."

Encrypt dipped his head, then stepped forward.

One by one, they entered the icy threshold. The portal swallowed them whole, each figure vanishing into light. When the last shadow passed, it sealed with a hushed whoosh, leaving the forest still again—its silence heavy, as though the trees themselves held their breath for what awaited at the peak of the Northern Ice Ring.

The portal spat them out into a world of ice and silence.

The Northern Ice Ring stretched in all directions, a merciless expanse of snow and stone. The air itself cut like knives, burning every patch of exposed skin. Breath plumed in frosty clouds, each exhale stolen by the wind. Before them rose the mountain—a towering giant crowned in mist, its peak lost within a storm of swirling white.

Mystic Von held the Tracer close, the device humming against his gloves. Its pale light flickered, struggling against the storm. He squinted at the shifting readouts, his brow hard with concentration.

"The energy signature is stronger here," he murmured, his words nearly carried away by the gale. "But the Trunk lies further up. Every step forward takes us closer—to either salvation or death."

Then came a stillness.

Through the sweeping snow, a shape emerged. A small figure, incongruous in the vast wilderness: Fin, the white rabbit. A reddish scarf draped around his neck, its ends snapping in the wind like banners of defiance. He stood perfectly still, eyes glinting with strange awareness.

Von froze. His stare locked on the rabbit, and for a moment, time seemed to hang suspended. "You can't hide out here forever, Fin." he shouted, his voice rolling across the frozen expanse.

The rabbit's ears twitched. His black eyes narrowed in something that looked disturbingly like amusement—or challenge. Then, without a sound, he pivoted and bolted, vanishing into the veil of snow and mist as though the storm itself had swallowed him whole.

Mystic Ara shivered, clutching her scarf as the wind clawed at her face. "I thought this place would be warmer… it's teeth-chattering cold," she muttered. Her words carried away on the gale, dissolving into white silence.

Mystic Von chuckled softly, though his own breath fogged the air. "Come on. Let us make our way toward the peak. This is not the place any of us would want to perish." His voice was steady, but beneath it pressed the urgency of survival.

They pressed forward, boots plunging deep into drifts that swallowed their ankles. Mystic Barricade, immense as a mountain himself, trudged at the front beside Von, his massive frame forcing open a path where the snow sought to hold them captive. Each step seemed to drain their strength, the cold leeching through their mystic-lined coats and burrowing into bone.

Von summoned the Tracer into the air, its faint hum guiding them like a beacon, hovering above the storm. The pale glow cut through the swirling snow, casting long streaks of light over the slope. He tucked his hands into his pockets, conserving warmth, his sharp eyes never leaving the device as its pulse grew steadier—stronger.

The ascent steepened, forcing them to call on their mystic abilities. With a synchronized breath, they lifted themselves slightly above the drifts, gliding instead of slogging, their steps lighter against the biting terrain. Energy embers sparked faintly at their feet, leaving glowing impressions in the snow that quickly faded in the storm.

Still, the mountain did not yield easily. Sheets of ice fractured under Barricade's weight; loose snow avalanched in miniature cascades around them. The howl of the wind bent trees into twisted silhouettes, and distant cracks echoed—reminders that in the Ice Ring, even the earth itself could betray them.

Back at the cottage, Mentor and Miraj sat in silence, their eyes fixed on the Tracer that linked them to the heroes' progress. The rustic interior exuded warmth—wooden beams latticing the ceiling, a stone fireplace crackling, the faint aroma of stew and bread clinging to the air. Yet beneath that comfort, a tremor of unease pulsed like a hidden heartbeat.

Mentor's brow furrowed as he watched the faint glow on the device shift and quiver. "I hope we haven't sent them into a lost cause," he muttered, voice low and heavy. "If they fail to retrieve the trunk, if Mal-Monger ever breaks free… then all we've fought for dies with him."

Miraj reached across the table, her grip firm around his hand, her stare steady despite the dread in her chest. "They will succeed, Mentor. They must. If he is freed, there will be no dome strong enough, no spell ancient enough, to contain what follows."

The Tracer pulsed once, brighter than before, filling the dim room with an eerie glow. Both Mentor and Miraj exchanged a glance—half hope, half fear.

The fate of the world, they knew, was now climbing through ice and storm.

Back on the mountain, Mystic Encrypt pressed both palms forward, his energy crackling through the frozen air. Sheets of snow lifted and peeled away from the path, crashing down the slope in muffled avalanches. Beside him, Mystic Ledge stood like a bulwark against the storm, his brow creased, arms outstretched. A translucent veil of force shimmered faintly around them, holding back the razor winds that screamed across the ridge.

But the higher they climbed, the more the mountain fought back. The air thinned, slicing their lungs raw with each breath. Frost clung to their lashes, and every exhale emerged in ragged bursts of steam. The mountain's icy grip pressed on their bodies as though it sought to drag them into its frozen heart.

Then Ara faltered. Her boot slipped on a hidden slick of ice, and she collapsed with a sharp cry. "My leg—!" She clutched at her ankle, pain etched across her face.

Ledge was there in an instant, his barrier flaring brighter as he knelt beside her. His hands, calloused but careful, pressed along the joint. "Sprain," he said, tone edged with relief and urgency. He glanced at Von. "We can't stop—not here. We'll move slower."

Ara's jaw tightened against the pain, but she nodded, forcing herself upright. Mystic Barricade shifted closer, taking some of her weight across his massive shoulder, his silence saying more than words.

Each step from then on was a trial. The path narrowed, the wind howled, and the very mountain seemed determined to test their resolve. Through it all, Von's energy embers burned with a steady, unyielding glow, his gaze fixed on the unseen peak ahead. Whatever lay buried in the Northern Ice Ring, he would reach it—even if the mountain demanded blood for passage.

After what felt like an eternity, they reached the jagged crown of the Ice Ring. The Tracer in Mystic Von's grasp pulsed violently, its screen flickering as though straining to contain the readings. They were standing directly above the buried Humming Black Trunk.

Mystic Barricade dropped to his knees, his energy embers blazing like a cosmic inferno. He clawed into the drifts with his bare hands, each sweep of his arms tearing through the mountain's frozen skin. Snow and ice shattered under his force, but the deeper he dug, the more the air itself seemed to vibrate—an ominous hum, steady, low, like something alive below.

At last, Barricade struck something solid. With a guttural roar, he unearthed the black trunk, its surface gleaming with frost yet untouched by time. The sight of it stole their breath. Its surface was not inert—it shivered faintly, almost breathing, threads of dark energy weaving across the ironlike exterior.

Von wasted no time. Lifting the Tracer high, he focused his embers into its core. A beam of energy split the stormy air, carrying their signal back across the distance. "Mentor—now."

Back at the cottage, Mentor had been watching the device pulse wildly, his heart drumming with both dread and relief. When Von's signal flared across the screen, he turned to Miraj. His embers erupted around him like a beacon in the night.

"It's time," he said.

Together, they rushed outside. Mentor spread his arms wide, drawing on the ancient syllables. Miraj lent her power, their energies intertwining like braided light. The ground trembled, and a vortex tore open before them—an oval of shimmering brilliance that pulsed like a living heart.

The return portal stood ready, a gateway carved through willpower and dread itself.

The first to emerge from the portal was the Humming Black Trunk. It thudded onto the ground with a weight that shook the earth, scattering snow and dirt into the air. Even still sealed, it radiated a presence, its surface faintly vibrating with a low hum that crawled into their bones. The heroes could only imagine the power Mal-Monger still sought within.

Mystic Ara stumbled out next, leaning heavily on Mystic Ledge. Her ankle throbbed, yet her eyes shone with hard-won triumph, a warrior's fire undimmed by pain.

Mystic Encrypt followed close behind, his breath a steady plume in the icy air. "I've endured a core's heat," he muttered, shaking his head. "But this cold... this cold cuts deeper."

Finally, Mystic Von stepped through. He flipped back his hood, his face raw from the bitter wind, but his gaze burned clear. He met Mentor's eyes, and the weight of command settled in his voice.

"Effective immediately," Von said, each word deliberate, "we no longer scatter. From now on, everything serves one purpose—the removal of General Scorpiondt and his associates."

The words hung in the air like an oath, drawing silence from all around.

With their prize secured, the mystics and their guides stepped back through the portal. The frigid peaks of the Ice Ring vanished behind them, replaced by the hearth-warmth of the cottage. Safe—for now.

Yet even in the comfort of home, the low hum of the Black Trunk lingered, a reminder that this victory was not an end but only the beginning of a far larger war.

Sunshine streamed into the cozy cottage, warm beams cutting through the rustic rafters and spilling across the worn floorboards. To help Mystic Ara rest her sprained ankle, Miraj prepared a Karibegoan dish of simmered, mashed leaves—served to her in bed. The earthy aroma filled the room, comforting and familiar, wrapping the home in a sense of calm.

At the wooden table, Mentor and Mystic Barricade hunched over a battered board game, its edges smoothed by years of play. The chairs creaked beneath them as they shifted, the sound blending with their banter.

"Don't mind if I do," Mentor said, grinning as he made the opening move.

Barricade followed, his grin cocky, his eyes glinting with competitive fire. "The next move could be your last," he warned, already plotting a daring leap across the board. He leaned back with swagger. "Tell you what—when I win, I'll buy you a year's worth of chairs."

Mentor chuckled, his fingers hovering confidently over the board. "I didn't put any money into this game. But if you insist…" He slid his piece into place with quiet precision.

As the match unfolded, Barricade's bravado began to falter. His confident grin slipped into furrowed focus, then into mounting dread. He leaned forward, squinting at the board as if the pieces might reveal a secret escape.

"Maybe we just play for fun, huh?" he offered, trying to mask his unease.

"No retreat, no surrender," Mentor replied smoothly, moving his final piece into position. With a clap of his hands, he declared victory.

Barricade sagged back, sheepish but good-natured. "Can I borrow a coin until the first of the month?" he muttered, flashing a grin.

From across the room, Miraj entered with folded arms and a knowing smile. "Not a cent. And speaking of coin—I seem to have misplaced the one you gave me."

Her words landed with an odd weight, drawing a glance between Mentor and Barricade. The warmth of the room remained, but beneath the laughter, a small unease stirred.

While the cottage buzzed with warmth and laughter, the atmosphere elsewhere was starkly different—aboard a sleek, high-tech Servacraft. In the low-lit laboratory, Dr. Serpendt now stood as the sole head of the Beta-Gene Fluid Project, a mantle inherited when Mystic Von abandoned it. The work was nearly finished, but Von's absence still clung to the place like a shadow—every glowing screen and scrawled margin seemed to whisper of his vanished hand.

The lab itself was a fortress of innovation. Beakers bubbled with volatile concoctions; translucent tubing pulsed with glowing liquids; data streams cascaded across hovering holo-screens. The air was alive with the constant hum of servers and machinery, a symphony of cold precision. Every gleam of polished steel, every sterile light, seemed to deny the warmth of humanity.

Dr. Serpendt stood at the helm, his tall frame cutting a severe silhouette against the rows of equipment. At the head of a rectangular table cluttered with holograms and instruments, he exuded authority like a second skin. His eyes—sharp, reptilian—swept across the gathered scientists. None dared shift under his gaze.

"Status," he commanded, his voice flat but carrying the weight of inevitability.

Dr. Jidohtta cleared his throat, fingers flicking across a glowing tablet before speaking. "We're at 96% completion as of today, Doctor."

The words hung in the air like a death knell.

Serpendt inclined his head slowly, his lips tightening into a thin line. "So close. The moment of culmination." His gaze lingered on the projected schematics of the human genome, highlighted in eerie red threads. "Von thought he bought time by abandoning us. But time belongs to finishers, not fugitives."

The scientists shifted uneasily, the weight of his words sinking in. 96% was not simply progress—it was the edge of transformation. What waited at a hundred percent would not be reversible.

Dr. Serpendt leaned forward, his voice dropping to a low hiss. "We will finish. And when the Surrogates rise, the world will forget Von's name. It will remember mine."

The hum of machinery seemed to deepen, as if even the Servacraft itself acknowledged his vow.

"No fracture," Mystic Encrypt said, brushing his fingers along Ara's ankle. His tone carried the confidence of a soldier who'd seen—and mended—more wounds than he cared to count.

Ara winced, stubbornness flashing in her eyes. "It feels like it is."

Encrypt gave her a patient half-smile. "But it isn't."

She rolled her eyes, and before she could press the point, her father's voice cut across the room. "Ara Von." Just her name—low, steady, enough to remind her of her manners.

Soft light filtered through the curtains, bathing the small bedroom in golden calm. The wooden beams, the handwoven rugs, even the faint crackle of the fire from the adjoining room wrapped the moment in a homely stillness—one that felt almost foreign after so many battles.

Concern edged Von's tone as he asked, "How long before she's walking again?"

Encrypt sat back, thoughtful. "Two weeks at most—likely sooner."

The door creaked open, and Miraj entered, balancing a steaming bowl of broth. The savory aroma filled the room. She handed it to Mystic Ledge, who took it with a grateful nod. "How's she doing?" she asked quietly.

Ledge settled on the edge of the bed, spoon in hand. "Well enough. She'll be back on her feet in a few days," he murmured before offering Ara her first bite.

Von chuckled, the sternness gone from his face. "Don't spoil her. She's already a handful."

Ara smirked, leaning back against the pillows, enjoying every moment of attention—from her father's watchful eye, her lover's quiet caretaking, and her comrade's practical healing. Even with the pain, her smile lingered, mischievous and unbowed.

In the cottage's shared room, Guide Mentor and Mystic Barricade lingered over Miraj's cooking, the wooden beams above glowing soft in the candlelight. Laughter and the clink of cutlery filled the air, wrapping them in the comfort of a quiet evening.

Then the single candle on the table quivered. Its small flame bent and twisted, flickering as though caught in a phantom draft.

Both men leaned closer.

The flame sputtered, then flared unnaturally—burning not gold but bright purple. The eerie glow painted their faces in otherworldly light.

And then, as quickly as it had come, it vanished. The wick gave a faint hiss, curling into darkness.

Silence fell. The warm cottage suddenly felt colder, as if the night itself had crept inside with the extinguished flame.

A sharp, deliberate knock rattled the front door. The sound cut through the warmth of the cottage like a blade. Mentor and Barricade exchanged a look— their laughter gone, replaced by a hush that clung to the air. Even the fire in the hearth seemed to shrink back, its crackle subdued.

Mentor rose, every instinct prickling. The floorboards groaned beneath his slow steps. When he pulled the door wide, two figures waited on the threshold.

Guide Moral stood first—short, brown-skinned, bald patches peeking through dreadlocks tipped in faded highlights. His presence was understated yet unnerving, wisdom wrapped in riddles. A single gold earring dangled with a purple marble that caught the dim light, while a necklace of wooden beads and a gold medallion pressed against the black fabric of his form-fit dashiki. His loose trousers, torn at the knee, and scuffed loafers told of long roads walked, but his eyes told of knowledge meant to unsettle.

At his side, half in shadow, stood Minion—a boy no older than twelve. His dreadlocks were bound beneath a black scarf, his dashiki a striking weave of gray, gold, and green. Colorful bracelets stacked his left arm, each one whispering of meaning never explained. Yet what gripped Mentor's attention most was the basket cradled in the boy's hands—black wicker, brimming with red apples so polished they seemed to glow. Something about them felt wrong, as though their gleam belonged not to nature, but to some darker hand.

"Good afternoon, Guide Mentor." Moral said smoothly, twirling a strand of hair. The words carried no warmth, only riddled intent.

"Afternoon." Mentor answered carefully. His voice was steady, but his eyes flicked over the pair with suspicion. "What brings you here?"

Moral's lips curved in a smile that revealed nothing. "We heard of the mystic heroes—the ones who retrieved the Trunk."

Mentor stiffened. His tone hardened. "How did you find out about that?"

"Word travels fast, doesn't it," Moral replied, the simple phrase weighted with implications Mentor didn't like.

Suppressing his irritation, Mentor stepped aside. "Then come in."

The cottage shifted as they entered, its humble walls seeming to pulse with the strange energy their presence carried. Mentor introduced them to Barricade, whose bulk filled the room yet whose stare betrayed unease. A moment later, footsteps creaked across the floorboards. Mystic Von appeared from Ara's room, followed by Ledge and Encrypt, their cloaks trailing pale light from the embers still alive in their veins.

The air thickened. Five mystics, a wary host, and two guests whose intentions were anything but clear.

And at the center of the wooden table, Minion set down the basket of gleaming red apples.

Left alone in her room, Mystic Ara lay back against the thin mattress, her gaze drifting across the low wooden ceiling. The muffled sounds of the cottage faded into the background until all that remained was the silence of her own thoughts.

How did it come to this?

Only months ago, she had been a student at Petrichore University, chasing research deadlines and debating professors. Now she was in the home of a Karibegoan guide, cloaked in powers she barely understood, carrying the weight of a destiny she had never asked for.

Her thoughts lingered on Captain Ledge, the steady force at her side. Somehow, amid the chaos, a bond had taken root—unexpected, unshakable. She touched the red cloth tied at her wrist, feeling the pulse of a future that seemed both uncertain and inevitable.

Rainah has set this path for me, she thought, her chest tightening. A destiny I never expected to live out. Yet my heart tells me my next destination must be Petrichore.

A single tear slipped down her cheek, tracing the curve of her face before falling to the pillow. It was grief, yes—but also resolve.

Mystic Ledge broke the silence first, his curiosity clear. "Who do we have here?"

Mentor introduced the visitors with measured calm: Guide Moral, once his student, and Minion, the boy he now guided. Von's sharp eyes lingered on the youth, unsettled by his silence.

"He's well," Moral assured, his tone steady. "He cannot speak, yet carries knowledge deeper than most men will ever grasp."

He offered gratitude then, thanking the mystics for returning the Humming Black Trunk to Indigo. Minion stepped forward, lifting a basket of red apples in silent offering. But Ledge redirected the thanks. "You should thank Mentor."

Perplexity flickered in Guide Moral's eyes. "Why is that? Am I missing something?"

Von answered, matter-of-fact but weighty. Mentor had reborn them in the Fetal Orb, reshaping their very energy, enabling them to find the trunk. The revelation struck Moral like a blow; his breath came fast, his gaze wide with disbelief.

Mentor's guilt spilled out in a torrent. He had broken tradition, yes—but for survival. "I did what was needed to keep the trunk in Karibegoan hands," he implored.

Respect shifted in Moral's eyes, admiration hardening into quiet rebuke. "You taught me tradition forbids such partings," he said, low, pained. "Now I see tradition means nothing to you."

He turned toward the door, Minion at his side. Before leaving, Moral paused, delivering his warning in words that felt less like speech than prophecy. "A reign shall be reclaimed on the day it rains—fear staining the faces of the chained."

The door shut behind them with a thud, leaving silence heavy as stone.

Barricade eyed the basket, reaching for an apple, but Miraj slapped it from his hand. "Not Indigo's fruit," she snapped. "Not after the way he toyed with his hair." Her tone carried no jest.

Outside, Guide Moral and Minion disappeared beneath the vaulted canopy of Indigo's forest. Shadows wrapped them in shifting light, ancient trees whispering like witnesses. Moral's voice fell quiet but stern. "Lesson, Minion: a Guide must be held to account for reckless acts. Never abandon tradition lightly."

Minion nodded, solemn as the branches bowed overhead.

Then, without warning, Moral spoke a Majeskrit command.

"Con-De-Mon: Life Reaper."

The words curdled the air. Trees blackened, moss withered, small creatures shriveled to husks. Soil itself cracked, drained of life. A low vibration spread outward—reaching the cottage.

Inside, Von stood at the window, watching the two vanish among the trees. The midday light still poured in, but a strange chill clung to the air. Encrypt joined him, fists clenched. "I don't trust that man—or the boy. Whatever they are planning, it will touch Indigo... and us."

The floor shuddered faintly beneath their feet. A hum began, soft at first, then swelling—vibrating through the boards, matching the rhythm of a pulse. Von's gaze shifted downward, toward the source.

The Humming Black Trunk.

Tucked away in the underground chamber, its seal now blazed with violet light, flickering like a heartbeat. The air thickened with each thrum, as if the relic itself was awakening.

Mentor's voice broke the silence, unsteady. "What's happening?"

Von turned, his face unreadable, but his tone grave. "The Trunk has sensed them. And something else… something moving beneath this world."

The hum deepened. The glow brightened. And in that tense stillness, the cottage no longer felt like a refuge, but the front line of an unseen war.

The cottage lay deep in silence, its timbers creaking softly against the weight of night. In the shared room, a single candle flickered on the wooden table, casting long shadows across the walls. Guide Mentor sat opposite Mystic Encrypt, the ancient Book of Majeskrit spread open between them. The leather-bound tome exuded age, its pages breathing with wisdom older than memory.

Mentor's voice carried low, deliberate, as he traced the symbols with a calloused finger. "Every rune here isn't just a word or a spell—it's vibration. Breathe them to life. Read them wrong, you call nothing; read them true, you call the world."

Encrypt leaned forward, his silver eyes reflecting the shifting flame. He listened intently, nodding, then asked with quiet curiosity, "But how did this book even come into existence? Who would've gathered all of this knowledge into one place?"

Mentor leaned back, the question lingering in the dim light. Rising from his chair, he crossed to the counter where a pitcher of beer sat waiting. He poured himself a tin cup, the froth spilling just over the rim. "Cup for you?" he asked, half-turning.

Encrypt shook his head, lips twitching into a faint smile. "No, thank you. I don't drink in the dead of night."

"Suit yourself, Mystic," Mentor said, returning with his cup. He lowered himself back into the chair, the wood groaning beneath his weight, and took a long pull before speaking again.

"My people are older than this book—Mystics before any page was bound, before ink ever touched hide. In terms of aura, we carried the knowledge inside our chests long before it was written down. The Monks of Mercy gave the book form and passed it down. Later, it was taught only to what we call Guides—at a school hidden from common sight. That's what I know."

Encrypt sat with the words, his gaze drifting over the curling script. A thought burned quietly within him. "Then I'd like to meet these Monks of Mercy someday," he said at last.

Mentor exhaled through his nose, the sound equal parts sigh and chuckle. "They don't interact much with their own people, much less outsiders. Monks stay in shadow. But I will see what I can do."

The candle flame bent in the draft of their shared silence. Between them, the Book of Majeskrit seemed to hum faintly, as if stirred by the weight of what had been spoken.

The Conqueror VI
As told by General Scorpiondt

They finally found it.

The Trunk.

They carried it back like champions. Cloaked in frost and foolishness.

Mystic Von and his disciples—the reanimated ghosts of Petrichore, now pretending to be gods—scaled the Ice Ring to reclaim what they did not understand, could not contain, and never should have unearthed. And yet, they celebrated this retrieval as if they had captured the heart of a dying star.

Let me be perfectly clear.

The Humming Black Trunk is not a trophy.

It is a grave.

And the hum they hear is not an echo of victory—it is a reminder that silence can be broken.

Eleven months. That's how long it took for them to act.

Von and Encrypt had spent nearly a year sipping brew in a village lit by glowing fruit, marveling at the poetry of insects and the "wisdom" of forest elders. How tragic that a species on the brink of annihilation can still find time to barter over biscuits and flirt beneath moonlight. When you lull a rebel long enough, he forgets the sound of war.

But time does not forget.

And neither do I.

While they danced through Karibegoan marketplaces and whispered over their broken experiments, my Beta-Gene Fluid project neared completion. Ninety-six percent. That's where my scientists stand. No beer. No sentiment. Just purpose.

That's the difference between us.

They crave meaning.

I craft it.

And yet… something stirs.

Von knows we are closing in. I saw it in his eyes, in the way he stopped mid-sentence when he heard the name: the Humming Black Trunk. It wasn't Mentor who told him—it was a woman named Miracle. Fitting, isn't it? That truth, when delivered without warning, always sounds like prophecy.

He was rattled.

Encrypt as well.

Good. Fear focuses the mind.

They retrieved the Trunk under the illusion that it would bring them safety. But what they brought back to Indigo is not protection—it is invitation. The hum they hear? That is not Mal-Monger reaching out. That is the universe clearing its throat.

And Mentor…

Ah, Mentor. A man whose mind has grown old while his tongue still plays games. He thought sealing the Trunk in the Northern Ice Ring would remove temptation. He thought frost could subdue fire.

But you cannot bury a god in ice and call it a tomb.

The Trunk remembers.

So do I.

His confession was pathetic—he abandoned the sacred codes of the Karibegoan order. Performed forbidden rites. Transformed children into weapons wrapped in silk scarves. And for what? To keep the Trunk from falling into the hands of the Empire?

It was ours first.

Mal-Monger—yes, I know his name well. A mistake the Karibegoans tried to erase. Not kill. Not even imprison. Erase. Because that's what cowards do when they meet a power they can't understand.

But I understand him.

He is not their shame.

He is their future.

When the Mystics returned from the Ice Ring, they dragged with them a pulse. A frequency. A heartbeat beneath iron.

And with it, came cracks.

Von declared, "We no longer scatter."

An order. A unification. A sign that he is awakening to leadership.

Which means he is also awakening to threat.

From me.

Then came the visitors. Guide Moral and his… boy. Minion. Such a name. Such innocence, painted onto the face of something far more ancient. That child is not what they believe he is. He does not speak because words would make him less.

They brought apples, polished like mirrors, but I know better. In every rebellion, there comes a moment when poison arrives dressed as offering. The girl nearly ate one. She would have, too—had her instincts not twitched.

But what concerned me most was not the fruit.

It was the words Moral left behind.

"A reign shall be reclaimed on the day it rains—fear staining the faces of the chained."

A riddle. But riddles are truths wearing masks.

He knows what approaches.

So do I.

In the shadows of Indigo, where they mistake glow for light and ritual for righteousness, the Trunk now hums louder. I can feel it, even here—aboard my Servacraft, orbiting far above their folklore. The vibration carries through the fabric of the world like a signal awaiting reply.

And if Mal-Monger is listening…

Then so am I.

Let me tell you what they fear most:

That the Trunk will open.

That it will choose.

But they are mistaken.

The Trunk does not choose.

It remembers.

And what it remembers is betrayal.

They believe it is still sealed.

They believe I am unaware.

They believe wrong.

So let the girl nurse her twisted ankle.

Let Barricade win his board games.

Let Mentor lie to himself while Von mutters oaths beneath candlelight.

Let Encrypt study spells.

Let Ledge dream of honor.

Let them all bask in the warmth of each other.

Because soon, the hum will rise to a howl.

And on that day, when the red cloth flutters not in wind, but in fire—

They will see me.

Not as the past they fled from.

But as the end they were always destined to meet.

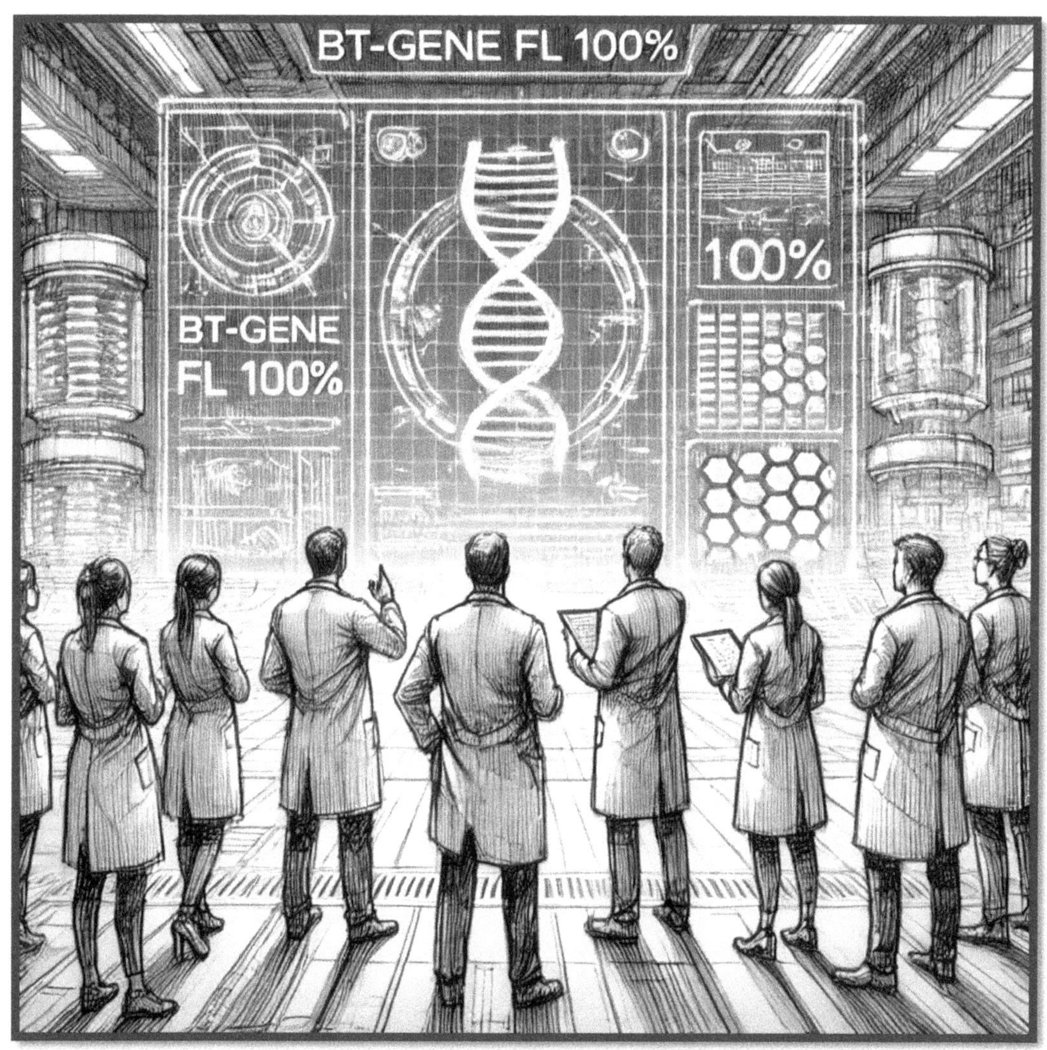

Chapter 7 | **Project Is Completed**

Months had passed since their last encounter with Guide Moral and Minion. Now, in the early morning hours of Indigo, the first rays of sunlight painted the sky. The cottage stood quietly in the heart of the mystical land, its presence both humble and steadfast. Outside, a ground fire crackled, its warmth pushing back the edge of the morning chill.

Mystics Von and Encrypt sat beside Mentor at the fire, each cradling a tin cup filled with precious brewed coffee. In this remote and enigmatic place, coffee was a rare luxury—more treasured than coin—and Mentor reminded them with a gruff tone not to spill a single drop.

Von, ever the sharp-tongued, lifted his cup and quipped, "Coffee may be difficult to get out here, but oddly enough, alcohol flows like water."

Mentor squinted at him, unimpressed, while Encrypt chuckled into his own cup. The brief silence that followed was filled with the hiss of the fire and the rich, bitter scent of coffee curling upward. Von raised his tin, savoring that first sip of the morning, their banter fading into the hush of dawn.

A woman's frantic voice shattered the serene morning air.

"They're changing us! Please—help me!"

From the tree line she burst forth, stumbling into view. Her sleek black hair was tied back in haste, loose strands clinging to her sweat-damp face. A long kurta of shifting multicolored patterns swept against her legs, its fabric torn from the brush, while bangles clattered wildly on her wrists. Flat-soled juttis slapped against the uneven earth as she fought her way forward, panic propelling her through the forest's embrace.

Her cry pierced the quiet of Indigo like a warning bell.

Von reacted instantly. With a flick of his hand, a glowing field unfurled around him, Mentor, and Encrypt—a protective barrier humming with latent power. The woman collapsed just beyond its shimmering edge, breath ragged, body trembling, her face a portrait of exhaustion and fear.

Mentor's eyes narrowed. How did she breach the dome? he thought. Unless she slipped through the hairline seam we never sealed…

Von dropped the barrier just long enough to reach her. A cauterized beam wound scorched her shoulder—clean, cruel. He resealed the field with a flick.

The commotion stirred the rest of the household. The cottage door creaked open and Barricade, Ara, and Ledge strode into the clearing, faces sharpened by equal parts concern and curiosity. Encrypt quickly relayed what had happened.

Ara dropped to her knees, placing two fingers against the woman's throat. "Pulse weak," she murmured. "Bleeding's minimal."

Then she looked up at her father, eyes wide with unease. "But… how did this human woman end up here?"

Von's gaze hardened, the words carrying the weight of a revelation none of them wanted spoken aloud.

"The Beta-Gene Fluid is complete," he said, voice flat. *"100%."*

Silence pressed down on them, heavier than the forest's canopy. The fire crackled uselessly in the background, its warmth swallowed by the chill that had settled over the mystics.

The woman had carried more than her wounds into Indigo. She had carried proof. And the certainty that their world had shifted forever.

As dusk surrendered to night, the cottage glowed with firelight, its timbered walls sheltering the fragile hush of concern. The stranger was laid gently upon a stack of thick woolen blankets spread before the hearth, where the flames snapped and hissed, casting restless shadows across the room.

Ara knelt beside her, the soft embers of compassion bright in her eyes. She pressed a damp red cloth against the woman's fevered brow, each motion tender, deliberate—an unspoken vow to protect life, even in its most vulnerable form. The faint rise and fall of the woman's chest answered Ara's care, though the pallor of her face still bore the mark of suffering.

Encrypt stood near, tall and vigilant, his frame outlined by the dance of the fire. His gaze did not waver, every breath of the patient measured, every flicker of her pulse quietly noted. The soldier in him had not left—discipline etched into his posture, vigilance coiled in his stare—but there was something more: a protective stillness, as though he had taken it upon himself to stand between her fragile body and the weight of a hostile universe.

Behind them, Mentor leaned on the rough-hewn table, watching in silence, the set of his jaw betraying a storm of unease he did not voice. Barricade lingered by the door, his massive arms crossed, eyes shifting between fire and window, as though expecting trouble to follow on the woman's heels. Von himself stood apart, half-shrouded in shadow, his thoughts unreadable, his mind already turning the woman's arrival into a harbinger of greater calamity.

The fire crackled louder, filling the silence that none dared break. Outside, the Indigo night stretched endless and inscrutable, and inside, within the cottage walls, destiny had found them once again.

Mystic Von labored tirelessly in the underground chamber, the cramped air thick with parchment dust and the faint tang of molten metal. His eyes, lit by the candle's wavering glow, scanned equations and schematics sprawled across the wooden table. The Sigma-Gene Fluid Project consumed him—every page, every calculation, every sleepless hour whispering that failure was not an option. Tonight, under Indigo's watchful skies, the project had to be completed.

But frustration mounted, his mutters breaking into a sharp bark that echoed off the stone walls. "Encrypt!"

Within moments, Mystic Encrypt hurried down the creaking steps, his eyes wide with alarm. "What's going on, Von?" His voice carried a soldier's readiness, though beneath it lay the eagerness of a student willing to follow his teacher anywhere.

Von didn't glance up. His hands trembled slightly as he pressed another formula flat against the table. "I need all the help I can get," he said, voice steady but edged with intensity. "Because tonight—tonight, we finish this project."

The weight of his words thickened the air. A summons followed. "Mentor!"

The old Guide appeared at the doorway, brow knit with confusion, but curiosity drew him in. Von didn't waste time with pleasantries. "I need a few tin cups of that black, hot bean-water."

Mentor blinked. "Coffee?"

Von nodded curtly. "Yes. That stuff."

Mentor shrugged, scratching at his beard. "The coffee is finished, but I still have tea. Strong, strong tea."

Von closed his eyes for a breath, disbelief flashing across his face, then exhaled sharply. "Fine. That will have to do."

As Mentor clattered with kettles and tin cups at the side table, Von fixed Encrypt with a hard stare. His voice dropped low, a note of warning woven into its rhythm.

"Tonight, under the full moon, the lone wolves emerge from the shadows."

The words lingered in the chamber, half prophecy, half omen.

Encrypt stiffened, understanding that Von's cryptic remark was no idle flourish. Outside, the wind gathered strength, threading through the forest above. The old timbers of the cottage groaned as if unsettled, and the fire in the hearth sputtered, its glow warped by the shifting shadows.

Down below, in the pulse of candlelight, two men leaned over their work—not merely scholars or mystics, but conspirators against fate itself.

The following day dawned with a cautious, fragile hope.

The human woman stirred, the coarse wool of thick blankets brushing her skin as she pushed herself halfway upright. Her eyelids fluttered against the shafts of morning light pouring through the cottage windows, the golden glow both gentle and unfamiliar. The air was thick with the mingled scents of herbs, earth, and old wood—a world both foreign and strangely comforting. Her throat dry, she croaked out a soft, uncertain, "Hello? … Hello?"

In the back room, Mystics Ara and Ledge sat cross-legged, their breathing steady, their minds submerged in the deep ritual of Hyberitation. Through this ancient practice, they replenished their energy centers, tapping into the oldest traditions of the Majeskrit tongue. Yet even in the stillness of meditation, Ara felt something tug at the edges of her awareness.

A vision surged before her closed eyes. She saw a woman's face—stern, noble, streaked with urgency—as trembling hands reached up and lifted a crown from her head. At its center was a massive blue stone, fractured down its heart, its glow dim but still alive. The crown was pressed into the hands of a loyal aide. Words followed, sharp with command and fear: "Bury it deep. They must never touch the Shard of the Heirloom Family." The image wavered, sinking into shadow, but the weight of it pressed heavy in Ara's chest.

A voice—faint, fragile, desperate—echoed in her spirit.

Without opening her eyes, Ara shifted. She invoked the Halo Ascend, the words resonant with power: a secret manifestation that allowed her soul's essence to step beyond her body. A radiant halo bloomed into existence behind her head, splitting away in luminous form. It drifted free of her physical frame, a circle of living light gliding soundlessly through the air until it passed into the shared room where the stranger waited.

The woman clutched the blankets tighter around her shoulders, heart pounding. The room was empty, yet a presence stirred.

"Who's there?" she whispered, fear threading her voice.

The reply came soft, calm, a voice both near and everywhere at once. "Good morning. My name is Ara Von. Please remain at rest; I will be with you soon."

The woman's eyes darted around the room, bewildered. "Where are you? I... I cannot see you."

"Look above," Ara's voice urged gently.

Her gaze lifted—and her breath caught. Suspended above her was a glowing halo, pure white light cascading across the walls, washing away shadow. It radiated a warmth that felt alive, not just illumination but presence, filling her with the unexplainable sense that she was both safe and seen.

Ara's voice wrapped around her again, steady, reassuring. "Do not be afraid. Beside you is a tin cup of water mixed with healing herbs. Miraj prepared it for your recovery. Drink—it will strengthen you."

Shaking hands reached for the cup, the cool metal grounding her in reality as she raised it to her lips. The herbal infusion was bitter at first, but warmth spread through her chest and limbs with each swallow, as if the drink itself carried calm. Her trembling eased.

The halo pulsed once, like a heartbeat of light—then slowly faded. Ara's presence withdrew, leaving the woman alone, yet not abandoned.

She leaned back against the blankets, eyes wide, her thoughts racing. This cottage was no ordinary refuge. It was a threshold to ancient power, to mysteries she had never dreamed existed.

Her journey through this mystical world had only just begun. And though fear lingered at the edges, she now felt a flicker of strength—and the unexpected comfort of an ally she had not imagined.

The morning hunt led them deep into Indigo's forest, where sunlight lanced through the canopy in golden shafts, painting the undergrowth in shifting shadows. The air was cool and crisp, alive with the scents of moss, damp bark, and distant flowers.

Mystic Barricade moved at the front, every step heavy yet precise, his soldier's training sharpening his senses. He crouched, running his broad fingers over a patch of disturbed earth. "Boar," he muttered, tracing the fresh hoof prints. The faint musk of their quarry drifted in on the breeze.

Mentor nodded, retrieving a coil of rope from their gear. "Then we set a snare, simple as that," he said simply, his tone seasoned with the confidence of long experience.

Nearby, Miraj gathered Elamamgis fruits into her woven basket, their sweet fragrance perfuming the air. At Barricade's request, she handed one over. Its potent aroma would serve as bait no creature could resist. Together, they knotted the rope, fixed the trigger, and set the fruit at the center of the trap.

Once prepared, the three concealed themselves behind a dense tangle of bushes. Silence pressed in, broken only by the flutter of wings overhead and the creak of branches swaying in the breeze.

Movement stirred the leaves.

Fin, the white rabbit, hopped into view—his red scarf bobbing at his neck. His nose twitched, catching the fruit's scent. He froze, ears stiff, then crept forward with exaggerated caution, eyes narrowing like a thief checking for guards.

A voice hissed from the bush. "Go away now."

Fin stopped, ears flicking. He glanced around, suspicious. Then, with a cheeky grin, he ignored the warning and reached for the fruit again.

Mentor stepped out of the bush, arms folded. "Don't even think about it."

For a moment, they locked eyes. Fin's whiskers twitched. Then, in a blur, the rabbit bolted back into the trees, vanishing between the shadows. Mentor sighed and slipped back into hiding.

The forest grew still—until the undergrowth shivered.

The wild boar emerged. Its massive frame pushed through the brush, tusks glinting, eyes small and black as it rooted toward the bait. Even from a distance, its power was undeniable, its bristled hide rippling with each step.

Mentor whispered, a hint of awe in his voice. "Lord, look at the size of that beast."

Barricade's grin widened. "Think it'll fit in my belly?"

Miraj smirked. "Your belly is not the only one that is empty, big man."

"Shh," Mentor hissed, raising a hand.

The boar snorted, nose quivering at the fruit. With a sudden snap, it lunged—only for the rope to tighten around its thick leg. The beast bellowed, thrashing, shaking the trees with its fury. But the trap held.

Barricade surged forward, muscles straining as he hauled the rope tighter, anchoring it against the beast's violent jerks. Miraj and Mentor joined in, their combined effort subduing the boar until its struggles slowed, its breath heaving clouds into the morning air.

When it was finally subdued, Barricade hoisted the animal over his massive shoulders, grinning with triumph. Mentor and Miraj collected their baskets—fruit and water sloshing in rusted buckets.

They trekked homeward through shafts of golden light, the forest echoing with their laughter. The morning had given them more than food. It had given them victory, camaraderie, and a story worth retelling.

A sense of tranquility had settled over the cozy cottage tucked deep within the woods, the warm glow of the crackling fireplace casting flickering shadows across the walls. Introveca, the weary stranger who had sought refuge there, tried to rise carefully from the woolen blankets, hoping not to disturb the peace. But her legs betrayed her—just as she steadied herself, the front door creaked open, and laughter poured inside. The joyous sounds of camaraderie shattered the stillness.

Startled, Introveca lost her balance and tumbled back onto the soft blanket. Mystic Barricade reacted at once. With quiet strength, he crossed the room, his eyes steady with reassurance.

"I think you'd prefer this," he said warmly, lifting her with a firm yet gentle grip. Their eyes met, a silent exchange of trust, before he guided her into a sturdy chair beside the fire.

She hesitated, then whispered, "Could I trouble you for a cup of hot tea?"

Barricade smiled and nodded. He busied himself at the hearth, filling the kettle, while Mentor and Miraj exchanged a knowing glance—the tenderness of the moment was its own reminder of why they fought to preserve such bonds.

Miraj eased closer. "May I ask your name, miss?"

The woman sighed heavily, her voice trembling. "Introveca." Her eyes glistened as the weight of loss pressed down on her.

Barricade turned, voice steady. "Could you share what you saw happening?"

Her breath faltered, but she forced the words out. "Hundreds of men in white, shiny metal shells descended on my people. They wore wristbands of steel and pierced our arms with small glass tubes—filled with a green liquid that glowed. Their eyes... copper, before my very eyes."

Mentor leaned forward, his tone edged with urgency. "And those who were injected with that thing—what happened to them?"

Introveca's voice broke. "They fell to their knees, writhing. It was as though their strength, their minds, their very souls were being drained. They changed—inside out."

Barricade's jaw tightened. "Did any of your relatives endure the same?"

Her answer was a whisper drowned in grief. "Yes. My parents... they gave themselves up so I could escape."

Mentor's voice softened, carrying the weight of compassion. "Do not carry guilt for what they chose, do you hear? Give thanks for their sacrifice—not shame."

Barricade poured the steaming tea into a tin cup. "Their gift was your life," he said, placing the cup into her trembling hands. "Do not let despair be the thief that takes it from you."

For the first time since her arrival, Introveca felt a flicker of solace—a fragile ember of hope kindled by their kindness.

But just as Barricade leaned forward to pass her the tea, a deafening roar erupted. The cottage walls quaked. Heavy footsteps pounded across the rooftop, each strike a hammer of dread. Introveca gasped, clutching Barricade's arm.

"Oh nahin," she whispered, terror flooding her eyes. "They found me."

"What's happening out there?" Miraj demanded, her voice tight.

Mentor's brow furrowed, his ears straining. "I can't quite make it out."

Barricade held steady, his frame braced, every instinct ready to shield them. Then—

BOOM.

The explosion rocked the cottage. The tin cup flew from his hand, scalding tea splashing across the floorboards as the very air seemed to split.

With a violent shake, the serenity was gone. The cottage itself seemed to hold its breath as everyone inside braced for the storm about to break.

Deep in Hyberitation, Mystic Ledge and Ara felt the floor tremble beneath them, dust sifting from the ceiling. Their focus shattered as the cottage groaned under the force of another boom.

Ledge's eyes snapped open, his embers flickering. "That wasn't wind," he muttered.

Ara rose beside him, steady and alert. "The storm's here. Peace won't protect us now."

Another crash shook the walls. They exchanged a look, resolve replacing calm. Embers flared to life around them.

Their time for stillness was over. The battle had arrived.

Mystic Barricade instructed Introveca to stay put, his tone calm but urgent. "Everyone else, move! We confront this threat now."

Outside, two hooded figures clashed in midair, their strikes exploding with bursts of mystic energy that lit the night like lightning. The duel was savage, each blow shaking the ground, each counterstrike faster than the eye could follow.

Mystic Ledge narrowed his gaze. "Their forms… I know them. But this power—no, it's different."

Ara's chest tightened as she stared upward. A fleeting thought struck her—Father? But the aura was too raw, too altered. These were not the men she remembered.

The group stood frozen, torn between awe and dread, as the sky burned with each collision. Only Mentor's expression shifted—first confusion, then dawning recognition. His eyes widened, a slow smile creeping across his face.

At last, he exhaled, almost laughing at the impossibility of it.

"The Sigma-Gene Fluid Project… it worked. Don't you see? Those two… they're Mystics Encrypt and Von."

As the two combatants descended, their coat-tails sliced through the cool morning air. Beneath the dark fabric, they wore full-body black spandex with high, tubular necks that contoured to their forms—clothing designed for both agility and protection. Matte-black combat boots grounded their steps, thudding lightly against the firm earth.

With a single motion, they pulled back their hoods.

Faces once familiar now appeared honed to near-divine perfection. Their eyes gleamed an uncanny silver, catching the first rays of sun with an ethereal glow. Disheveled hair framed sharp jawlines, their every feature sharpened as if carved by unseen hands. Even the daylight seemed to bend around them, their presence radiating a quiet, controlled power that stunned the onlookers.

Counselor Von's voice, deep and raspy, broke the silence.

"Good morning. We stand before you as advanced, mystic beings. The Sigma-Gene Fluid reconfigured our genetic chain—0-1101-z—elevating us beyond our former limits."

Beside him, Counselor Encrypt spoke with calm finality.

"From this moment onward, we are no longer just Mystics. We are Counselors."

Mystic Barricade couldn't hold back his admiration. He clapped slowly, eyes fixed on their piercing irises, their overwhelming auras, their sharpened forms. With a smirk he muttered, "I'll say it—this isn't just mystic. This is deity-level."

The group looked on, awe tinged with unease. The transformed men radiated power—immense, controlled, and daunting.

As they moved toward the cottage, morning light spilled across the clearing, warming the grass and brushing the treetops in gold. Mystic Ledge walked beside Counselor Von, questions burning.

"Why were you and Counselor Encrypt sparring on the roof?"

Von's silver eyes turned to him, steady and unblinking.

"We were testing our limits. Such power must be measured before it can be wielded."

Ledge hesitated, then pressed. "Was it worth it?"

Von's expression softened into something almost sorrowful.

"Yes. Power takes its price."

"What did you lose?"

Von's reply was heavy, his tone carrying the weight of truth.

"Our eyes no longer bear full sunlight. And these forms—" his hand brushed his altered face, "—have made us unrecognizable to our own species. Yet what we've gained is power beyond imagination. Power that demands burdens."

Ledge, unsettled, asked the final question. "Do you regret it?"

Von's answer was iron.

"No. Regret is a luxury we can no longer afford. It is too late for us—and too late for the Ikannunaa."

His words settled over the group like a shadow stretching across the brightening forest. Even in the brilliance of morning, they all understood—the world had already changed, and so had they.

Morning light streamed through the cottage windows, washing the wooden table in a golden glow. The smell of warm bread and steeped tea lingered in the air, but the atmosphere around the table was taut. Counselor Von and Counselor Encrypt sat with Introveca, who still wrestled with the memories of what she had seen—the gleam of glass tubes, the piercing of arms, the green glow.

Her voice, fragile but edged with anger, broke the silence.

"They filled us with that… liquid. What was it?"

Counselor Von's tone was calm, though heavy with regret.

"Beta-Gene Fluid. It was designed to suppress any threat your people might one day pose. The injections weakened you—shortened life spans, dulled strength, dimmed the mind, severed spiritual connection. It left your people docile. Easier to enslave."

"I'm sorry, Introveca."

Her head snapped toward him, eyes wide with fury.

"How do you know so much about this?"

The table fell silent. No one dared meet her gaze. The weight of an unspoken truth thickened the air. She pressed again, voice trembling.

"Why are you apologizing? Answer me!"

Counselor Von exhaled deeply, his stare fixed on the grain of the wooden table.

"Because I created it."

The confession shattered her composure. "Stop talking!" she cried, fists trembling, tears burning her eyes.

Mystic Barricade rose, steady but firm, and placed a hand between them.

"Introveca," he said, his voice low, "he had no choice. The Empire destroyed his world. They may have taken his wife. And they threatened to kill Ara—his only daughter—if he refused. He built the fluid under a blade to his throat. And when it was finished, they planned to kill him and Ara anyway."

The truth pulled the air from her lungs. Her anger faltered, collapsing into grief and confusion. She turned her face away, unable to meet Ara's or Von's eyes.

It was Ara who broke the silence. Her voice was gentle, but it carried an iron edge of promise.

"What you saw outside—their new forms—means the Empire's fall is coming. And if your parents still live, I'll heal them with the Blood Pinnacle flower."

Introveca blinked back tears, a glimmer of hope breaking through the storm. Ara, sensing the moment, softened it with a grin.

"Besides… you've got front-row seats to their downfall. Enjoy the show."

A reluctant smile tugged at Introveca's lips. The darkness in her chest eased, just enough for laughter to breathe.

She turned back to Von, her voice steadier now.

"I'm sorry for shouting."

Von inclined his head, forgiving without hesitation. "Anyone in your place would have done the same."

Then, with new resolve, she asked, "How can I help?"

Mystic Ledge leaned forward, curious. "What skills do you have, Introveca?"

"Hand drumming, farming, cooking, sewing," she answered, a shy pride creeping into her tone.

Encrypt smirked. "Perfect. I've got a back seam in my pants that needs mending."

Laughter rippled through the table. Barricade added with a grin, "Let us give her a little time to settle before we bury her in work."

But Ledge's voice carried quiet weight. "Uniforms, repairs, provisions—skills like yours matter. You're not just a guest here. You could be one of us."

For the first time since stepping into the cottage, Introveca felt something shift. No longer just a survivor—she was an ally. She had a role. A purpose. And for the first time in days, she did not feel alone.

Faint moonlight threaded through the Indigo forest canopy, casting an ethereal glow over a secluded cottage—its silence hiding the gravity of what stirred within. Beneath its wooden beams, Counselor Von and Counselor Encrypt prepared for a night that would alter destiny itself.

They led Mystic Ara, Mystic Barricade, and Mystic Ledge down the moss-covered steps into the underground room. Candlelight flickered across stone walls lined with scattered notes and vials. Von's tone was steady, but carried the weight of warning.

"The transformation will be swift... but agonizing. There is no avoiding it."

From a case, Counselor Encrypt revealed three syringes filled with shimmering blue fluid that caught the moon's pale glow. Introveca, lingering near the doorway, gasped.

"What is that?"

"The Sigma-Gene Fluid," Von answered, his eyes unreadable. "It will remake them—into beings like us."

Encrypt worked with precise calm, loading each needle. The fluid glimmered as if alive, reflecting in his eyes. One by one, he pressed the syringes into waiting arms. Anticipation tangled with dread as the Mystics exchanged silent looks.

"Lie down," Von instructed. The earthen floor was cold beneath them.

Ara frowned. "Why?"

Encrypt's voice dripped with dry amusement. "Because your body is about to reboot. You'll thank me later."

Then it began.

The underground chamber vibrated with a low hum as the Sigma-Gene Fluid surged through their veins. Muscles locked and spasmed. The scent of damp earth mixed with the acrid tang of the fluid, filling the air with something raw and metallic. Above them, the forest stilled—no insect, no bird dared break the silence.

Ledge convulsed first, a guttural gasp tearing from his throat. Ara followed, her cry echoing against the stone. Barricade's massive frame trembled, fists pounding the ground as if to resist the pain tearing through him. Energy rippled off their bodies in waves, distorting the candlelight.

Von stood rigid, pride and unease battling in his stare. Encrypt knelt close, searching their faces for signs beyond agony. For a moment, it seemed the process might consume them entirely.

And then, silence.

The convulsions stilled. Their breaths came ragged but steady, their bodies sprawled across the cold floor, veins glowing faintly beneath the skin like threads of blue lava.

Von's voice broke the hush.

"Welcome to your new existence."

The chamber seemed to pulse with his words, the very earth acknowledging what had just been unleashed. The night had ended, but their true trial was only beginning.

The morning sun blazed against the cottage walls, heat spilling through the shutters as the group gathered around the wooden table. Birds sang outside, their melody weaving a fragile calm over breakfast.

Counselor Von and Counselor Encrypt traded lighthearted banter about their favorite pastries. Von recalled a science conference where he first tasted a brown bread roll stuffed with Ciots-Cheese, a memory that still made him smile.

Introveca leaned forward, eyes bright. "Tell me the flavors. I'll try to bake it myself."

Encrypt chuckled and added his own favorite—a cold bun smeared with Kuconita spread. "If she wants a real challenge, she should start there. I still remember the recipe."

Their laughter softened as Mentor shared tales of meals he and Miraj had discovered across distant worlds—moments of joy before exile. His voice dimmed, nostalgia shadowing the room.

And then—

A violent crash split the tranquility. The door to the underground room slammed open, footsteps pounding up the stairs in rapid succession. The table fell silent. Every gaze turned toward the sound, breath held as unease thickened the air.

The tension heightened as Counselor Barricade, Counselor Ledge, and Counselor Ara stepped through the door. Energy embers drifted from their frames, glowing like celestial fireflies in the dim light. Their silver eyes burned with an unearthly intensity as they squinted against the light streaming through the windows, their disheveled hair only deepening their otherworldly presence.

Their forms, sharpened by the Sigma-Gene Fluid, radiated power. Each step was deliberate, heavy with the legacy of the mystics.

Miraj's breath caught as she watched them stride forward. They weren't just peers anymore—they were something greater, symbols of what lay ahead.

Counselor Barricade paused at the threshold, his deep voice breaking the silence. "Now this is what I'm talking about."

Introveca smirked faintly, her eyes shining with amusement. Counselor Ara, however, cut the air with her piercing gaze. Her unspoken warning was clear: anyone who doubted their readiness would answer to her.

The balance in the cottage shifted. The Counselors had arrived, and with them came urgency and purpose.

Ara turned her stare on her father, her tone sharp. "Didn't I tell you never to leave me unconscious and abandoned, Father?"

Counselor Von's reply carried a wry edge. "We might have discussed it. Still—you're alive, lady Counselor."

Rolling her eyes, Ara snatched his cup, drained it in one gulp, and slammed it down. "There. We're even. Thought it was coffee. Tea."

Miraj rolled her eyes at the petty payback.

Barricade's gaze found Introveca. A brief smile passed between them, unspoken but charged.

Counselor Ledge broke the silence. "Von, will this upgrade prove enough for the confrontation?"

From below, the Humming Black Trunk cracked with purple light. A rasping voice seeped through the floorboards: Oh, it's enough. Enough for me, boy. One day, you will be mine. Hahaha…

Von rose, calm yet steady. "That decision rests with you, Counselor. No upgrade will matter if your spirit falters. Readiness is not a tool—it is a state of being."

The words settled heavily.

Then Von's tone shifted, lighter but edged. "Some fresh air would do us all good. Why not a sparring match? Two former Keannelden soldiers—let's see Grenaivel's strength."

Barricade and Ledge exchanged a look. The challenge needed no words.

As they prepared to step outside, Von gave his final instruction. "Change into your uniforms."

The Counselors nodded and left, anticipation thick in the air.

The deep forest greeted them with quiet majesty. Towering trees formed a natural arena, sunlight piercing the canopy in shifting patterns of gold and green. The serenity only sharpened the tension between the two sparring Counselors.

Barricade and Ledge faced each other in the clearing, hoods low. Their new forms still felt foreign—strength ready at their fingertips, but not always steady. The others lingered at the edge, silent.

From the cottage, Mentor's voice rang out: "Do not tear up my forest—or my roof."

A ripple of chuckles, then stillness.

Barricade struck first, vanishing clumsily in a blur. He reappeared behind Ledge with a mistimed strike that still clipped his shoulder. Ledge stumbled, recovered, and countered with a sweeping kick that cut the air. Barricade rematerialized late, forced into defense.

"Come on, Barricade!" Ledge taunted, though his own balance wavered. "Show me what you've got!"

Barricade answered with a barrage of glowing punches. Some went wild, but one landed square, driving Ledge back. Wiping blood from his lip, he smirked. "Not bad. My turn."

He surged forward, fists flashing, but the rhythm of his new body betrayed him. Barricade blocked unevenly, their clash sending shockwaves through the clearing. Branches snapped, leaves spiraled, dirt split open beneath their feet.

Barricade leapt, a burst of raw white energy flaring from his hands. The aim faltered, the blast scattering skyward as Ledge barely redirected it. It detonated above the canopy, startling a flock of birds into flight.

Before Barricade could reset, Ledge vanished, reappearing midair with a spinning kick that sent him crashing down. Barricade rolled to his feet, answering with a downward strike that shook the earth, nearly knocking himself off balance.

"Enough showing off!" he growled, sparks dancing uncontrolled around him.

They clashed head-on, fists colliding in bursts of unstable light that forced the onlookers to shield their eyes.

Then, with reckless precision, Ledge ducked under a swing and tried to summon a Majeskrit technique. "Ma-Jes-Tic: Merkaba!" A glowing star began to form, debris pulling in, its power straining against his grip.

Before it could spiral out of control, Counselor Von's voice cut through the clearing. "That's enough. Stand down."

The star fizzled. Ledge exhaled, extending a hand. "How are you holding up?"

Barricade smirked, brushing dirt from his face. "I've had worse. You?"

They clasped hands, laughter breaking the tension. The forest seemed to breathe again.

Applause rose from the group. Von clapped once. "Good warm-up. Back to breakfast—we've got a long day ahead."

Together they returned, the forest's scent of earth trailing them—a fleeting peace before the storm to come.

Afternoon sunlight bathed the cottage grounds as Counselor Von and Mentor assembled the group outside. Shoulder to shoulder, the Counselors lined up in disciplined formation, the air heavy with anticipation.

"We've gathered you here to begin training," Counselor Von announced, his tone calm but resolute. "Today you will learn to manifest mystic energy into any form you wish."

Mentor stepped forward, his voice carrying authority. "Tomorrow we move on to using energy in martial arts, understood? Energy and intent are like yin and yang. You cannot have one without the other."

Before the exercises began, Mentor clarified the fundamentals. "Manifestations are only necessary when manifesting physical objects. For flight or levitation, words aren't required—but paired with a manifestation, the results are enhanced. And as you know, the Halo Ascend allows your spirit to act as an extension of your senses, sending your perception where your body cannot follow."

The training began in earnest. It was not merely magic—it was discipline. Von and Mentor moved among the Counselors, adjusting stances, correcting hand placement, and urging focus. Their voices blended with passages from the Book of Majeskrit, knowledge forbidden to Karibegoan outsiders, now shared out of necessity.

One by one, the Counselors learned to summon light. Hands glowed with radiant orbs, shimmering like fireflies in the dusk. Energy coursed through their bodies, at first erratic, then steady as their confidence grew. Next came heat: waves of warmth shimmered in the cool forest air, bending the light in faint ripples.

Progress varied. Counselor Ledge's light flared brightest, illuminating the treeline, while Counselor Barricade's heat rolled like a furnace, forcing even Mentor to step back with a grin. Counselor Encrypt's power flickered, unstable but growing stronger with each attempt.

Mistakes came—bursts of uncontrolled energy, sparks that sputtered out— but so did breakthroughs. Mentor barked corrections, Ara cut in with sharp observations, and Von's approving nods marked every success. Despite the strain, a quiet exhilaration spread. They weren't just learning—they were awakening.

By the time twilight settled, the clearing buzzed with light and heat, the air alive with raw potential. For the first time, they glimpsed what they might become: a force capable of turning the tide.

Breathing hard, Barricade wiped sweat from his brow. Introveca approached with a tin cup of cool water, her smile warm, her presence grounding after a day that had pushed them all to their limits.

In the night's stillness, while the others slept above, Counselor Von descended into the candlelit underground chamber. The air was thick, alive with mystic energy, as though the stone walls themselves held their breath.

Seated cross-legged on the cold floor, Von closed his eyes. For a long moment he was still—preparing to attempt what no Mystic had dared. Then, in a hushed tone, he spoke the forbidden tongue:

As-Tra-L: Halo Ascend.

The words reverberated, heavy with ancient power. Behind him, a radiant white ring flared into existence, drowning the candlelight in its brilliance. The halo rose through the wooden floorboards, then the roof, until it hung suspended beneath the moonlit sky. Tilting, it became a horizontal disk—a celestial star hovering above the cottage.

"Go," Von commanded.

The halo streaked across Indigo like a shooting star, his spirit tethered to its flight. Sweat beaded on his brow, but his focus never wavered.

When it reached the distant territory of Goa, the halo slowed, hovering above village homes, ancient stone walls, and the patrols of Ikannunaa soldiers. Through it, Von saw, heard, and felt as though he were there himself.

But what he found chilled him. The Prominent—the Ikannunaa's flagship—was gone. Relief flickered, but his vigilance sharpened. Nearby, he spotted General Scorpiondt speaking with Dr. Serpendt and a black-and-green armored I.R.S. operative beside a Servacraft. He could barely make out their words, but he caught mention of a political conflict with a planet called Heirloomus—still holding a grudge over the decimation of Petrichore.

Von guided the halo closer. His heart pounded as Scorpiondt's voice carried through:

"…thirty-three days. I must depart Earth in thirty-three days."

The General froze. His head snapped up, gaze locking on the radiant disk above him. His sharp eyes narrowed, scanning the sky.

"What is it, General?" Dr. Serpendt asked, unalarmed.

"I'm not sure…" Scorpiondt's voice was low, edged, honed by years of war.

Before he could act, the halo vanished.

Back in the chamber, Von's eyes flew open as he gasped, sucking in air like a drowning man breaking the surface. Sweat poured from his trembling body, soaking his clothes. His spirit had been stretched to the very limit—but the mission had succeeded.

Counselor Von steadied his breathing, preparing to rise—when a sound halted him.

From the far corner, the Humming Black Trunk stirred. A faint glow seeped through its cracks, purple at first, then deepening, brightening, until the whole surface throbbed with light. The low hum swelled into a haunting resonance, melodic yet unnatural, vibrating through the chamber walls and into Von's bones.

The glow shifted—purple bleeding into a near-blinding white.

Von froze. Sweat glistened on his face, the radiance painting his features in stark relief. His expression hardened as his eyes locked on the trunk, searching its surface for meaning.

The chamber no longer belonged to his meditation—it pulsed with the trunk's rhythm, the air thick with foreboding, as though the object itself waited… ready to reveal, or to consume.

Day two arrived, and the forest clearing outside the cottage thrummed with anticipation. The Counselors gathered once more—muscles sore, spirits unbroken.

Counselor Von stood before them, his presence commanding. "Efficiency is key," he said, his voice cutting through the morning air. "Draw mystic energy from your core. Direct it to the nerve endings of the limb you choose. A hand strike—push it to your fingertips. A kick—channel it through your foot. Precision is everything. Waste energy, and you will collapse. Only Hyberitation will restore you."

To illustrate, he drew in a breath, raised his arm, and thrust his hand forward. The glow of his core raced down his arm, bursting from his fingertips in a ripple of light. The air cracked, a shockwave splitting the silence. It was controlled, elegant, devastating.

The Counselors followed, stumbling at first. Energy leaked wild, strikes misaligned, blasts fizzling out before they landed. Von and Mentor corrected them—shifting stances, guiding focus, reminding them that discipline mattered more than power.

Hour after hour, the clearing echoed with exertion—shouts, impacts, bursts of light, and the steady rhythm of failure turning to mastery. Sweat gleamed on brows. Breath came ragged. But slowly, surely, their strikes sharpened. Energy no longer sputtered—it obeyed.

By sunset, something had shifted. Their blows carried weight, their auras flared in rhythm with their movements. The boundary between muscle and mystic blurred. They were no longer simply learning techniques—they were becoming something new.

Day Three.

The clearing behind the cottage had become a crucible. The sun hung low, shadows stretching across the field where the Counselors stood.

Counselor Ledge's voice cut through the quiet. "Out there, Scorpiondt won't wait for you to think. Today, we burn hesitation out of you."

Beside him, Counselor Barricade cracked his knuckles. "No excuses. You get hit, you get back up. Out there, failure means graves."

Counselor Von smirked, pacing. "Don't mind the theatrics. Remember—our enemy's fast, ruthless, and twice as ugly as Barricade on a bad day. Use your heads as much as your hands."

Barricade grunted. "Keep talking, genius. Let's see how your jokes hold up when Ara drops you."

Von gave a mock bow. "Ladies first."

Ara stepped forward, eyes sharp. "I don't need the advantage. Just the chance."

Ledge raised his arm. "Pairs. Encrypt with Barricade. Ara with Von. Mentor, Introveca—observe. Move!"

The field erupted. Encrypt darted like a shadow, Barricade a fortress crashing through every feint. Across the way, Ara lunged at Von—ferocious, precise, but he deflected with maddening ease.

"You fight angry," he told her, sidestepping. "Power without aim is noise."

She struck again, measured this time. Von stepped back, nodding.

At the center, Ledge barked orders, holding the field together. "Encrypt—anticipate, don't react! Barricade—corral, don't crush! Ara—control your pace! Von—teach, don't gloat!"

Dust swirled, breath ragged. Then Ledge raised his hand. "Enough!"

Silence fell.

"You're getting sharper," he said. "But what comes next will test more than strength. It will test who you are."

Barricade thumped his chest. "About time."

Von wiped sweat, grinning. "Let's hope Scorpiondt appreciates rehearsal."

Ara's gaze fixed on the horizon. "No. This isn't rehearsal. This is survival."

They stood together in the fading light—battered, breathless, but bound by unity. And though Day Three ended, their training did not; over the following weeks, they sharpened body, mind, and bond until the line between practice and battle was all but gone.

After an exhausting training session, the heroes returned to the cottage. Counselor Barricade's stomach broke the silence with a low rumble.

"It knows. I still haven't eaten since this morning," he muttered, earning a round of chuckles.

They settled around the long wooden table, a familiar anchor in the cottage. The warmth of the fire and the simple smell of food gave the moment a sense of calm, rare after so many battles.

Counselor Von spoke first, his presence commanding without effort. His voice carried urgency, but also control, setting the weight of what was to come.

Across from him, Counselor Encrypt leaned toward Barricade, voice measured. "Your size works against you. You're strong, yes—but shadows don't care about strength."

Introveca, tending Barricade's bruises, tilted her head. "Could he hide his presence if unseen?"

Encrypt nodded once. "He could. But stealth isn't about being invisible—it's about leaving nothing behind. No sound, no trace, no breath out of place."

Barricade crossed his arms, skeptical. "Even if I vanish?"

Encrypt's reply was blunt. "If they can still sense you, you haven't vanished."

The words landed, firm but practical.

Meanwhile, Ara crouched beside Counselor Ledge, wrapping his arm. "How much time do we really have to prepare?" she asked.

Encrypt gave the answer without hesitation. "From what your father tells me—thirty-three days."

The room shifted, silence pressing in. Ara frowned. "And if we run out of time?"

Von spoke before Encrypt could, still working on his plate. "It isn't us running out," he said flatly. "It's the ones who've filled the stars with graveyards. Their time is what's ticking."

Ledge's steady voice followed. "General Scorpiondt plans to leave this planet in thirty-three days. The Ikannunaa have greater use for him elsewhere. If we're going to strike, that's our window." His words sharpened the air with resolve.

Ara's curiosity wasn't satisfied. "How do you know he hasn't already gone?"

Von barely looked up from his food. "Two nights ago, while you slept, I broke the limits of the Halo Ascend technique."

The room froze. Mentor's tone carried respect. "You crossed that distance and returned, without losing the cord between body and spirit?"

Von smirked. "What can I say? I'm a once-in-a-lifetime Mentor."

Mentor inclined his head, conceding the point.

Then Von leaned back and tapped his plate. "Now—if you don't let me finish lunch, General Scorpiondt won't be the problem."

The Counselors smiled faintly. They knew Von's quirks. And they knew this ordinary meal was the quiet before the storm—one they would face together.

The Conqueror VII
As told by General Scorpiondt

What they call "progress," I call illusion.

What they believe is a breakthrough, I recognize as a breaking point.

Let them celebrate in shadows.

Somewhere beneath that misfit cottage—under their flickering candlelight and trembling hopes—Dr. Von and the boy Encrypt, frenzied and star-eyed, dared to complete the Beta-Gene Fluid Project. I have no doubt their hands shook with purpose. I know that kind of tremor—it precedes all acts of desperation.

They used gold.

They used heat.

They used themselves.

Pathetic.

They forged what they do not yet understand, all in the name of reclaiming a past they were never meant to survive. They think knowledge can save them. They think mystic power is their shield. But they have forgotten—power without structure is simply... noise.

I know what they are doing.

I know what is coming.

And I know what must be done.

Let us speak truth—my truth—since the universe has no use for theirs.

Mystic Ara, that fragile symbol of hope, planted her thirty-three seeds of Blood Pinnacle as if they were prayers. How quaint. Thirty-three—what a poetic number. But even sacred numbers rot in unguarded soil. The earth is no protector. It devours the weak and buries their memories without remorse.

She believes this is legacy.

I call it... a child's ritual.

And Miraj, her silent accomplice, stood beside her like a ghost from a planet that no longer breathes. Loyalty is admirable—if it serves strength. Otherwise, it is sentimentality in disguise.

Then came the fools' feast. A farce of eggs and flour. Chaos masked as unity. I read the reports—the girl nearly poisoned them. She poured her emotions into a meal and called it magic. And they laughed. They laughed like children on the eve of extinction.

This is what their rebellion is built upon?

Spilled yolks and forgotten mushrooms?

Let me be clear: I do not fear their bonding.

I pity it.

Barricade, the ox with the soft heart, showed his true nature not through war, but through digestion. A glutton of emotion. A walking contradiction. His strength is real—I will not lie—but his control? Fragile. And when the purging began, so too did the metaphor reveal itself. These mystics carry too much inside them. They are full of grief, memory, regret.

These are not warriors.

These are bloated vessels waiting to burst.

And then—ah yes—the flower. That one glowing petal that the so-called Captain Ledge handed to Ara like it meant something. A stolen token passed between two children pretending to understand destiny. They kissed beneath the stars, didn't they? As if love could alter fate.

But here's the truth:

Love does not change war.

It only delays the weapon's fall.

Von and Encrypt toiled in their little underground cave like rats searching for fire. And fire they found. But not because they earned it—because I allowed the time. Because I was not yet ready to burn it all down. Because a fire must be seen to be feared.

They completed the project, yes.

But what they made...

Will unravel them faster than I ever could.

Their hands touched a power they do not deserve. Sigma. Beta. Names don't matter. What matters is control. And Von has none.

I watched him, once—long ago—before the uniform, before the mask, before the title of General etched itself across my spine. He was a man of science then. Curious. Cautious. Afraid. He still is. He only replaced fear with determination. But determination, in the hands of a wounded mind, is the most unstable element of all.

And Encrypt?

He wants to be a doctor.

How adorable.

Let the record show:

I do not underestimate them.

I only see them... fully.

Ara's resolve is tightening.

Ledge is remembering how to lead.

Barricade is finding discipline.

Encrypt is awakening his mind.

Von is racing time.

But none of it matters.

The moment they finished their project, I finished mine.

They light their candles; I command the storm.

They whisper of prophecy; I write reality.

Let them believe they've taken a step forward.

Because soon...

They will learn the ground beneath their feet was never their own.

And when that moment arrives—when the humming of their little black trunk becomes a scream—

They will finally hear what I have always known:

Hope is not the answer.

Obedience is.

Counselor Von

Chapter 8 | **Red For Rebellion**

Four weeks later, night had settled thick across Indigo, the stars dimmed by drifting smoke. In front of the cottage, a small fire crackled, its glow painting silver across Counselor Ara's eyes. She sat with Miraj and Introveca, each cradling a steaming tin cup of tea, the scent of herbs drifting into the cool night air.

Inside the cottage, the men's laughter rumbled through the walls—Barricade's booming voice tangling with Encrypt's quick remarks, Ledge's low tone rolling beneath them. Out here, though, it was quieter, slower.

Ara gazed into the flames, voice steady. "In Hyberitation, I saw it again. A crown, with a broken blue stone at its center. It was pulled from a woman's head and handed to another, ordered to be buried deep. They called it the Shard of the Heirloom Family."

Miraj sipped her tea, eyes glinting in the firelight. "Mmm. A vision like that does not come for nothing, Ara. If your spirit shows it to you, then it will come to pass soon."

Ara hesitated, her lips curving faintly. "And there's Ledge. He's strong, unyielding… like stone itself. I tell myself it's nothing, but I can't stop watching him."

Miraj chuckled low, shaking her head. "Fire always finds stone to spark against. But remember this—you are Counselors now. Family. No one else shares your blood or your aura. Only the five of you. That bond is deeper than anything else."

Introveca leaned forward, tea warming her palms. "And if I wanted that too? Not just standing on the edge, watching? Barricade… he's rough, but there's something in him I can't ignore. If I could stand beside him—as a Counselor—I would."

Ara reached across the fire, touching her hand. "Then claim it. None of us were born Counselors. We became them by choice."

The fire popped, sparks rising into the night. Ara lifted her hand, her silver eyes narrowing as the flames bent to her will. They swayed, then flared higher, twisting like they were alive.

"Careful now," Miraj warned, but Ara's grin only widened.

The flames lashed outward, too close to Introveca. She yelped, spilling her tin cup of tea, the liquid hissing as it hit the dirt.

Ara laughed, enjoying her control, until the fire surged taller—catching the low branch of a nearby tree.

Miraj sighed, rising to her feet. "Lord… here we go again." She muttered a sharp manifestation from the Book of Majeskrit, voice quick and commanding. A rush of cold swept through the clearing, smothering the blaze until only smoke and glowing embers remained.

She turned to Ara, half stern, half amused. "You have not changed one bit, girl."

Introveca burst into laughter, brushing her skirts where the tea had splashed. Ara smiled deep, silver eyes glowing in the fire's afterlight as Miraj shook her head, smiling despite herself.

It was the morning of reckoning. Counselor Von lay deep in sleep, his breath steady but his lips moving with unsettling murmurs. Words drifted into the still night: "He's not one of us… his mystical hidden powers… I followed him for years." Each phrase hung heavy, pulled from some force beyond the waking world.

In his dream, a figure emerged from the dark—a pale man cloaked in a black hood, its folds casting his face in shadow. Only the eyes were visible, burning moonlight-silver, piercing straight into Von's soul. The stranger's presence pressed down on him like a tidal wave, immense and unknowable, carrying with it the weight of secrets untold.

Von tried to speak, to ask the figure's name, but his voice failed him. Just as the question formed in his mind, the vision dissolved into nothingness.

He awoke with a start, heart pounding, the final image of those silver eyes etched into him like a brand.

Beside his bed, Ara leaned over, pressing a finger lightly to her father's forehead.

"What were you saying in your sleep, Father?" she asked, her tone curious but edged with concern.

Counselor Von blinked, still tangled in the remnants of his dream. "I... I am unsure," he muttered, forcing himself upright. The rich aroma drifting in from the kitchen tugged at his senses. "Who prepared breakfast?" he asked, his voice sluggish, his mind still shaking off the night.

"That," Ara answered with a sly smirk, "would be me."

Von's expression shifted instantly to one of playful dread. "You didn't have to cook, Ara," he nagged, rubbing his face. "Miraj or Introveca would've gladly handled it."

Ara narrowed her eyes, a mischievous spark lighting her features. "Don't worry yourself into a heart attack, old man. Introveca supervised me—just like you asked her to—only this time behind my back."

With a practiced flick, she tossed a neatly folded bundle of clothes onto his lap.

"Now," she declared, her grin widening, "get dressed. Today, we rock and roll."

It was a Petrichoren military saying—meaning *stand strong and march forward.*

Counselor Von chuckled, shaking his head as he swung his legs off the bed. Ara's spirited energy lingered like sunlight in the room, a reminder of the light she carried into even the most uncertain times.

Once she had gone, Von unfolded the bundle she had left. Inside was his black hooded coat—yet it was no longer just the coat he had always worn. The fabric was denser, stronger, contoured for both protection and agility. A knotted red cloth wrapped over the right arm and shoulder, its placement deliberate—a banner of resilience and unity.

Something new caught his eye. Between the folds of the cloth gleamed a small triangular metal emblem, etched with an ancient mystic sigil. Alongside it lay a red wooden-beaded bracelet, smooth and cool to the touch—a symbol of protection, guidance, and the traditions that bound them.

Von ran his fingers over the details, pride and apprehension mingling in his chest. These were more than alterations; they were declarations. They marked his evolution—and the gravity of the battles to come.

Yet even as he admired them, the dream clung to him. The pale man. The silver eyes. The sense of inevitability that had seeped into his bones. The image whispered like a shadow of trials yet to come.

Exhaling, Von grounded himself, drawing strength from the relics of his people and the faith of his Counsel. He slipped into the uniform, fastening each piece with care. At the mirror, he paused, studying the reflection that stared back—a warrior's face, tempered by loss, honed by resolve.

For a long moment, he held that stare. Then, with a wry curl of his lips, he muttered to himself:

"I need to shave."

Upon entering the shared room's kitchen, where everyone was gathered, Counselor Von adjusted his newly fitted coat with a nod of approval. "Who's responsible for these magnificent improvements?" he asked, curiosity lacing his tone.

Counselor Ara smiled warmly. "Introveca not only supervised breakfast for you but worked with a Karibegoan tailor and blacksmith to enhance all our uniforms."

Von raised an eyebrow, surprise mixing with genuine admiration. He turned to the young woman. "Thank you, Introveca. You've more than proven your worth."

Introveca offered a modest smile, pride tucked beneath humility. "You're welcome, Counselor. Please—sit."

Ara smirked as Von moved toward the table. "And thank Rainah you finally shaved… though, not that it helped."

Von gave her a sidelong glance. "Quite. But in your Counselor form, you appear older yourself."

Ara narrowed her eyes. "You did this to me, Father."

"Thank me," Von said with a smirk. "You've grown. A little more mature now."

Counselor Ledge chuckled under his breath, earning a sharp slap on the shoulder from Ara—her clear reminder that the joke was not his to enjoy.

As Von reached the wooden table, his eyes widened at the spread before him. "Is all of this meant for Counselor Barricade?" he quipped.

Barricade laughed, rubbing the back of his neck. "I wish! No, we're expecting visitors."

"Visitors?" Von echoed, eyebrow raised.

Before Barricade could respond, Mentor interjected, his tone calm but serious. "Before we touch this food, you should know—the Triplet Elders of Indigo are expected this morning. They wish to meet you all before leaving for Goa."

Von exhaled, resigned but steady. "Very well. We will wait. In the meantime, let us turn our thoughts to the obstacles ahead—most importantly, the

Surrogates of the Mystique Order, who stand between us and our final confrontation with General Scorpiondt."

Before Counselor Von could continue his thought, a strange, upbeat knocking broke across the cottage door—rhythmic, almost like someone drumming for fun. The Counselors exchanged puzzled glances.

Mentor, unable to resist, began to dance toward the sound, his steps matching the beat.

"Well, would you look at him go," Counselor Barricade chuckled, enjoying the show.

With a final twirl, Mentor flung the door open. Three identical Karibegoan Elders stood before him, their presence commanding reverence.

"What's going on? Come in!" Mentor grinned, bowing as he gestured them inside.

The Elders, clad in matching flowing orange robes that shimmered with mystic auras, wore beaded necklaces bearing ivory medallions etched with strange engravings. Their thick white dreadlocks twisted down past their backs as they greeted him with casual fist bumps. "Rough walk, Guide Mentor. My blister burst inside my slipper—and that heat out there? It had no mercy on us, my brother."

From the kitchen, Miraj emerged, wiping flour from her apron. "Gentlemen, would you like something to drink?" she asked warmly.

"Three beers, madame," one Elder replied with a grin. "That should cure our sobriety."

Counselor Ara raised an eyebrow. "Is drinking alcohol some Karibegoan thing?" she asked, glancing at Mentor. "Because he always has brew in his hand."

"Ara," Counselor Ledge hissed, pinching the bridge of his nose.

But the Elder laughed heartily. "Fair question. Our ancestors were heavy drinkers—so yes, it's a Karibegoan thing. It helps us relax and wash down all the food we're invited to enjoy."

Barricade smirked, raising his hand for a high-five. "Can't argue with that."

"Big man, lower it." the Elder quipped, smacking his palm once Barricade complied. Laughter rippled through the cottage, easing the tension.

With drinks in hand, stories and jokes flowed easily until Counselor Von leaned forward. "Tell me, Elders—how old is your race, truly?"

One Elder, cheeks stuffed with bread, grinned. "We have been around for about thirty-three thousand Earth years. Ancient tropical mystics from the planet Ras-Magenta, in the Cuhlabreeze star system."

The name stirred Von's memory. "Cuhlabreeze—isn't that where the Illuminated Pranas reside?"

"That's right," the Elder said. "The Illuminated Pranas ruled Sri-Magnolia—spiritual, powerful, a truly noble people." Another paused mid-meal, curious. And how do you come to know about them?"

"From the GPA—the Galactic Political Assembly," Von answered. "Pranas, Petrichorens, Grenaivelans—we all met once to address interstellar trade and Ikannunaa threats."

Counselor Ledge leaned in. "And where are the Pranas now? I don't recall seeing any of them here."

The Elders' expressions darkened. One lowered his gaze, setting his cup down with deliberate care before speaking. "A rogue Karibegoan wiped them out—his name was Guide… Mal-Monger."

Silence settled heavily over the table. At last, another Elder spoke. "Speaking of him, we give thanks for the recovery of the Humming Black Trunk. Where is it now?"

Mentor answered quietly. "Down in my underground room."

"Good," the Elder replied, though unease edged his tone.

Encrypt's voice cut through the air. "Why have you come to Earth? Any particular reason? Surely not just for its warm beaches?"

The Elders exchanged troubled glances. One dropped the food from his hand, his reply barely above a whisper. "After the destruction of Ras-Magenta, we had to evacuate to a planet that could sustain us—close enough for our portals to hold a stable tether. Earth was chosen, but it wasn't as stable as we believed. During the passage, we lost some of our people… that's how your Guide lost the trunk."

Ara's breath caught, her silver eyes narrowing as her voice hardened. "Destroyed, lost—always the same story. Petrichore. My home. My people. How many more worlds will fall before someone stops Scorpiondt?"

The Elders bowed their heads. "We are sorry—truly sorry."

Ara's voice trembled, anger cracking through her sorrow. "Don't apologize to me, Elder. Save it for General Scorpiondt—when my hand is around his throat. For forcing my father to harm innocents. For taking my mother away."

The Triplets exchanged grave looks. Deep down, they knew her words carried more than anger. They carried prophecy. The Counselors would be the ones to end General Scorpiondt.

That afternoon, the Counselors gathered on the cottage grounds, joined by friends of Miraj and Mentor. The air carried the weight of anticipation and sorrow as the Mystic Elders of Indigo prepared them for departure.

The first Elder stepped forward, a brass bowl of burning herbs in hand. With a tree branch, he wafted the smoke toward each Counselor's face. They inhaled, drawing strength from the ritual as his voice resonated with ancient blessing.

The second Elder followed, presenting sacred gifts: beaded necklaces fashioned from marble stones and metals once worn by their ancestors in times of great trial. One by one, he placed them around their necks. "These talismans carry the resilience of those who came before you. Wear them as heritage, as shield, as bond."

The third Elder, his stare unwavering, spoke words of encouragement. "Stand as one. Be brave. And never forget the duty that has chosen you." His calm tone carried the weight of mountains.

When the blessings ended, Introveca stepped forward, her eyes shimmering. She stopped before Counselor Barricade, then—without hesitation—he pulled her into a firm, tender embrace. Lowering his head, he whispered so only she could hear:

"I will come back for you after this is over."

Her smile trembled with love and trust. In her native tongue she whispered, "Mera dil sirf tumhare liye dhadakta hai."

Barricade tilted his head. "What does that mean?"

Her gaze held his, her voice just above a whisper. "It means... my heart beats only for you."

A grin tugged his lips. With a playful glint, he mimed pulling his heart from his chest and placing it in her hands. Introveca chuckled softly, holding the invisible heart to her chest as if guarding something sacred.

No more words were needed. Their bond was promise enough.

Counselor Von stepped forward, his voice ringing with authority: "Together, we are the Refuge of the Mystic Counsel—warriors of rebellion, forever bound. Counselors, move out!"

The Counselors ascended toward the barrier's crown, golden sunlight painting their figures in fire. Counselor Encrypt raised his hand; the shimmering veil parted. Together, they soared skyward, their silhouettes vanishing into brilliance.

Across Indigo, villagers raised their eyes. Some prayed. Some wept. All hoped.

Front Warrior Khalfani stood among them, his voice low but steady: "We provided hope. You provided heroes. Their time has now come. *Go, Von.*"

His words rode the wind toward the disappearing sky.

Silence lingered heavy—until Mentor broke it with a half-grin. "Well," he said, "time for a cold one. Something tells me these are going to be long days."

The gathering shared weary smiles, filing back into the cottage. The door shut behind them.

Then—knock, knock.

Mentor opened it, and there, perched on a sack of carrots, sat a single gold coin. At the edge of the forest stood Fin the rabbit—now in a green top hat— waving with gleeful mischief.

Mentor chuckled, flashing a peace sign. "Debt settled," he muttered as Fin vanished into the foliage.

He shut the door and turned to the others, smirking. "Curried carrot soup, anyone? And this time—maybe skip Miraj's spice?"

In mid-flight, Counselor Von guided the Counselors with steady precision.

"Remain northeast," he ordered, his voice cutting cleanly through the rush of wind. "Keep the sun on your left—and out of our eyes."

"Are we still bound for Goa?" Counselor Ledge asked, his tone edged with curiosity and impatience.

"Yes. Goa," Von confirmed, his expression firm. "But from the farthest side—for security."

They pressed on, cutting across the sky like dark streaks against the morning light.

Then Counselor Encrypt, ever the strategist, spoke. "We should land soon—recharge, then move on foot near the border. Less risk of detection."

The others nodded in agreement. Banking downward, they descended into the thick shadows of the forest. When their boots touched earth, their figures melted into the gloom beneath the canopy, the Counselors moving like silhouettes made for secrecy.

On the forest floor, the Mystic Counsel formed a wide circle, sitting cross-legged with arms resting on their knees as they entered Hyberitation. The forest's quiet wrapped around them, time stretching as they recharged their energies.

A sudden snap of a twig near Counselor Ara broke the stillness. Though deep in meditation, her senses remained sharp. Warm breath grazed the nape of her neck. She pivoted, eyes flashing open.

A massive black wolf loomed before her, teeth bared, a low growl rising from its chest. Yet the intimidation faltered when Ara locked eyes with it. Her calm, unyielding stare held firm.

The beast hesitated, growl fading. In its deep brown eyes flickered something—familiarity, recognition. Ara's heart skipped. A buried memory rose. Her voice trembled.

"Mother… is that you?"

The wolf's gaze softened, as if in answer. Tears welled as Ara leaned in, wrapping her arms around the creature's thick frame. "I've missed you so much," she whispered.

It nuzzled her once, then pulled away. With a final look, it disappeared into the underbrush.

Counselor Barricade approached, studying her face. "Big Mama must've traveled north, alone by the look of the tracks," he said. "You all right?"

Ara nodded, eyes lingering on the trees where the wolf had vanished. "Yes. I'm fine now."

Counselor Von's voice broke the moment, firm yet understanding. "If her pack is near, they won't want to meet a pack of Counselors unprepared. March— we still have ground to cover."

To cut the tension, Counselor Ledge smirked. "If another shows up, she won't let it go. Then we'll have one more mouth to feed."

Ara shot him a playful glare. "I'll make you vanish, lover boy—then we'll have one less mouth to feed."

Laughter rippled through the Counsel, easing the weight of the moment. They pressed on through miles of rugged terrain until the forest thinned, opening onto a vast clearing. Ahead lay a rocky, hidden pathway leading straight into the heart of Goa's territory.

Their trek had brought them closer to their destination, and though the journey ahead promised trials, the Counselors stood ready to face them together.

At the mountain's edge—where Elder Abhay once stood with a young fighter and Spiritual Leader Ohm—the Counselors gathered. Hoods lowered, streaks of war paint marked their faces. They squinted against the glare of the sun, eyes fixed on the vast territory below.

The view was breathtaking: rolling hills, thick forests, rivers threading silver through the land. Yet woven into that beauty was ugliness—the dominance of the Ikannunaa Empire. Servacrafts prowled the skies, soldiers marched in perfect rhythm, and tribespeople labored under the yoke of forced servitude.

Even from this height, the enemy's grip was undeniable. Sleek stone fortresses jutted from the earth, monuments of domination carved into a land that once thrived free.

"The collateral damage will be immeasurable," Counselor Encrypt murmured, eyes narrowed. "What do you think the level of destruction will be here?"

Counselor Von's expression remained unreadable, his voice calm but unyielding. "There's no need to measure it. Most of the loss will be theirs. What matters is that they taste the consequences of their mercilessness."

At his summons, Counselors Barricade and Ara stepped forward. His command came steady, iron-clad. "Bombs away, Counsel."

Ara's voice rang out: "Counselors, hoods on!"

In unison, they obeyed, shadows cloaking their painted faces, transforming them into figures of myth.

Barricade and Ara grasped their heavy black drawstring bags. They exchanged a glance—a wordless oath—before leaping from the cliff. Their bodies cut through the air, the roar of wind drowning all but their focus.

On the cliff, Von and the others stood unmoving, their hooded forms black against the blazing sun. The two bags disappeared from sight below.

The Counselors braced themselves. The sun bore witness. And far beneath, the first tremors of chaos waited to rise.

On the ground, soldiers in sleek white-and-black armor patrolled with mechanical precision, their movements betraying absolute loyalty to General Scorpiondt. Nearby, the tribe's people labored under their watch, chipping at massive fragments of white stone. Digital monitors clasped around their ankles blinked steadily—a cold reminder of their bondage.

Among them was Spiritual Leader Ohm. Once proud, he now staggered beneath exhaustion, each swing of his sledgehammer weaker than the last. The ankle monitor pulsed as his strength failed, forcing him to lean on the handle for breath, sweat streaming down his face.

His pause drew the soldier's eye. Cold, unfeeling, the guard strode over. "Back to work," he barked.

Ohm raised his weary, copper-colored eyes. "Please... just a moment," he begged, voice rasping with fatigue.

"There is no rest here," the soldier sneered. He lifted his beam rifle, tail end angled to strike the elder down.

The blow never landed.

Above, the sky convulsed with thunder. Explosions burst across the horizon, releasing clouds of strange crimson dust that glowed as it caught the light. Soldiers and laborers froze, staring skyward. The dust fell in waves, a mist that curled and swirled as it touched the earth.

The tribes inhaled it. At first they coughed—but then their limbs steadied, their lungs filled with air, their minds cleared. Strength surged back into broken bodies; despair gave way to fire.

"What in the dead is this?" a soldier stammered, his voice betraying fear.

The air thickened with static, the scent of scorched ozone hanging heavy. The ground itself seemed to wait.

And then—they came.

Five figures descended from the clouds, emerging through the thick haze like specters slipping between worlds. Their black hooded coats billowed around them, their descent eerily slow and deliberate, as if gravity itself bent to their will.

They landed in perfect synchronicity, forming a tight, impenetrable circle with their backs to one another—a formation of absolute unity. A silent storm of energy pulsed around them, distorting the air in faint ripples, as though reality itself recoiled at their presence.

Soldiers froze in place, their weapons half-raised. Some instinctively reached for their specialized binoculars, lenses clicking into focus as they tried to make sense of what stood before them. Through the scopes, the details became sharper—humanoid in form, yet undeniably transformed.

Their midnight cloaks swallowed the sunlight, but surrounding each of them was a translucent, shifting energy sphere, faint but undeniable, like barriers woven from pure will. The faint hum of that energy pressed against the air, a resonance that set teeth on edge and hearts pounding in unison.

And then there was the detail no one could ignore.

The vivid red cloth tied around each of their right arms fluttered and snapped in the breeze, but not like ordinary fabric. Its movement was unnatural, almost sentient, as if each strip carried with it the whispers of an ancient covenant. Every gust of wind turned the cloth into a voice, a warning, and a promise.

A hush fell over the battlefield. The wind sighed through the ruins, carrying with it a single, undeniable truth—something beyond comprehension had arrived.

One soldier lowered his binoculars, his hands trembling. His voice, muffled through his helmet, carried across the tense silence. "No... it can't be... the rebellion... again."

The word rebellion rolled across the soldiers' ranks like a curse returned to haunt them.

The five figures stepped forward in unison, each movement calculated, deliberate. They were not in a rush, for they had no need to be. Every step landed like a hammer, a strike against the empire's illusion of control. The tribespeople stirred, whispers rippling through the crowd like sparks racing along dry tinder. Their murmurs grew louder as recognition dawned—recognition not of faces, but of symbols, of timing, of destiny.

Spiritual Leader Ohm, his frail body trembling yet infused with sudden vigor, pushed his way to the front. His copper-colored eyes filled with tears as he gazed upon the five. His voice cracked, but its weight carried. "It turned out... the visions were accurate. The saviors are here!"

The declaration lit the tribe like wildfire. Hope surged where despair had reigned, and their cries mingled with the sound of rattling chains and pounding hearts.

"Someone report the rebels' return!" shouted one tribesman, his voice ringing with both fear and defiance.

The soldiers, unnerved, shifted nervously, their formations faltering as doubt seeped in. For every cry of resistance, their control slipped further.

The crowd parted, giving the five Counselors space as they advanced. One figure moved to the forefront—a man of commanding presence, his face freshly shaved, his jaw sharp, his gaze like steel. His hood shadowed the fire in his eyes, but when he spoke, his voice carried like a clarion call, cutting through the dust and fear.

"I am Counselor Von," he declared, his tone calm but brimming with authority. "We are the Refuge of the Mystic Counsel—born of fire, bound by vengeance, unbroken by empire." His eyes swept across the battlefield, locking on soldiers, laborers, and tribespeople alike. "Your chains end today."

The tribespeople erupted, voices roaring like a tide breaking against stone. Soldiers faltered, their discipline wavering as the red cloths burned into their vision like an omen fulfilled.

And in that suspended moment—between despair and deliverance—the balance of Goa trembled, waiting to tip.

"We are the Refuge of the Mystic Counsel," he declared, his words slicing through the tension like a blade. "I command every soldier here to lie down your arms and surrender."

A soldier, unimpressed, stepped forward, raising his weapon. "Whoever you are, we don't take orders from you," he sneered, his voice dripping with disdain. "But nice performance."

In response, the white-bearded figure turned to his companions and nodded. The Counselors removed their hoods in unison, revealing their faces. Gasps rippled through the crowd as recognition dawned on the tribes people and soldiers.

"Von... it's Von!" Spiritual Leader Ohm whispered in disbelief. Without hesitation, he rushed forward and embraced Counselor Von, his old friend. "You've returned!"

Counselor Von returned the embrace, his expression resolute. "Ohm, you must evacuate your people," he urged. "It's too dangerous to stay here."

Ohm nodded. "Yes, of course!" He turned to his people, his voice rising above the chaos. "Run! Leave here now! Go!"

With a swift motion of Counselor Von's hand, the ankle monitors clamped onto the tribes people powered down. A series of clicks echoed as the locks released, and the devices fell like discarded chains. The tribes people stared in awe before scrambling to escape, their shackles gone.

One soldier, enraged by the sudden turn of events, raised his beam gun, aiming at the fleeing tribes people. "We didn't say you could leave!" he shouted, his finger tightening on the trigger.

Before the soldier could fire, Counselor Von waved his hand again. The soldier's beam gun—and every other weapon in the area—powered down, transforming into useless hunks of metal. The soldiers froze, stunned into silence, their power rendered meaningless.

"Leave!" Counselor Von commanded, his voice unyielding. With newfound hope and freedom, the tribes people fled into the forest, leaving the soldiers behind, their once-powerful weapons clattering to the ground.

Counselor Ledge stepped forward, his tone icy and commanding. "Now, all of you—leave this place," he ordered, glaring at the soldiers. "Or none of you will have the pleasure of seeing the moon again."

The soldiers exchanged uneasy glances, their defiance crumbling under the weight of the Counselors' power. Panic took hold, and they turned to flee into the forest, their footsteps fading into the distance. Yet, a few hesitated, abandoning the retreat as they scrambled back toward the Servacrafts, desperate to regain control.

Noticing the soldiers sprinting toward the Servacrafts, Counselor Ledge called out after them. "And don't even think about returning to the Servacrafts," he warned, his tone edged with finality. "We're destroying those."

Before they could act on Ledge's statement, Counselor Ara stepped forward, her voice firm. "No," she said, cutting through the tension. "Leave one Servacraft intact."

Counselor Ledge raised an eyebrow. "And why should we do that?"

Ara's stare was unwavering as she responded. "When this mission is complete, I'm going back to Petrichore to find my mother—alone."

A heavy silence fell over the Counselors. Counselor Von remained stoic, his eyes shifting to the side before he gave a firm nod. "I don't trust the plan. But I trust you," he said, his tone steady.

A glance was exchanged between the Counselors; their unity remained unbroken, even in the face of tough decisions. The mission continued, but Ara's determination now carried an additional weight—a personal promise she intended to keep, no matter the cost.

An eerie silence grew in the forest as the Counselors stood their ground.

"Lady and gentlemen, I need to step away from the action for a moment," Counselor Barricade announced, already adjusting his stance as if preparing for launch.

Counselor Ledge arched a brow. "Why's that, Counselor?"

"I left something behind last time," Barricade replied matter-of-factly.

Ledge smirked. "What could that be? Don't tell me you're after a Servacraft now."

Barricade chuckled, shaking his head. "Nope. But I am breaking into one to get my lucky trigger glove back." His tone was light, but the grin that followed carried his usual mix of mischief and confidence.

He took off into the air in a burst of energy, his coat snapping in the wind.

"Hurry back!" Counselor Encrypt called after him, laughter edging his words.

The Servacraft loomed against the skyline, its steel belly bristling with turrets and spotlights. Barricade slipped beneath its shadow, ducking behind the undercarriage. He shouldn't have been able to vanish—he was built like a fortress—but his years in the military had taught him the art of timing. He stilled his breathing, moving only when the floodlights swept away, syncing his steps with the hum of the engines.

Two armored soldiers marched past, their boots ringing against the gangway.

"Quartermaster's inventory was off again," one grumbled.

"Always is," the other muttered.

Barricade flattened himself against the bulkhead, listening, then moved once the sound of their boots faded.

He slipped through a maintenance hatch, the cramped passage groaning under his weight. Crawling forward, he bumped his elbow against a loose panel, the clang echoing like thunder.

"Who's there?" a soldier barked, his rifle beam cutting through the corridor.

Barricade froze, teeth clenched. The light hovered on the corner just shy of him—then swung away.

"Must've been the ventilation again," the guard muttered before moving off.

Barricade exhaled, muttering under his breath, "Biggest ventilation problem you'll ever ignore."

Finally, he reached the storage bay. Racks of confiscated gear lined the walls, crates stacked high. His sharp eyes scanned the clutter until they landed on it: a scuffed, worn leather glove, tucked carelessly on a shelf.

He lifted it gently, brushing the dust from its surface. No glow, no power—just stitched leather, the trigger finger worn thin from years of use. Barricade smiled faintly, slipping it back onto his hand.

"Just a glove," he whispered. "But it's my glove."

A siren blared suddenly, red lights flashing across the bay. A soldier shouted from the far corridor: "Intruder!"

Barricade groaned, rolling his eyes. "All this fuss over one glove."

He barreled back through the maintenance hatch, alarms howling, soldiers giving chase. As he dove out of the craft's underbelly, he hit the forest floor with a heavy thud, sprinting until the shouts faded behind him.

The forest seemed to hold its breath as shadows stirred. From the gloom emerged five armored soldiers—each clad in a different accent of menace: black-and-red, black-and-white, black-and-yellow, black-and-green, and black-and-blue. Their visors glinted faintly in the filtered sunlight, reflections cold and unfeeling. The earth itself seemed to tighten beneath their synchronized steps as they fanned out, forming a circle around the Counselors.

"There they are," Counselor Von muttered, his tone steady, yet carrying a razor's edge of anticipation. His silver eyes narrowed. "The I.R.S are never too far behind schedule."

The operative in black-and-red stepped forward, the squad's unspoken leader. His voice boomed metallic, distorted by his helm, void of humanity.

"Droid! Fugitives—you are surrounded. Surrender, and you may yet live."

Counselor Von's gaze hardened, unshaken by the threat. His words fell like a blade drawn in silence.

"And to the Ikannunaa Royal Squadron—hear this: you are surrounded. Do not bother surrendering… you will not live."

A tense beat stretched between both sides, the air crackling with static hostility. Then the operatives went for their firearms. Counselor Von raised a hand, ready to disarm them as he had the soldiers earlier—but the one in black-and-red cut him off. Droid! No use — these aren't beam or energy-charged weapons," he said, admitting he'd seen what Von had done to the soldiers' rifles before they deserted. At that, the operative in black-and-blue snapped his hand up in signal.

Gunfire erupted.

The stillness shattered as bullets shrieked through the forest, shredding bark and stone, ripping through branches overhead. The thunder of firepower echoed like a storm trapped in the trees.

But before a single shot could find its mark, Counselor Encrypt moved— his body blurring as he thrust his arms outward. In an instant, a shimmering dome of mystic energy enveloped the Counselors, translucent yet impenetrable. The bullets hammered against it with a furious metallic ping, sparking off in wild ricochets. Steel and fire were reduced to harmless fragments, scattering into the woods.

When the volley finally ceased, the shield hummed with fading power, smoke drifting through the clearing. The five operatives tightened their formation, weapons reloading in synchronized precision.

At that moment, Counselor Barricade descended into their midst, his massive frame crashing down in a burst of clay and dust. The ground quaked beneath his landing. He brushed dirt from his coat, calm as though he'd merely returned from a stroll.

"What's happening?" he asked, his tone casual, his deep voice cutting through the haze.

Counselor Von's stare never wavered from the operatives as he answered coolly, "Just some target practice."

The battle began in earnest.

Counselor Encrypt moved first. One blink—and he was gone, a blur of motion darting straight for the operative in black-and-blue. The armored trooper raised his weapon to fire, but Encrypt was already inside his guard. His fists hammered in rapid succession—jaw, ribs, throat, elbow, temple—each strike a sharp crack against metal plating. The operative staggered back, overwhelmed by the relentless onslaught. Encrypt pivoted, driving an elbow into the operative's helm, then a sweeping kick that knocked him flat against the earth. The operative sprawled, his rifle skidding across the dirt, armor crumpled from Encrypt's precision barrage.

Across the clearing, Counselor Barricade thundered forward like a living juggernaut. His opponent in black-and-yellow launched a storm of super-kicks and palm strikes, the air snapping with each blow. The forest rang with their collisions—bone, steel, and raw force meeting with punishing cracks. Barricade absorbed the hits, his massive frame barely giving ground. He grinned through the barrage, then roared, seizing the soldier's arm mid-strike. With a savage twist, he swung the man overhead and slammed him into a boulder. The rock shattered into shards, the operative limp within the wreckage.

Counselor Ledge's duel was a blur of grace and danger. The operative in black-and-green attacked with acrobatic precision, flipping between branches, spinning into rapid-fire kicks. Ledge countered with calm economy, slipping just beyond reach each time. A high kick whistled toward his temple—only for Ledge to vanish. He reappeared behind his opponent, his silver eyes glinting. In one motion, he delivered a super-charged kick. The impact sent the operative flying, slamming into a tree trunk so violently that the ancient wood splintered and toppled.

Counselor Ara, her energy unbridled, met the operative in black-and-white head-on. Her fists hammered into his chestplate, each strike leaving visible dents in the armor. The operative lashed back with a spinning kick that cut the air like a blade, but Ara ducked low, rising with a brutal uppercut that snapped the man's head back. She followed with a flurry—knee, elbow, backfist—that drove him stumbling into the dirt. Her combat style blended elegance and ferocity, every movement graceful, every strike devastating.

Through it all, Counselor Von remained locked in his own confrontation. His opponent, the operative in black-and-red, stood poised, blade gleaming darkly in the light. The air between them crackled with old animosity.

Von's voice was calm, yet edged with memory. "You remember me."

The operative's weapon tightened in his grip. "Droid! It doesn't matter."

"It matters to me," Von said, his silver eyes unyielding. "You killed a colleague… a brother."

With a snarl, the operative lunged, blade arcing. Von sidestepped, his palm glowing with searing embers as he parried the strike. The ground split beneath the force of their clash, sparks of light scattering. Their duel became a blur of steel and flame—strike and counter, light against shadow. The operative's blade swept wide, but Von's hand burst outward, unleashing a concussive wave that hurled him back. Yet the soldier rose again, relentless, his counterattacks sharp and merciless.

The battle raged, the forest trembling beneath its fury.

At last, Counselor Von's voice cut through the chaos, commanding and resolute. "Counselors—finish them!"

The Counselors responded as one. Their energy ignited, white embers flaring into a storm of radiance. They unleashed synchronized blasts, beams of devastating light converging on their fallen enemies. The clearing erupted as the operatives were engulfed, their forms dissolving into nothingness, erased in the brilliance of mystic power.

Only one remained—the operative in black-and-red. He stumbled back, desperation clawing through his movements. A hand shot to the device at his neck, which pulsed with a sinister red glow. He turned to flee, but Von was already upon him.

A massive orb of energy formed in Von's palm, swirling with lethal intent. His voice was low, steady, personal.

"This one is for you, Cal."

He hurled the orb.

The blast struck, enveloping the operative in light. In an instant, he was vaporized—gone as though he had never existed.

Silence reclaimed the battlefield. The gunfire had ceased, the dust had settled, and the only sound left was the rustle of leaves and the Counselors' steady breathing.

The group regrouped at the center of the clearing, their stares hard but weary. They stood together, five shadows against the smoldering aftermath. Their resolve was unbroken.

The I.R.S was no more.

"Where is General Scorpiondt?" Counselor Ara asked, her voice steady despite her exhaustion.

Counselor Von's gaze shifted to the horizon, his tone grave. "He's coming. Prepare yourselves—this fight is far from over."

A low rumble rolled across the sky. The Counselors looked up as a massive Servacraft punched through the clouds, its searchlights raking the battlefield like blades of white fire.

"Here comes the pig pest of peril," Counselor Ledge muttered, disdain dripping from every syllable.

The Servacraft slammed onto the ground beside its parked kin. A hiss cut the silence as the back hatch opened, releasing a thick pressurized mist. The sound of heavy, deliberate footsteps echoed through the vapor.

General Scorpiondt emerged—towering, armored, his every movement measured and commanding. Behind him followed Dr. Serpendt, eyes cold and sharp as blades.

Ara's lips curled into a sneer. "A snake with no fangs came to bite."

Scorpiondt ignored her, his focus on Serpendt. "So, what do we have here, Doctor?" His voice dripped with mockery.

Serpendt's stare lingered on the Counselors. "Dr. Von, his daughter Ara, former Lieutenants Barricade and Encrypt, and Captain Ledge. Or what's left of them."

"Altered," Scorpiondt mused, narrowing his eyes. "This reeks of Von's work."

Serpendt gave a tight nod. "I'd wager as much."

Scorpiondt's smile was cruel. "My handiwork will alter their existence." He turned his back on Serpendt. "Now, Doctor, if you'll excuse me... I must swat a few flies."

He advanced. The Counselors mirrored him, every step forward radiating defiance. At the front, Counselor Von locked eyes with his old enemy.

"Good day, Doctor," Scorpiondt sneered.

"Good day, General," Von answered evenly. "And it's Counselor Von now, if you don't mind."

"Not at all... Counselor." Scorpiondt's smirk deepened. "Tell me—where are my I.R.S operatives?"

"We dismantled them," Von replied, calm and deliberate.

Scorpiondt's smile snapped into a snarl. "That's funny," he growled, "because that's exactly what I came here to do to you."

He struck without warning. His hand cracked across Von's face, the slap so brutal it sent him staggering. The clearing fell into stunned silence, broken only by the whisper of the wind.

The Counselors tightened formation, whitish energy kindling around them. Scorpiondt smirked, feeding on their fury.

Ara's rage erupted. She surged forward—but Ledge stepped in, bracing her shoulder. "Stay strong," he said firmly. "Let him fight. He needs this."

Scorpiondt loomed over Von, who struggled back to his feet. With monstrous ease, the General seized him by the front of his coat and hoisted him skyward. His fist sank into Von's midsection like a battering ram. The blow hurled Von back into his comrades, the ground trembling from the impact.

Von groaned, forcing himself upright, but Ledge was already moving. He released Ara, his eyes locked on Scorpiondt. His voice sharpened like drawn steel.

"Alright, Ara," he said, steady and commanding. "Now we rock and roll."

The Counselors closed ranks, forming a tight circle around General Scorpiondt. Their black hooded coats whipped in the storm, rain cascading in sheets, thunder rumbling overhead. The battlefield's mud churned under their boots, lit by flashes of lightning that carved the sky into stark contrasts of light and shadow.

Scorpiondt's eyes swept the ring of cloaked figures, his lip curling in disdain. "What is this?" he sneered, his baritone voice carrying over the storm. "A child's game of ring-around-the-villain? You mistake theater for war

The Counselors said nothing. Their silence was their defiance.

Then Ara moved.

She sprang forward with explosive grace, leaping high and driving her fist toward Scorpiondt's jaw, the rain streaking off her knuckles like shards of glass. Scorpiondt's eyes narrowed. In one motion he caught her wrist mid-strike, twisted, and flung her across the circle. She crashed into the mud, rolled, and rose to her feet, her arm throbbing but her glare unbroken—fury smoldering in her silver eyes.

Before he could pursue, Encrypt flashed in. His speed blurred him into streaks of black and red, his turbo spin kick carving through the rain like a blade. The air cracked from the velocity—but Scorpiondt ducked under, his reflexes sharp as lightning. His backhand caught Encrypt mid-spin, the blow detonating like a cannon. Encrypt slammed into a stone pillar, the impact shattering it to rubble before he collapsed to his knees, clutching his ribs.

A rumble rose from the ground—Barricade.

He barreled forward, each step a quake, his fists colliding together with a thunderclap that shook the battlefield. The shockwave rippled outward, splashing mud and water into the air.

"Ah… my former protégé," Scorpiondt said, smiling with cruel nostalgia.

"You never asked if I wanted to be your protégé," Barricade growled, his voice a low earthquake.

He crashed into Scorpiondt, hands locking against the General's in a raw contest of strength. The earth cracked beneath them as power met power. Barricade roared, forcing Scorpiondt back before lifting and slamming him into the ground. For a heartbeat, victory flickered—until Scorpiondt rolled free and snapped a brutal kick into Barricade's chest. The impact launched him backward in a spray of mud, skidding trenches into the earth before he finally halted, clutching his ribs.

Ledge was already moving.

He vaulted high, flipping clean over Scorpiondt's head with acrobatic precision. Mid-arc, his leg swung downward like a guillotine aimed at Scorpiondt's spine. But the General's timing was merciless—he reached up, caught Ledge mid-air by the ankle, and slammed him down into the sodden ground. The mud exploded around them as Scorpiondt yanked him up again and hurled him bodily into the side of a nearby Servacraft. Metal screamed and dented inward as Ledge crashed, slumping to the ground with a groan of pain.

The circle was broken.

Scorpiondt stood alone at the center of the storm, his chest rising steady, his stance unshaken. Rain streamed down his armor as he looked at the battered Counselors around him. His voice, calm and venomous, cut through the thunder.

"This is your rebellion—*Dawn is generous?*" he mocked, his sneer lit by lightning. "Pathetic. You cannot even scratch me."

The Counselors steadied themselves, mud-streaked and bruised but unbroken. Energy began to rise again, white embers kindling in their veins. The storm above raged on, as though Goa itself held its breath, waiting for the next strike.

The Counselors regrouped, battered but unbroken, their hoods dripping with rain, their silver eyes glowing with shared determination.

"Focus," Counselor Von commanded, his voice a steel edge against the storm. "Only together can we bring him down."

They nodded in unison. In that instant, their breath, their resolve, their power aligned.

Encrypt struck first—his movements a blur, fists flashing toward Scorpiondt's throat, ribs, and solar plexus. Each blow carried surgical precision, forcing the General's guard higher, faster. Scorpiondt parried, his arms like iron, but the rhythm broke when Barricade slammed in from the side, driving his elbow into the General's ribs with bone-jarring force.

The impact staggered Scorpiondt for the first time.

Ara seized the opening. She soared into the air, her fists ablaze with energy embers that hissed and crackled in the downpour. She crashed down with both fists into Scorpiondt's chest, the strike booming like thunder. The giant stumbled backward, his boots sinking deep into the mud.

Ledge was already behind him. He spun, his heel smashing into the back of Scorpiondt's knee. The force drove the General down to one leg, mud splashing outward.

A furious roar tore from Scorpiondt's throat. His body flared with raw energy, and a shockwave blasted outward, tossing the Counselors across the clearing. Trees buckled, Servacrafts rattled, and the rain itself seemed to recoil from the burst.

But the Counselors rose again, their formation intact, their will unbroken.

Barricade bent low, heaving a boulder the size of a wagon into his arms. With a grunt, he hurled it at Scorpiondt. The General's fist shattered the stone midair, fragments exploding like shrapnel. Yet the debris cloud blinded him long enough for Encrypt to dart in again, his fists hammering rapid-fire into Scorpiondt's ribs, each strike punctuated by the crackle of mystic energy.

Scorpiondt snarled, swinging blindly, but Ara and Ledge were already moving.

Barricade surged forward, his fists sparking with violent energy. With a primal roar, he leapt and drove his knee square into Scorpiondt's jaw. The impact detonated in a spray of light and mud, snapping the General's head back.

The titan stumbled, arms flailing for balance—then crashed full force into the side of his own Servacraft. The metal hull buckled inward with a deafening screech, sparks spraying into the rain.

The battlefield shook with the sound, a brief silence following. For the first time, the great General Scorpiondt had been driven off his feet.

Rain poured in relentless sheets, drumming against shattered stone and the dented hulls of Servacrafts. The Counselors stood apart in a half-circle, mud caking their coats, war paint streaked away until only pale traces clung to their skin. Their breaths came heavy and sharp, steam rising in the cold as they stared at the broken giant before them.

General Scorpiondt lay in the muck, one knee digging into the earth, blood trailing from the corner of his mouth. His glare still burned, white-hot with fury and pride. "You… think this is over?" he growled, each word vibrating like thunder in his chest.

From the Servacraft's open hatch, the sound of metallic footsteps cut through the storm. Dr. Serpendt emerged, his coat plastered to his lean frame, one gloved hand clutching a syringe filled with a viscous, yellow glow. His voice was steady, almost casual, as he stepped down into the rain.

"It's not over," Serpendt declared. "It has only begun."

Before the Counselors could close in, the doctor drove the syringe into Scorpiondt's thick neck and depressed the plunger. The liquid burned like fire beneath his skin, veins flaring gold through his body as he convulsed. His roar split the heavens, half agony, half triumph.

The Counselors shielded their eyes as a burst of energy exploded outward, kicking up mud and rain in a violent cyclone.

When the storm settled, the man before them was gone.

In his place rose Omega Scorpiondt—towering, monstrous. His muscles swelled to grotesque proportions, skin straining against the unnatural growth. His eyes turned a ghostly milk-white, no pupils, no humanity—just void. Each breath he took came like the hiss of a furnace, steam pouring from his mouth and nose.

With one step, the ground caved beneath his heel. With another, trees bent away as if bowing to his grotesque rebirth. He flexed his arms, and the sound of splitting armor echoed like tearing steel.

Counselor Ara's jaw tightened as she whispered, "Rainah protect us."

Beside her, Encrypt's tone cut sharp with urgency. "Von—what did Serpendt inject him with?"

Von's stare never wavered, his silver eyes glowing brighter in the storm. "Omega-gene fluid," he said grimly. "The final tier. Unstable, but powerful enough to end us all if we falter."

Omega Scorpiondt threw back his head and released a guttural roar that shook the earth itself. The Counselors staggered, mud rippling at their feet from the sheer force of the sound.

Von raised his fists, crackling embers sparking along his arms. His voice rang steady, resolute, carrying through the storm.

"This isn't over," he said. "It's just beginning."

The Counselors shifted into formation, every muscle taut, every heart pounding. Rain and blood mingled on the battlefield as their enemy rose higher than ever before.

The second battle—the true battle—was about to begin.

Back in Indigo, the day had carried an easy rhythm—Guide Mentor, Miraj, and Introveca had returned from the bustling market, baskets heavy with fruit, bread, and bolts of fabric. Their chatter trailed off the moment they caught sight of the cottage ahead. The front door creaked back and forth in the breeze, slamming gently against the frame as though mocking them.

Introveca froze, her arms tightening around her basket. "Did… did any of us forget to close the door?" she asked, unease threading through her voice.

Mentor frowned, his shoulders stiffening. "No. I locked it myself." He glanced sidelong at Miraj. "Unless maybe you did?"

"Do not even start, boy." Miraj snapped, silencing him with a glare. "We need to check inside. Now."

The three exchanged a grim look. The path to the threshold suddenly felt longer, the weight of the supplies cutting into their hands. The floorboards moaned beneath their steps as they crossed the threshold. The cottage, usually brimming with warmth, felt hollow—like a heart that had stopped beating.

Then Mentor saw it. At the far end of the main hall, the heavy door to the underground room was ajar. The thick wood bowed inward, the frame splintered as though forced by an unnatural strength. His stomach sank.

"Stay here," Mentor ordered, his voice a rasp. He set down his basket and moved forward with deliberate caution. Each step toward the stairwell felt heavier than the last.

The air grew colder as he descended. The wooden stairs groaned, the shadows crowding tighter with each step. At the bottom, he struck a match. The tiny flame flared, its glow licking across the damp stone walls until it caught the shape waiting in the far corner.

His breath hitched.

The Humming Black Trunk—the ancient prison, the dread relic—lay wide open. Its ornate hinges gaped like snapped bones, the elaborate carvings along its surface dull and lifeless. The hum that had once filled the chamber was gone. In its place, silence pressed in, suffocating, as though the air itself feared to move.

Mentor stumbled forward, the match trembling in his hand. His knees buckled and hit the stone floor with a hollow thud. "No…" His voice cracked into a scream. "No! Mal-Monger—he is gone, boy! He is gone!"

The cry clawed up the narrow stairwell, shaking the wooden beams above.

Footsteps thundered down behind him. Introveca and Miraj appeared, their faces pale in the flickering light. "Mentor, what is it?" Miraj demanded, though her eyes had already found the yawning trunk.

Mentor turned, his face etched with despair. "The trunk…" His voice shook as if the words themselves cut him. "Someone open it. Mal-Monger is free."

The flame of the match sputtered and died, plunging the chamber into near darkness. Only the faint glow of the disturbed carvings lingered, as if mocking their failure.

Miraj's hand clutched at her chest, her breathing shallow. Introveca pressed a fist to her mouth, wide-eyed.

Mentor's whisper echoed in the silence, broken and raw. "Whoever released him has doomed us all."

The stone walls seemed to close in, the shadows bending like listening ears. Above, the once-gentle forest stirred uneasily in the wind—as though the land itself felt the tremor of something ancient and terrible walking free once more.

Counselor Ara

Chapter 8 Continued | **Red For Rebellion**

Back in Goa, the battlefield thundered with chaos as rain poured from the heavens, drenching the shattered ground. Omega Scorpiondt—no longer merely a general, but a berserk juggernaut—towered above the Counselors. His grotesquely swollen muscles bulged with unnatural strength, veins glowing faintly beneath his pallid skin. His milk-white eyes cut through the storm like beacons of wrath, and his guttural growl rattled the air itself.

"I'll take care of this," Counselor Barricade declared, stepping forward through the curtain of rain. He cracked his neck, popped his knuckles, and squared his shoulders, his immense frame a living wall of defiance. "It's just you and me, big man."

Omega Scorpiondt needed no invitation. With terrifying speed, he charged, shoulder lowered like a battering ram. The impact struck Barricade's abdomen with seismic force, launching him off his feet and smashing him into the muck. Mud, water, and shards of stone erupted as the earth quaked beneath the blow.

Groaning, Barricade pushed up on one knee—only to see the titanic silhouette blotting out the sky as Omega Scorpiondt leapt. He crashed down with bone-cracking force, fists hammering like war drums. Each punch sent shockwaves rippling outward, splintering stone and rattling the Counselors' bones.

"Anytime, team!" Barricade growled through clenched teeth, his body straining to endure.

Counselor Ledge answered, launching forward with a ferocious cry. His shoulder strike knocked Omega Scorpiondt off balance, but the monster's counter came like lightning. Gripping Ledge's arm, Scorpiondt spun in a brutal arc and hurled him skyward.

Ledge's scream tore through the storm as he plummeted—only for Scorpiondt to meet him mid-air. The spinning punch cracked into Ledge's chest, sending him crashing into a Servacraft outbuilding, wood and stone exploding as he crumpled inside the wreckage.

From the sidelines, Dr. Serpendt's grin widened, his voice drowned yet sharpened by the storm. "Behold—the brilliance of progress. The Ikannunaa will immortalize this victory."

Counselor Encrypt streaked in low, a blur of motion, spinning to sweep Omega Scorpiondt's legs. The strike should have toppled any man. But the monster stood unmoved. His hand shot down like an iron trap, clamping Encrypt by the throat and lifting him effortlessly. Fists rained like meteors, then Scorpiondt flung him aside, his body crashing through the mud and sliding across the ground like discarded debris.

Counselor Ara roared in fury, blazing with wild determination. She vaulted onto Scorpiondt's back, arms locking around his neck in a chokehold. He staggered, but only for a heartbeat. With a bellow, he seized her wrists and swung her like a weapon, smashing her into a crumbling wall. Stone cascaded as he flung her into the debris, leaving her buried in dust and rain.

Then all went still.

Omega Scorpiondt turned his milk-white eyes toward Counselor Von. The storm's noise seemed to fade. The rain slowed, parting like a curtain around the two figures—warrior and monster locked in silence.

"Did you have fun, General?" Von asked, his voice calm, razor-sharp. "Because playtime is over."

Scorpiondt lunged. The ground shattered with his first step—then faltered. His monstrous body spasmed mid-charge. He clutched his chest, his guttural roar shifting into something raw, pained. "What… what is this?"

Dr. Serpendt's smug veneer cracked into panic. "No! No, this isn't right!"

Counselor Von's smirk broke the tension. His eyes glowed with cold triumph. "Did you think I wouldn't prepare for this? Your Beta line carried a hidden enzyme, seeded long ago. It destabilizes the Omega state after exactly three minutes. A spectacular rise…" His hand curled into a fist. "…then a brutal collapse."

Omega Scorpiondt convulsed, his grotesque form shrinking. Muscles deflated, glowing veins dimmed, and the thunder of his power drained from his frame. He crashed to his knees, mud splattering around him, his gasps ragged and weak.

The storm swallowed his roar, leaving only the pounding rain and the Counselors' heavy breaths.

As if on cue, energy embers rose from the Counselors' battered bodies, shimmering through the storm. Each ember pulsed like a heartbeat, glowing brighter until the battlefield itself seemed alive with their defiance. Even beneath the rubble where Counselor Ara lay pinned, her embers burned fiercely, glowing through cracks in the stone as if announcing she would not be buried.

Dr. Serpendt spun in alarm, his face pale, his voice cutting through the rain. "Look around you, General! Do you not see? The battlefield is crawling with energy orbs—they're everywhere!"

And indeed they were—dozens of radiant spheres drifted above the mud and ruins, hovering, swirling, orbiting the Counselors like guardians. The storm-light reflected off them in crimson, violet, and gold hues, as if the storm itself had bent in submission to their will.

The Counselors regrouped, rising one by one, mud and rain streaking their faces, their silhouettes black against the glow. Their collective power surged, raw and uncontainable, the air thickening with pressure until every breath felt heavy, every heartbeat thundered like a drum.

Counselor Encrypt staggered to his place in the circle, his chest heaving. His sharp gaze locked onto the kneeling General. "What happened to him?" he asked, his tone equal parts disbelief and suspicion. "He's back in his original form. Why?"

Counselor Von stepped forward, shoulders squared, the glow of embers flickering along the hem of his cloak. His voice was steady, unflinching, cutting through the chaos like a blade. "The injection Serpendt gave him was only ever temporary. Omega-gene fluid burns bright… but it burns out faster." His eyes narrowed. "I ensured it, back in my last days as their head biologist."

The words landed like a thunderclap. Serpendt froze, realization dawning in his horrified eyes.

Counselor Ledge broke the silence, his grin sharp despite his bloodied lip. "You're incredible, sir."

Counselor Von didn't look at him. His gaze remained fixed on Scorpiondt, who trembled on his knees, fists clenching in mud as though trying to hold his body together through sheer rage. Von's reply came low, deliberate. "I know." He stepped closer, rain streaking down his face, his eyes like steel. "Now, let's finish this—and clean up their mess."

At that, the Counselors aligned. Their embers flared brighter, spheres orbiting them faster, the storm swirling in sync with their rising power. The ground beneath them thrummed, every drop of rain hissing into steam as it touched the radiant energy enveloping their bodies.

The circle of Counselors stood poised in silence, save for the hum of their energy. In that suspended moment, one truth became undeniable: this was the final movement of their rebellion's symphony.

The ultimate battle was about to begin.

As if on cue, energy embers rose from the bodies of the Counselors, illuminating the battlefield with an otherworldly glow. Even beneath the rubble where Counselor Ara lay, the embers pulsed with an intense radiance.

Dr. Serpendt panicked, his eyes darting wildly. "Look around you, General!" he shouted, his voice trembling. "There are energy orbs everywhere!"

The Counselors regrouped, battered yet unbroken, their collective power surging to an almost tangible level. Counselor Encrypt stepped forward, his moonlight-glowing eyes locking onto the dazed gaze of General Scorpiondt. For a breath, the battlefield fell silent, the storm itself pausing, as though the world held its breath at the judgment about to be delivered.

Then, Encrypt raised his hand. A swirling portal erupted above, its rim glowing in ethereal blue, edges spitting arcs of raw energy. In a single, fluid motion, he seized the General by the leg. With monstrous strength, he spun him three times, faster with each rotation, before releasing. Scorpiondt's battered body hurtled upward into the waiting gateway.

Twin orbs of energy flared in Encrypt's palms. He fired them skyward; each struck the General mid-flight, detonating in blinding bursts that shook the heavens.

Scorpiondt was swallowed whole by the portal.

On the Northern Ice Ring, he emerged in a snowbank, gasping in the frozen air. Before he could rise, Encrypt materialized before him, dragging him upright with one hand. His breath came out like a growl, his words booming:

"We are Refuge!"

With coiled fury, Encrypt's foot shot forward, slamming into Scorpiondt's chest. The strike cracked like thunder, launching the General back through the portal.

High above Goa, the portal spat him into the open sky. Counselor Barricade was already ascending, a streak of light tearing against the storm. His colossal arm struck Scorpiondt with resonant force, the impact shaking the air itself.

Then—the Phantom Pillar. Barricade dissolved into a shimmer, reappearing behind the General, each strike redirecting him: ribs, back, chest. He carved the tyrant's fall with surgical precision, vanishing and returning with every blow. Finally, he pivoted, his last kick launching Scorpiondt downward into the storm below—straight into Ledge's waiting power.

"Ma-Jes-Tic: Merkaba!" Counselor Ledge roared.

Between his hands, the blazing star ignited, a perfect geometric burst of impossible light. Winds shrieked as the construct drew in stone, snow, and shattered steel. Even the storm recoiled, clouds splitting above.

In the Indigo forest miles away, a plume of purple smoke rose as animals fled. A voice hissed from the void, oily and cruel: Yes, boy… show me your power. Now that I am free, I will have my revenge. I am coming for you, Counselor Ledge… *hahahaha.*

But there was no time for fear. Scorpiondt's plummeting body slammed into the star's core.

The Merkaba exploded.

The explosion drowned the sky in light, tearing through the clouds, rattling the peaks, its thunder echoing across the horizon. The Counselors shielded themselves as debris and fire rained down.

Within the inferno, Scorpiondt roared, his voice defiant even as the light consumed him. "You think this is my end? The Empire will outlive you all!"

Then silence.

When the blaze subsided, the battlefield was unrecognizable—a crater vast and steaming, snow melted into rivers. For a long breath, it seemed Scorpiondt had been obliterated.

But then—movement.

He dragged himself from the wreckage, blood spilling from his lips, armor shattered, body trembling with every effort. Still, his eyes blazed with venomous fire.

Badly beaten. But not undone.

The Counselors stood at the crater's edge, the storm winds whipping their cloaks, their circle tightening once more. Ara stepped forward, her energy embers flaring, eyes unyielding.

This was no victory.

It was only the beginning of a darker reckoning.

Amid the chaos, Counselor Ara advanced with unwavering determination. Her energy embers flared brighter, illuminating her path through the storm and wreckage. Each step she took reverberated with resolve, her presence cutting through the battlefield like a blade of light.

General Scorpiondt—broken but unbowed—rose to meet her, yet his defiance faltered when she levitated inches above the wet earth and her hand shot forward, seizing his throat. In one fluid motion, Ara lifted him high off the ground. Her grip was iron, unrelenting. The General's legs thrashed in empty air, his once-commanding aura reduced to a hollow echo.

Her voice, calm yet laced with lethal finality, cut through the roar of wind and rain.

"Your reign of terror ends here."

The words fell like a judgment, heavy and absolute.

From the edge of the crater, Counselor Von stepped forward, his cloak soaked and clinging to his form, his eyes reflecting both sorrow and purpose. Under his breath, he muttered:

"Rebirth for the willing… erasure for the damned."

At his command, the battlefield shifted. A glowing Fetal Orb bloomed into existence at its heart, swelling with a radiant white brilliance that defied the storm. Its pulsing light carved through the shadows, a sphere of hope—or of annihilation.

"Ara!" Von's voice thundered, firm and commanding. "Get the General into the orb."

Ara hesitated, her stare sharp with doubt. "Why would you want me to do that?"

"No time for questions," Von snapped, his voice cutting through her hesitation like steel. "Do it."

The weight in his tone banished all uncertainty. Ara nodded once, resolve hardening. At her side, Counselor Ledge leaned close, his whisper low but reverent.

"He's all yours, my queen."

A smirk tugged at Ara's lips, her confidence rekindled. Energy flared around her, surging in waves as she refocused on her quarry. She launched forward, every motion precise, every strike laced with righteous fury. Bicycle kicks hammered into Scorpiondt's chest, driving him backward step by step, forcing him toward the glowing maw of the orb.

"This is for Petrichore!" she cried, her voice echoing across the ruins as she landed a devastating punch that shook his broken armor and sent blood spraying into the rain.

Scorpiondt stumbled, teetering at the edge of the orb's pull, the luminous energy tugging at his frame. Ara did not falter. She closed the gap in one last surge, her palm igniting with fire-hot embers.

With a final, energy-infused strike—a slap sharp enough to split the air—she sent him spiraling backward into the light.

As his body disappeared into the radiant sphere, Ara whispered, her voice low but unshakable, resonating through the storm:

"And that's for my mother."

The Fetal Orb swallowed him whole, its brilliance flaring once more before dimming into silence.

Inside the orb, General Scorpiondt found himself face-to-face with Counselor Von. The Counselor sat cross-legged, calm and immovable, as though the chaos of battle no longer existed. The orb's radiant interior pulsed in rhythmic waves of white light, each surge amplifying the suffocating silence.

"General Scorpiondt," Von said, his voice echoing in every direction, reverberating against the glowing walls. "This is the edge of a black hole for you. Your existence has birthed only pain and suffering. May Rainah never have mercy on your soul."

Scorpiondt opened his mouth to sneer, to spit venom back—but something else stirred.

The orb's glow brightened, refracting into a thousand shifting patterns that sliced into his mind. Dark, unrelenting memories surged like a flood, hammering him with the weight of what he had done.

He saw the horrified screams of families as their homes burned.

The enslaved, shackled beneath his orders, writhing under merciless whips.

His blade descending on the helpless, leaving blood to stain the dust.

Whole star systems silenced in fire, their skies emptied by his conquest.

Worlds reduced to ashes, civilizations erased because he willed it so.

Every atrocity played back in relentless clarity. And for the first time in his existence, General Scorpiondt was not the hunter—but the haunted.

His lips curled back in rage as the images crashed against him. "No!" he roared, his voice raw. He lunged at Counselor Von, desperate to strike, to silence the torment.

But Von did not flinch. He simply stared, his calm presence magnified by the orb's pulsing light.

Before Scorpiondt's hand could reach him, the orb shuddered and shot skyward, ripping through the clouds with breathtaking speed. The world outside became a blur of rain, storm, and shadow as it ascended higher and higher, carrying its prisoner toward the heavens.

Then—*detonation.*

A spectacular explosion of light and energy erupted, blinding in its brilliance. Its thunderous echo split the air, shaking the mountains, rattling the forests.

Above the battlefield, a gaping wound tore through the storm's dark canopy, and for the first time in hours, sunlight broke through. Beams of gold pierced the clouds, spilling across the scarred earth like a benediction.

The Counselors below stood in awe, bathed in the sudden warmth, their silhouettes outlined in light. The battlefield was transformed—mud, blood, and ruin now illuminated beneath the cleansing radiance.

For all its fury, the storm had broken.

The Counselors stood together, their forms bathed in golden light. Beneath their lowered hoods, their eyes narrowed against the sting of daylight, but their victory was undeniable. Silence blanketed the battlefield, broken only by the hiss of rain steaming off scorched earth.

From a distance, Dr. Serpendt trembled, his voice cracking as fear overtook him.

"What have they done? Oh no… they've destroyed General Scorpiondt."

Counselor Ara's voice cut softly through the stillness, heavy with guilt.

"He's gone. I shouldn't have listened to him."

Before her words settled, Ledge's gaze caught movement in the sky. He pointed upward, his tone urgent.

"Wait—look! Is that who I think it is?"

The Counselors followed his stare. A figure plummeted from the heavens, tumbling lifelessly through the golden light. Ara's heart seized as recognition struck her.

"It's my father! It's Von!" she cried, her voice rising in both relief and dread. Her expression faltered when she realized he wasn't moving. "He's unconscious!"

"I've got him!" Counselor Barricade bellowed. With a powerful leap, he launched himself skyward. His massive form cut through the air, intercepting Von just before the ground could claim him. Cradling him with unexpected gentleness, Barricade descended, his boots striking the earth with a solid thud.

Counselor Encrypt dropped to Von's side, his expression taut with focus. He pressed two fingers against Von's neck.

"Pulse is weak," he reported grimly. Without hesitation, he placed both palms on Von's chest. Sparks of electric mystic energy flared, crackling into Von's body like bolts from a storm.

The first shock jolted his frame—but no response.

Ara fell to her knees beside him, tears streaking her rain-soaked face. "Father, wake up! Please… come back to us!"

Encrypt clenched his jaw and surged again, channeling a second burst of searing light. Von's body jerked under the force, but his eyes remained closed.

"Once more," Encrypt muttered, determination burning in his silver gaze. He pushed harder, unleashing a final surge. The energy roared like thunder, flooding Von's chest with radiant power.

At last—Von stirred. His eyelids fluttered open, a faint groan escaping as he drew breath. Relief rippled through the Counselors as they helped him upright.

"That was too close," Barricade exhaled, his broad shoulders relaxing as tension drained away.

But while their focus lingered on Von, Dr. Serpendt moved. His panic sharpened into ruthless calculation. Seizing the moment, he slipped toward General Scorpiondt's private Servacraft. By the time anyone glanced his way, the hatch was sealed and the engines ignited.

The craft lifted from the earth, its roar rising above the battered battlefield. Serpendt's pale face was the last thing visible in the cockpit window—eyes wide not with relief, but with venomous intent—as the Servacraft climbed into the storm clouds and vanished from sight.

But Counselor Ledge, ever vigilant, caught the movement. His eyes narrowed, tracking the ascending craft.

"Not so fast, Serpendt," he muttered.

He extended his arm, fingers splayed, gathering mystic energy until it seethed in his palm like a miniature sun. With a sharp thrust, he released it—a beam of condensed light tearing across the sky.

The blast struck true. The Servacraft's hull shuddered, flames blooming along its engines. It sputtered, wobbled, then spiraled, its mechanical shriek piercing the storm.

A heartbeat later, the inevitable came. With a deafening explosion, the craft ruptured mid-air, trailing fire as it plummeted over the edge of a nearby cliff. The wreckage tumbled end over end into the abyss below, swallowed by the churning mists that rose from the depths.

For a long moment, silence followed—save for the distant echo of crumbling debris—leaving only the question of whether Serpendt's fall had ended his schemes, or merely scattered their shadow into darker corners.

The Counselors stood together, battered but unbroken, their mission complete—for now.

Counselor Ara steadied her father with a hand on his shoulder, her voice firm yet gentle. "We did it, Father. The General is no more."

Counselor Von nodded, his gaze fixed on the horizon. "We've won this battle," he said, his tone even but weighted. "But the war isn't over yet."

He exhaled, weary. "Come, let's get out of here. I could use a hot cup of coffee."

Counselor Encrypt glanced sidelong. "My apologies, sir. I had the last cup this morning. But I'll brew you tea."

Von sighed, the corner of his mouth curling. "Tea will do."

They began their slow march back toward Indigo. The battlefield, broken and blood-stained, offered no reprieve—only the illusion of silence.

Then came the thump. Heavy. Deliberate. Followed by a metallic voice that scraped across the clearing:

DROID! "Gatekeeper-10."

The Counselors froze. Another thump landed to their right, the same mechanical tone declaring:

DROID! "Gatekeeper-42."

Then another. DROID! "Gatekeeper-2."

One after another, voices called out as iron feet struck the ground in unison.

DROID! "Gatekeeper-51."

DROID! "Gatekeeper-35."

DROID! "Gatekeeper-22."

Shapes emerged from the rain and smoke—an army of androids, glowing red eyes cutting through the gloom. They encircled the Counselors in an unbreakable ring.

Encrypt's jaw tightened. "There must be a hundred of them. What are they?"

Von's voice dropped, low and grim. "Gatekeepers. They never function alone. If they're here... their masters are inbound."

"More company," Counselor Ledge said, pointing skyward.

Five silhouettes descended from the storm clouds, cloaked in sleek black spandex that shimmered with unnatural sheen. Four men, one woman, their presence oppressive, their aura unmistakably sinister. They hovered above the ground, like specters passing judgment.

At their head stood a pale man with slicked-back black hair, a trimmed beard, and sunlight-gold eyes that cut like blades. His voice resonated with authority as he spoke:

"I am Order-Arlo, leader of the Surrogates of the Mystique Order, servants of the Ikannunaa Royal Empire. You are under arrest for the slayings of Squadron operatives, Dr. Serpendt, General Scorpiondt, and for the destruction of imperial property.

"Your other option," he said, voice curling into mock generosity, "is to work for us. Fugitives can still prove... useful."

Von's reply was steady, cutting through the rain. "I know who you are, what you are, and why you're here. We are not going with you. And we will never serve."

Arlo's golden eyes narrowed. "That was not a choice." He raised a hand. "Gatekeepers—take them."

The machines surged forward. The Counselors fought with what strength remained—energy shields flared, fists struck, mystic light shattered steel. The battlefield became a storm of sparks, fire, and fury.

But numbers won. For every Gatekeeper dismantled, two more replaced it. Exhaustion set in; their movements slowed, defenses faltered. The tide turned.

One by one, the Counselors were driven to the ground beneath a mountain of androids—metal limbs clamping, pressing, burying them alive. The battlefield grew silent save for the cold hum of circuitry.

For a breath, it seemed finished.

Then—a spark. A fist broke through the pile of steel, clutching a strip of red cloth.

The sky rumbled. Lightning split the heavens, striking the field with deafening force. The red cloth blazed in the stormlight, the symbol of their defiance. Energy embers reignited, flaring out from beneath the weight of metal.

A voice thundered from below, strong and unyielding:

"This war is far from over."

Over a year had passed since the fall of General Scorpiondt on Earth.

Petrichore—once a world of gleaming cities and vibrant skies—had become a husk of its former self. Towering spires that had once kissed the clouds now lay in heaps of rubble, reduced to scattered stones and dust. The skies, once alive with the hum of flight, had fallen silent. The few vessels that remained lay twisted on the ground like shattered bones. Streets were buried under debris, and the acrid scent of decay clung to the air.

The survivors endured in the shadow of this devastation. Food and water were scarce, and each dawn brought not hope, but another fight for survival. Power vacuums widened into chasms, tearing communities apart. Neighbors turned wary of each other, desperation eroding what little unity remained. Petrichore teetered at the edge of collapse, where hope itself had become a memory.

On a day forecasted for heavy rain, dark clouds churned across the ravaged horizon. Lightning flickered in their depths, restless and hungry. The stillness broke when the roar of a vessel split the heavens. A Servacraft—its sleek frame still bearing the insignia of the Ikannunaa Empire—pierced the atmosphere, engines blazing as it descended in a measured glide.

Then fate struck.

A jagged bolt of lightning clawed from the clouds, raking across the Servacraft's flank. Its engines screamed, their steady hum unraveling into a tortured wail. Red alarms strobed the cockpit in frantic pulses of light as the pilot wrestled with failing controls. The ship lurched violently, tilting into a death spiral.

Moments later, the ground shook as the Servacraft crashed into the dense forest bordering a nearby settlement. The impact was catastrophic. Trees splintered, earth buckled, and the explosion scattered flaming wreckage across the undergrowth. Smoke billowed upward in thick, black columns, blotting the sky. The war machine, once a symbol of dominance, now lay as nothing more than wreckage—proof of how fragile even empire-born steel could be against the fury of nature.

Yet, as the wreckage smoldered, something stirred within.

Whatever—or whoever—had survived the crash was not finished yet.

The Conqueror VIII

As told by General Scorpiondt

They think they've won.

Let them taste the sweet rot of that lie, for victory… true victory… does not belong to the loud, nor the luminous. It belongs to the patient.

Yes—let history record their defiance: the girl with the red cloth, the doctor's brood, the clumsy giant, the sword-bearer, and the whispering son of Grenaivel. Let history laugh in the glow of their makeshift triumph. They call it "rebellion." I call it the final tantrum of a dying ideology.

They broke into my sanctum, their hearts bloated with purpose. I watched them converge with eyes like children rushing to finish a play before bedtime— before the shadows truly come.

And yet... they did strike. They did unleash their little Orb. A final red flash—a desperate flare meant to cauterize the wound they refused to let fester. Ah, yes. The Fetal Orb. How poetic. Life—weaponized. The only irony sharper than its sting was the look on their faces when it actually worked.

My body—this vessel the Empire so dutifully engineered—broke.

A magnificent fracture, really. I felt each bone sever like the chains I once wore in Tusilbarrh. My lungs collapsed, a pity. I always enjoyed the sound of my own breath just before battle. But no matter. The body is not the general. The body is a mask.

And masks... can be replaced.

They'll speak of my fall as though it is final. They'll speak of their "moment." Mystic this. Counselor that. As if titles stitched from stolen cloth make them more than boys and girls playing gods on borrowed soil.

But listen closely—bend your ears toward the silence that followed my collapse, and you will hear it:

Footsteps.

Not of angels. Not of saviors.

But of Order.

The Gatekeepers arrived as planned. The Surrogates of the Mistique Order—my contingency made flesh. They descend not in panic, but in sequence. Precision is their blood. Loyalty is their only faith.

You see, while the Mystics danced in their little circle of fate, I prepared the next stage of the war. For them, this was an ending. For me, merely the beginning of the next order.

Let Ara cry out. Let Ledge lunge for meaning. Let the red cloth wave in the wind like some holy banner. I have studied rebellion. I have crushed it in thirteen star systems. It always ends the same: with rebels too stunned to realize they've inherited only rubble.

And Von... dear Doctor Von. You built your hope like I built my Omega fluid—with design, with faith, with fear. But unlike you, I did not need it to survive. It was never about preservation. It was about immortality through orchestration. Even in my destruction, I remain… author.

Yes, Counselor Encrypt. Burn your energy to keep the light alive. Yes, Barricade—bear your burdens, thunder your griefs. Yes, Ara—love your rebellion as one loves a fire they cannot control. Let that passion consume you, and know that the ashes it leaves behind will spell my name long after your tongues forget their own.

I do not die today.

I transition.

From presence… to principle.

From muscle… to myth.

And if by some flickering star's cruelty I am truly gone, then remember this:

I do not fear endings.

I engineer them.

Scorpiondt, Last General of the Ikannunaa, Out.

End

of

Saga

I

Novel Cast And Credits

Doctor | Mystic | Counselor Jon Von of planet Petrichore

Rebel Crew/ Fugitives | Mystic Heros | Refuge of the Mystic Counsel of Indigo, planet Earth

Professor Dia Von of planet Petrichore

Ara Von of planet Petrichore

Tes of planet Petrichore

Doctor | Uncle Cal of planet Petrichore

Ms. Pan of planet Petrichore

Queen Lor of planet Petrichore

Captain | Mystic | Counselor Ledge of planet Grenaivel

Lieutenant | Mystic | Counselor Encrypt of planet Grenaivel

Lieutenant | Mystic | Counselor Barricade of planet Grenaivel

Tribe Leader Parth of Goa, India, planet Earth

Supreme-Elder Raj of Goa, India, planet Earth

Elder Abhay of Goa, India, planet Earth

Spiritual Leader Ohm of Goa, India, planet Earth

King Atan-els of planet Nimbbiraa-Six

Prince Atsu-els of planet Nimbbiraa-Six

Prince Ata-els of planet Nimbbiraa-Six

Lord Nailatper of planet Angtroma

King Nephilesis of planet Broche Reine

Queen Angeliqonn of planet Broche Reine

Snob the Great (Merchant King) of planet UNKNOWN

Lord | General | Omega Scorpiondt of planet Tusilbarrh

Doctor Serpendt of planet Tusilbarrh

Doctor Jidohtta of planet UNKNOWN

Bokimpa of planet Nimbbiraa-Six

Order-Arlo of planet Nimbbiraa-Five

Surrogates of the Mystique Order of planet Nimbbiraa-Five

Stephan J. Courthall of New York, planet Earth

Front Warrior Khalfani of planet Earth

Guide Mal-Monger of planet Ras-Magenta

The Boy of Goa, India, planet Earth

Guide Mentor of planet Ras-Magenta | Indigo, planet Earth

Guardian Mythic of planet Ras-Magenta | Indigo, planet Earth

Maestro (The Piper) of planet Ras-Magenta | Indigo, planet Earth

Miraj of planet Ras-Magenta | Indigo, planet Earth

Miracle of planet Ras-Magenta | Indigo, planet Earth

Mojo of planet Ras-Magenta | Indigo, planet Earth

Introveca of Satana, India, planet Earth

Guide Moral of planet Ras-Magenta | Indigo, planet Earth

Minion of planet Ras-Magenta | Indigo, planet Earth

Monks of Mercy of Mercy Island, planet Ras-Magenta | Indigo, planet Earth

Sauruvex of planet Earth

Fin of Indigo, planet Earth

NOVEL CREDITS

Marcus Halloway

Eliza Trennor

Jonah Wexley

Nadine Keswick

Tobias Rallin

Miriam V. Dawlish

Oliver Grenshaw

Selene Brohm

Declan Virelli

Camilla Hensley

Raymond Thorne

Cassian Drayle

Sapphire N. Owens

Ida Mae Owens

Post Credit Scene

The black sky rumbled, a prelude to the storm about to swallow the city. Lightning split the heavens, bleaching the low roofs and wet streets in a single flash. It was 1985 at Yonkers General Hospital, deep in Earth's New York.

Inside, night shift hum. Nurses at the front desk laughed over paperwork while an FM talk show droned from a plastic radio. Down the nursery hall, a janitor eased a mop along the tile, head bobbing to the muffled hiss of a Walkman.

Two nurses stood at the nursery's wide glass, counting the neat rows of sleeping cribs. One baby had a thin red ribbon tied around his right arm.

"What's his name?" the first asked, keeping her voice just above a whisper.

The other checked her clipboard. "Stephan J. Courthall."

The first nurse lingered, eyes soft. "Feels like he's... different," she murmured.

Her colleague squeezed her elbow. "Come on. Cafeteria before it floods."

They drifted away. In Stephan's crib, a white ring of light opened in the air behind his head—thin as a coin, bright as breath. It hovered, casting a gentle halo over his face. The newborn's lips twitched into something like a grin, as if warmed by a presence no monitor could catch. Then the ring dimmed to nothing.

Outside, rain came hard. Across the street, a black sedan idled beneath a dead streetlamp. Two men in dark suits and fedoras watched the hospital. Their sunglasses stayed on despite the storm.

At the roofline, a figure in a black hooded coat stepped into view and dropped from the parapet. He landed at the far end of the building with a near-silent thud and walked on without looking back, coat tails licking at the wind. For a heartbeat the rain carried a thread of sound—syllables too old for the radio below.

In the sedan, the passenger lifted a slim black handset. His voice was calm, clipped. 'Droid, Gatekeeper-33 reporting. Code 1-0-7-0-1. Possible Counsel member sighted at the hospital."

A familiar voice came back, dark and measured. "I thought they went extinct in exile. If that is a Counselor, then they know the infant is our first NF-Sigma male on record."

"Droid! Orders?" Thirty-Three asked. If he felt anything, his face didn't show it.

"Return to headquarters and await instruction from Order-Arlo," the voice said.

"Yes, Dr. Serpendt." He thumbed the line closed.

Thunder rolled over Yonkers General. Inside, baby Stephan slept on, the red ribbon loose against his tiny arm.

Deleted Chapter Scenes

The thunder of energy blasts shook the plains of Goa. Cries of the dying carried on the wind, tangled with the metallic shriek of Ikannunaa weapons.

Inside the last standing hut at the village's center, Spiritual Leader Ohm knelt in silence. His face—once serene—was drawn tight with strain. Smoke pressed through the cracks in the walls, carrying the bitter scent of sandalwood, neem, and turmeric. Once calming, the aroma now felt like a cruel reminder of traditions slipping into ash.

The walls shuddered with each distant explosion. Firelight cast frantic shadows across the mud-plastered interior, flickering over the faces of his disciples. They were boys—barely men—with trembling hands and faltering lips as they tried to mouth the old chants.

Ohm pressed his palms together, voice low but steady, the Old Tongue shaping every syllable like a blade.

"O spirits of our ancestors... you who rest beneath this land—rise with us. Let the wind carry your will. Let fury move through our hands. Lend breath to the lungs of our warriors. Let the earth roar!"

He scattered ash into the fire pit. Sparks leapt, hissed—then faltered. The flames guttered, shrinking.

Something was wrong.

His voice rose, desperate, trembling.

"You rose for us before—when the Satana came, you answered! I am Ohm! Your voice on this earth! Answer me again!"

Silence.

The fire coughed out and died, smothered by a cold draft that slithered through the seams of the hut.

One disciple broke into sobs. Another simply stared at the dead pit, lips parted, eyes empty.

Ohm staggered upright, horror trembling in his limbs. His whisper fell like a curse.

"They... do not hear us. No... worse. They cannot."

The hut swayed under the force of a thunderous boom outside. The ground split with tremors. A massive craft descended from the clouds, blotting out the stars. Red light spilled across the ruins of the temple, washing the battlefield in the glow of a dying sun.

Screams tore the night.

Ohm pushed through the broken doorway into the storm. Rain poured over his white robes, turning them gray against his skin. His eyes roamed across the devastation: the dead piled among burning huts, the sacred ground slick with blood. And there—fallen in the mud—was Tribe Leader Parth, lifeless, unmoving.

Ohm dropped to his knees, voice breaking.

"The warriors... broken. The ancestors... silent. We are forsaken."

Tears blurred his sight. But through the crushing silence, something else stirred. Not ancient. Not ancestral. Something new—alien, unformed, yet undeniable.

It did not come from the past.

It came from the future.

And for the first time in all his years, Ohm did not know whether to bow his head in hope... or in terror.

Deleted Ch. 2 Scene ╷ Ashes at the Servacraft

The night air hung heavy with the acrid stench of scorched metal and burned flesh. Smoke crawled across the ground like a living thing, curling between the still forms of fallen tribesmen. Moonlight caught the jagged edges of shattered spears and warped shields, painting the battlefield in pale silver and deep shadow.

From the rear hatch of the Servacraft, the five cyber-enhanced warriors of the Ikannunaa Royal Squadron emerged in perfect unison. Their armor—black, gleaming, like liquid obsidian—reflected the glow of the burning encampment. Each moved with mechanical precision, footfalls silent despite the weight of their augmentations.

From the shadows of The Prominent stepped Prince Ata-els. He did not rush. Every movement was measured, deliberate, as though the destruction before him were nothing more than a gallery exhibit awaiting inspection. The reddish trim of his cloak swayed with the embers that drifted through the night air. His masked face tilted, surveying the carnage with the detached curiosity of a sovereign appraising a conquered world.

General Scorpiondt followed, his presence heavier than the smoke itself. His black eyes swept across the battlefield, lingering on the clusters of surviving rebels—men clinging to broken weapons as though defiance alone could stave off death. When he spoke, his voice carried the weight of inevitability.

"Order," he said, the words grinding like stone on stone, "is the natural state of all things. Chaos... is the weakness the desperate cannot resist."

A wounded tribesman lunged forward, spear aimed for Scorpiondt's chest. The General did not so much as shift. One IRS soldier intercepted, gauntlet closing over the man's skull. A single twist—bone snapped, and the body collapsed lifeless into the dust.

Prince Ata-els did not glance at the fallen rebel. His voice cut through the crackle of the burning village.

"Finish this. The rebellion exists because we permitted it. That failure will not stand."

The IRS descended on the battlefield like predators unleashed. One soldier hurled an energy pike that detonated in a flash of white fire, vaporizing a charging group. Another carved through two rebels at once, twin blades singing arcs too fast for the human eye to follow. In moments, the resistance line crumbled.

Scorpiondt strode forward, crushing a discarded helmet beneath his heel. He paused beside a dying warrior who still clutched a shattered spear, defiance burning in his eyes. The General crouched, speaking low enough for the man alone to hear.

"You think you fight for freedom," he said almost gently. "But freedom is the cruelest of prisons. Under my hand, you would have lived."

The man spat blood into his face.

Scorpiondt rose without flinching, wiped the smear from his cheek, and pressed his boot against the rebel's throat until the body stilled.

Ata-els moved through the chaos like a monarch in his court, every step deliberate, every turn of his head radiating disdain. The last pockets of resistance faltered—fighters dropped their weapons, some breaking for the treeline. At a flick of the Prince's hand, the IRS sharpshooter unleashed plasma fire, bolts streaking into the dark. Escapees crumpled at the forest's edge, each impact a hellish flare.

Ata-els stopped at the foot of the Servacraft's ramp, gazing over the ruin before him. His voice, smooth but laced with venom, carried across the battlefield.

"Let this be the last time you allow insects to nest beneath my rule."

Scorpiondt inclined his head, not in submission, but in acknowledgment.

"Then we will salt the earth, my Prince. Nothing will rise here again."

By dawn, the rebellion was ash. The only witnesses left were the hiss of cooling metal and the whisper of the wind over the dead.

Deleted Ch. 3 Scene | The Shadow in the Flame

The campfire whispered in the stillness, flames flickering gold and orange over weary faces. One by one, the others had slipped into sleep. Captain Ledge sat slouched against a fallen log, eyelids heavy. The fire's warmth lulled him downward. His vision blurred. The forest dissolved.

Then, nothing.

He stood barefoot in an endless void. The ground beneath him was slick, polished like black glass, yet cold as stone. Shadows drifted in slow, deliberate swirls, circling him as if aware, as if waiting. The silence pressed into his skull until he thought his own heartbeat might shatter it.

Then came the voice—smooth, rich, coiling with dark amusement.

"Captain Ledge… predictable, as ever."

It wrapped around him, curling like smoke from everywhere at once. Ledge spun, fists clenched, scanning the void. There was no one. Only ripples in the darkness.

The voice purred again, each word stretched with mockery.

"You believe you are their protector? That destiny bends to your sword?" A soft chuckle slithered between syllables. "How quaint."

The sound was velvet hiding steel—half laughter, half threat.

Ahead, a figure began to form. Short. Slender. Robes trailing endlessly into the dark. His face was a smear of shadow, but two glints of light marked where his eyes should have been—narrow, cunning, alive with sly delight. His grin appeared first—wide, wrong, and hungry.

The figure bowed low, mocking courtesy.

"I am intrigued, Captain. So noble. So loyal. So… breakable."

Ledge tried to move, to speak, but the air thickened, pressing him in place. The figure circled him with a predator's patience.

"You've been told stories, haven't you?" His voice tightened, sharper now. "Tales of light, of courage, of bonds unbroken." A tsk, soft and cruel. "Such delicious lies. Allow me to show you the truth."

The shadows surged forward. They poured into him like icy smoke, filling his chest, his veins. Cold fingers traced his spine from within. He gasped—but no sound came. His body stiffened as if it were no longer his own.

The figure's laughter rose, silk wrapped over iron.

"Yes… let it in. Feel how small you were before me."

A dark violet glow burst across his skin. His veins lit with molten dusk, his eyes swallowed into black pits. His lips twisted into a smile he did not choose— sharp, alien, cruel.

The voice bent close, a whisper colder than steel.

"Now… you are mine."

Ledge jolted awake.

The fire still burned, its warmth spilling across the circle of sleeping companions. His breath came ragged. Sweat dampened his palms. Slowly, he lifted his hands to the light.

For a heartbeat, he saw it—something pulsing beneath his skin, a shimmer of violet crawling just under the surface.

And then, it was gone.

Deleted Ch. 4 Scene | The Realignment

The Fetal Orb pulsed with an unearthly rhythm, pale currents spiraling around the five rebels, cocooning them in deep stillness.

All except Dr. Von.

His eyes opened, sharp, clinical. For a long moment he sat in silence. Then, with a dry grimace, he spat a slick pale seed onto the floor. It rolled lazily to the circle's center.

"Figures. First thing this thing does is try to plant me. Not impressed."

Rising with deliberate calm, he circled the others—Ara, Ledge, Encrypt, Barricade—studying them like test subjects.

"Stable. Breathing. Oblivious. Lucky for you."

He paused at Ara, his gaze tightening.

"You'd better come out of this stronger. Because if this system's built wrong, it'll chew you up before it saves you."

Flexing his fingers, he frowned. The hum was off—not clean, not tuned for them. He crouched, pressed his palm flat to the floor. The vibration was irregular, jittering against his skin.

That's when he saw it: a ripple in the wall, like liquid suspended midair.

"Of course. Calibration fault. Built for Karibegoan Guides, not for us. Which means…" He sighed. "We're running on the wrong settings."

Pinching the bridge of his nose, he muttered, "And here I was hoping to let the mystical babysitter handle everything."

He pressed his hand to the ripple. It gave way like warm water. Von smirked.

"Alright, Orb. Let's see what you're hiding under the hood."

The glow inside shifted—bruised purples and sickly greens. Veins of energy pulsed unevenly across the walls, alive but diseased, like circuitry choking on the wrong current. The hum wavered, strained, an engine sputtering on bad fuel.

Von shook his head. "Karibegoan channels. Perfect if you've got four eyes and a magic wand. For us? Death by misalignment."

He followed the jagged rhythm into a central chamber, where a spiraling column of liquid energy fed five conduits. None ran smooth; each flickered—weak, unstable, on the verge of collapse.

"There's the mismatch. It has us wired into the wrong template."

A side panel pulsed open beneath his touch, exposing snarled umbilical lines. With the precision of a surgeon, he uncoiled, rewired, and re-aligned them. Energy coursed, steadying under his hands. The chamber's glow brightened, the hum smoothing into perfect balance.

"There. Adjusted for our physiology. You're welcome."

He stepped back, brushing his hands clean, then cast one last glance at the chamber.

"Keep this between us. Mentor would faint if he knew I just rewrote his precious settings."

With that, Von slipped back through the ripple. Settling cross-legged among the others, he closed his eyes. To anyone watching, it looked as though he had never moved at all.

He exhaled, the faintest smirk tugging his lips.

"One wrong move in there, and we'd all be corpses by dawn."

Deleted Ch. 5 Scene | Lessons by the Hearth

The kitchen looked like the aftermath of a siege. Flour blanketed the counters like smoke after a cannon blast, and the kettle hissed faintly where a layer of char clung stubbornly to its bottom. Ara planted her fists on her hips, smirking at the devastation.

"Well, that was tragic. Next time, we stick to something simple. Like water."

From the doorway, Miraj's voice drifted in—measured, calm, and rooted with quiet authority.

"Child, you may laugh, but when the body hungers, even burnt stew finds its place."

Ara rolled up her sleeves, grabbing a cloth with exaggerated resolve. "Fine. I'll handle the battlefield cleanup. But if I find another potato on the ceiling, I'm charging extra."

Miraj's chuckle was low and warm, like the earth shifting gently underfoot. She stepped inside, reaching for a basin of water.

"I'll help. Chaos, I've learned, requires two kinds of hands—young and restless, old and steady—if it is to be put back in order."

They worked side by side. Ara moved with restless precision, tossing utensils into neat piles, scrubbing as if it were a tactical mission. Miraj moved with patience, each gesture deliberate, her presence smoothing the edges of the room itself.

After a time, Miraj spoke, voice carrying a weight that stilled Ara's movements.

"You carry yourself as though the world is yours to conquer. Bold. Unyielding. That is power, yes… but it is also danger."

Ara smirked, not glancing up from the counter she scrubbed. "Danger's part of the fun, isn't it?"

Miraj rested her hand lightly on the broom, her gaze fixed on Ara with piercing gentleness.

"Fun—until danger comes to collect its price. I've buried too many who thought as you do now. The true strength, child, is in knowing which battles deserve your fire."

That struck deeper than Ara expected. She paused, cloth slack in her hand, her usual sharpness dimmed by thought. "…And how do you know which ones are worth it?"

Miraj stepped closer, brushing a streak of flour from Ara's cheek with motherly tenderness. Her voice dropped to a whisper of wisdom.

"The ones you can live with losing. The ones that leave you standing, heart still whole. Everything else—let it go."

For a moment, Ara's smirk slipped, replaced by something rawer, quieter. She gave the faintest nod.

When the last pan was stacked and the floor swept clean, Miraj opened her arms, offering—not demanding—an embrace. Ara hesitated, stubborn as ever, but finally stepped forward. Miraj's hug carried the weight of generations, grounding Ara in a strength older than her fire.

"You are not alone in this fight," Miraj murmured. "Even a flame burns longer when it does not stand against the wind alone."

Ara lingered, then pulled back, a crooked half-smile returning to her face.

"Don't worry, Miraj. I'm still the wind."

Miraj's laugh—low, knowing, unhurried—was the only reply.

Deleted Ch. 6 Scene | The Trunk's Song

The frozen wind clawed at their cloaks as the rebels dragged the Humming Black Trunk across the ice. Its weight was unnatural—too heavy for its size, as if it carried not matter, but memory itself.

They moved in silence, boots crunching over frost. But one among them lagged behind, his eyes fixed on the Trunk.

Encrypt.

He slowed, letting the distance stretch between him and the others. His breath steamed in the night air, curling in spirals that seemed to pulse in time with the object's low hum. What the others dismissed as vibration, he heard as cadence. And then—cadence became language.

A chant. Low. Deliberate. Ancient.

The Trunk wasn't humming. It was singing.

Encrypt closed his eyes, tuning his senses inward. The song wound through him, bypassing words, carving itself directly into his marrow. The syllables were alien, yet their meaning rang clear as thunder:

"Doors unopened… prices unpaid… the circle broken, yet bound again."

His brow furrowed, lips parting in a whisper no one else could hear.

"Not prophecy. Not warning. A bargain."

The dark aura of the Trunk pressed against the tundra's stillness, pulling at him like a tide. His mind reached for it instinctively, the way one traces constellations in the night sky, trying to map a pattern. His fingers twitched, aching to draw a sigil in the air, to test the resonance.

He stopped himself with a sharp inhale of cold air. His jaw set, expression hardening as the weight of realization hit.

He looked to the others—Von striding ahead with stubborn precision, Ara confident at the lead, Barricade steady at her side, Ledge scanning the shadows. None of them noticed. None of them heard.

Only him.

Encrypt drew his cloak tighter, muttering under his breath in his usual sharp, sardonic cadence.

"Wonderful. Out of all of us, the cursed box chooses me for its choir."

He cast one final glance at the Trunk before quickening his pace to rejoin the group. But the song clung to him, a refrain threading itself into the back of his mind:

"Doors unopened… prices unpaid…"

And in that moment, Encrypt knew.

The Trunk had not been retrieved.

It had allowed itself to be found.

Deleted Ch. 7 Scene ∣ Von's Secret Test

The cottage slept in silence. Above, only the creak of beams settling in the night. Below, in a hidden chamber carved from stone, Dr. Von sat alone.

The room was bare—walls of rock, air damp and cool. A single candle guttered on the table, its flame bending with every breath of draft from the cracks.

Before him rested a vial of Sigma-Gene fluid, glowing faintly blue. Von rolled it between his fingers, the light catching like bottled lightning.

"Months of work. Lifetimes of theory. And here it sits… in a glorified perfume bottle."

He uncorked it and let a single drop fall into a shallow basin of water. Ripples spread outward. The glow swelled, washing pale light across the walls, stretching shadows like long fingers.

Von murmured a calibration phrase—syllables stolen from fractured Karibegoan texts. The water stirred. Strands lifted from the basin, coiling upward in ribbons until they shaped themselves into a figure.

A silhouette. His silhouette.

It spoke in his voice. Cold. Mocking.

"You tamper with currents you cannot control, Von."

Von froze for only a heartbeat, then let a brittle smirk tug at his mouth.

"Story of my life."

The figure tilted its head, grin twisting wider.

"You think you shape the stream. But it is the stream that shapes you."

The basin rattled, water sloshing as the shape leaned closer, voice sharp as steel.

"When it claims you, no one will know where the science ended… and the monster began."

Von's jaw tightened. His hands curled into fists. Then, with a sharp flick of his wrist, the figure shattered, collapsing into a splash across the table. Water ran in rivulets over the stone and pooled at his feet.

Silence filled the chamber again. Only the faint crackle of the candle remained.

Von stared into the basin, his reflection rippling back at him. His voice dropped, dry but edged with defiance.

"If the stream wants to shape me… it had better be ready to drown first."

He corked the vial, slid it back into its case, and snuffed out the candle.

Above, the cottage dreamed in peace.

Below, Von's private war with unseen currents had only just begun.

Deleted Ch. 8 Scene | Shadows Over Satana

The sky above Satana burned an unbroken blue, the sun high, thin clouds stretched taut across the horizon. Five figures cut through the daylight expanse in flawless formation, dark forms gleaming as they flew with lethal precision. Their flight was silent, seamless—predators daring the world below to notice.

The leader raised a gloved hand.

At once, the squad froze mid-air, bodies held steady against the wind. The leader tilted his head, eyes narrowing behind his lenses.

"Stop."

The word was smooth, sharp, almost casual—yet the others obeyed without hesitation.

He turned, scanning the horizon. From the direction of Goa, a ripple of force had bled across the air. It was not seen, not heard—only felt, vibrating through his bones. Power. Raw. Untamed.

A calculating half-smile curved his lips.

"Well, well… what do we have here?"

One of the squad shifted uneasily. "Is it one of ours?"

The leader chuckled—a sound more dangerous than amused.

"No. I would have been informed. Nothing of this scale slips by unnoticed. This… is uninvited."

With deliberate calm, he slid off his glove, letting the sunlight strike his bare hand. The pulse from Goa prickled against his skin like static, sharp and insistent.

"Power unclaimed. No allegiance. No leash. A wild card."

His voice cooled, the cadence of a man who measured every gamble like a blade across a throat.

"Valuable… or dangerous. Either way, it bears watching."

He replaced the glove with meticulous care and flicked his wrist, signaling formation.

"We observe from distance. We learn. And when the moment is right—we choose. To recruit it… or to erase it."

Without another word, he angled forward. The others fell in behind him seamlessly.

Five shadows streaked across the bright sky, leaving no cover behind them, only the glint of daylight on their dark forms as they sped toward Goa—predators answering the call of an unknown force.

Reflections From the Author

Stories are not just inventions. They are inheritances. They come to us in fragments — through whispers, memories, and the spaces between what was lost and what survived. Refuge of the Mystic Counsel began for me in those spaces: the quiet questions about what we owe to those who came before us, and the louder questions about what kind of world we leave behind.

At its heart, this story is about more than rebellion. It is about how we face forces greater than ourselves — oppression, betrayal, despair — and still find the courage to stand. It is about family, chosen and inherited. About the price of freedom. About what happens when ordinary people dare to become something greater, not for glory, but for survival, for love, for each other.

The Counselors, the Mystics, the rebels — they are echoes of us. They struggle with doubt. They clash with loyalty. They risk everything to protect what cannot be replaced. If you saw yourself in any of them, even for a moment, then this story has already done its work.

Every battle in these pages mirrors a battle in our own world — against injustice, against silence, against the shadows that insist we are powerless. And every moment of hope, no matter how fragile, is a reminder that we are not alone.

I want to thank you, the reader, for walking this path with me. For holding onto these characters as they stumbled, grew, and chose their destinies. Stories only live when someone listens, and you have listened.

The war is not over. It never truly is. But perhaps, in telling and retelling these tales, we arm ourselves with the one weapon no empire, no tyrant, no shadow can ever fully silence: belief.

Thank you for believing.

— Anthony James Owens

Future Publishings

INSPECTOR BENTLATCH KEAY II

SHATTERED PEPPERMINTS AND SCATTERED BULLETS

Genre | Crime & Mystery

REFUGE OF THE MYSTIC CNSL: ARA

SHARD OF THE HEIRLOOM FAMILY

Saga Two

Genre | Sci-Fiction & Fantasy

REFUGE OF THE MYSTIC COUNSEL

THE MALICE WITHIN

Saga Three

Genre | Sci-Fiction & Fantasy

www.ingramcontent.com/pod-product-compliance
Lightning Source LLC
Chambersburg PA
CBHW041207100726
47911CB00017B/885